Seeing Green

by

Beth Hudson

This book is dedicated to my friends, who over the years have encouraged me; supported me; read, critiqued, and corrected my drafts; come to my readings; listened to me vent and panic; and helped me to refine my writing to the point where I would ever want anyone to read it. Thank you. I couldn't have managed without you.

Written under the influence of books, music, and art.

Table of Contents

The Felling of Wystwood

The forest was under attack.

Vyiliish watched, aghast, as humans swarmed into Wystwood, armed with spears, swords, and axes. She had never had dealings with humans; her ash tree was located deep in the forest's heart, and she seldom ventured to the outskirts. The other tree spirits had relayed the news, and Vyiliish had rushed to see if she could aid her brothers and sisters. She had not really believed their tales, but now she could see the truth with her own eyes.

The scene was terrible beyond anything she could have imagined. A hundred woodcutters, their blades bloody with sap, hewed at the trees that bordered Wystwood. Behind them lay dozens of fallen trunks, pointing inward toward the heartwood; beech and maple, pine and oak, all casualties of the terrible assault against the forest. Vyiliish had known many of them since she had sprouted.

She could not understand why humans were here. Wystwood was ancient, far older than they and their axes. Four Powers, tied to the seasons, guided and protected the plants and animals: the Oak Youth, the Summerchild, the Wolflord, and the Holly Queen. The fifth Power slumbered and seldom woke; the Earth Stone, from which the first tree had sprouted. Humans seldom ventured here. It was not their domain, and they had no kinship with anything in the forest.

The tree spirits were helpless against the axes; all of their substance was contained in wood and bark, and none in the forms which moved freely through the forest. Horrified, Vyiliish watched as a birch spirit, hair yellow with autumn, wrapped her arms around the bole of her tree and clung, perhaps hoping it would save her. It did not. Instead, two woodcutters attacked the ash spirit at once, their strokes cutting through her body. From their expressions, Vyiliish could tell that they saw the ash woman; tree spirits, unlike the great Powers, were visible to mortal eyes. The woodcutter's faces were grooved with harsh, angry lines. Vyiliish let out a small cry of despair.

Wystwood was not entirely defenseless. Vyiliish could see that. The Wolflord harried the invaders, followed by creatures that leapt, crawled, and flew. Magic eddied around his form: a black-coated wolf the size of a stag, an enormous rack of antlers splaying from his head. The Wolflord was wide awake at this time of year; he was the most active of the forest Powers, and the fiercest. Though he wore a glamour to veil human minds, they looked around, eyes wide and white, every time he neared them. To the creatures of Wystwood, his presence inspired a ferocity approaching madness.

In the Wolflord's wake, bees stung and died by the hundreds, embedding their stingers in human flesh; serpents risked their fragile backs to deliver venom; wolves bit and dodged and bit again. Stags, their antlers branching into twelve and fourteen tines, forgot the autumn rut and turned their strength against the attackers. Bears and boars slashed a bloody path through blood and bone; crows and ravens stabbed at the hands and eyes of the invaders. Vyiliish could hardly bear the knowledge that her insubstantial form could do nothing to help against the invaders. Distraught by the carnage, she ran long fingers through her leafy hair, pulling it tight enough to hurt.

Against the animals were ranged dozens of archers, firing longbows taller than they. Men in well-worn clothing wielded pitchforks and hoes. Most disturbing was the rank of armored knights behind them, wielding swords and boar spears against the defenders. The presence of these knights proved that this was truly an army, and the invasion had been planned as a focused and determined effort to destroy Wystwood.

Horrific sounds cut through the air; screams of men, animals, and tree spirits mingled in a miasma of agony that suffused the forest edge. Songbirds, unfit for battle, shrilled alarms. Beneath all were the steady rhythms of chopping. Vyiliish smelled the men; their scent was metal, blood, and the death of trees.

Unable to watch any longer, Vyiliish retreated, wondering when it would be her turn. That was a terrifying thought. It was only chance that these trees lay at the outer edges, and that her slender birch grew near to Wystwood's core. At the speed the woodcutters moved, they might near the forest's beating heart in a handful of days. She wanted to do something. She *must* do something.

Near her feet, a badger houghed, his muzzle caked with blood, taking no notice of her presence. She stopped for a moment and knelt by him, touched by his courage in defending their common home.

"Brother Badger?" she asked. "Are you hurt?"

The badger looked at her with a fierce gaze, and spoke to her as the animals did, without words. He was tired and in pain, Vyiliish understood, but he would continue to fight until the invaders were either driven off or until he died of his wounds. It was his right.

Impressed by the badger's sacrifice, Vyiliish continued on toward the heartwood. The sounds and scents dissolved behind her as she moved, swallowed by the blanket of pine needles and leaf mold on the forest floor, and the softness of what browning leaves had not yet fallen. The hush spilled over her like a rain of silence.

It was a fresh, frost-cooled morning, and the spears of late autumn sunlight streamed through leaves that readied the trees for winter's sleep. Despite the horror of the woodcutters, Vyiliish greeted the sun with a shake of her leafy golden hair; at least the daystar would never turn against them. Leaves rustled with her passage: beech and maple, and a scatter of glittering aspens. Vyiliish nodded to them silently as she passed, hoping that not all of them were doomed. If the Powers could not stop the assault, they would be.

As Vyiliish slipped through stripes of shadow, Amashi joined her, acknowledging her with a smile that barely showed in his eyes. Three days ago, that smile would have radiated out from his heart and through his bark, warming Vyiliish like the sun at midsummer. Now his eyes, evergreen dark in his pine spirit's face, were also shadowed with their common fears. Still, she was glad to see him; they were of an age, had grown up together, and their bond was deep.

"Amashi," she said, and touched the rough bark of his face. "Tidings?"

"Only what we already know." Amashi's voice was weary. "Another hundred trees, and dozens of creatures. We've lost two entire packs of wolves, and several hives. The humans are determined to destroy us utterly."

"I know." Vyiliish released a sigh like the barest hint of breeze. "I'm going to the heartwood, to ask the Powers what I can do to help." The words fell from her mouth almost without thought; until she spoke them, she had no notion of asking the Powers for any such thing. She examined the idea, and found it a revelation. They would tell her what to do.

That drew a surprised laugh from Amashi. "Vyiliish! I didn't know you were so resolute! You sound as brave as an oak!"

"Come with me," Vyiliish said. "Stand with me and speak with the Powers."

Amashi's green needle-hair crested like a ruffled grouse. "Me? Stand before the Powers?" He shook his head. "No, sister, not I. But come to me after, and I will help *you* if I can." He slid his hand down her smooth cheek, then turned and strode off toward his tree.

Vyiliish gathered as much courage as she could find in her own rings and continued toward the heartwood. The Powers were fearsome, surely, but she had never heard that they were unjust. What made them so imposing was the intense reality of their existence, a reality that made everything else seem like phantom shadows. Even an oak spirit might find it hard to stay mindful in their presence.

She felt them as she neared the heartwood. A man would not have known what he saw; a hedge of holly that sheltered under a half-moon of immense and ancient oaks, and the entire area webbed with creepers and matted with small plants and brush. In the exact center lay a boulder, its unremarkable mottled surface roughened with rain and wind, and stained with lichen. As she neared it, Vyiliish felt an eerie prickling, as if from incipient lightning.

"Vyiliish," a sweet woman's voice called. "Dear one. Come, step into the hedge."

It was the Holly Queen; Vyiliish knew this, though she had never before been in her presence. All in Wystwood was connected, and just as Vyiliish knew when spiders adorned her boughs with their weaving, and when birds took her twigs to use in their nests, she knew the Holly Queen. She stepped into the hedge, feeling it open to enfold her like an embrace.

The Holly Queen's hair was dark and green and glossy; in it red berries and white flowers twined together. Her eyes were bright, and she was very, very tall. Vyiliish shivered in the chilling presence and the comfort of her power. Here was a might no human could match.

"No single human," the Holly Queen said. "But hundreds? Perhaps." She dropped a kiss on the top of Vyiliish's head; it felt like the most refreshing rain a warm spring could provide.

Vyiliish was unsurprised that her thoughts were not private. It took her a moment to understand what the Holly Queen had said. As the words dropped into her consciousness, her eyes widened; could not even a Power hold off this mortal force? Tears of dew dripped from her eyes, and she gazed at the Holly Queen in shock.

The hedge rippled, and a tall, muscular youth, his skin a polished brown, entered. Acorns clustered in his hair, which was the color of old blood. *The Oak Youth*, she knew. Usually he would be drowsy in autumn. Now his acorn eyes were clear, and his step firm: fully wakened, Vyiliish guessed, by the onslaught of the woodcutters.

"The Summerchild will be here soon," the Oak Youth said. His voice was deep, sonorous, and thrummed all the way through the wood of Vyiliish's core. Vyiliish stared at him, feeling the sap that ran through her warming to his presence. Then she realized the implications of what he had said.

And that was even more of a shock. Normally the Summerchild would be deep in slumber at the precipice of winter, dreaming of green leaves and the frenetic industry of ants. Now the vines were dry, the ants were hiding deep in their hills, and frost sketched flowers every morning on the rust-hued fallen leaves.

"We know why you have come," said a young voice that seemed to come from all round them. The Summerchild drew itself up from the mesh of leaves.

The Summerchild was a gamin figure, leaves and vines stuck or growing to its skin, eyes a constant shift of green, blue, and mud. Though it stood on two legs, it moved in a fluid way, like the slither of a serpent, and its limbs had more joints than a man or a tree spirit. It barely came up to Vyiliish's waist. Nonetheless, like the other Powers, the contrast of its presence made other colors seem faded and sounds muted.

Three Powers seldom met in Wystwood; most were tied to the seasons, and rarely had a reason to stir when theirs was not in the ascendant, except when nature became unbalanced. That was a rare occurrence in Wystwood. The Wolflord, though he did not sleep away any seasons, reached his full might in winter. Together, the strength of these three drew her like water flowing downhill to a stream.

There was a fifth power, Vyiliish knew, but even the oldest trees did not remember the last time it had woken. She could feel the wellspring of power in the mottled rock, the power that fueled the deepest magics of Wystwood. The Earth Stone dreamed, and Wystwood grew out of its visions.

The Holly Queen laid her hand on Vyiliish's forehead; the touch prickled and burned, but it was not uncomfortable. "We know why you have come, Vyiliish."

"We know." The Oak Youth's sonorous voice made it clear that the three were in agreement.

Vyiliish believed them. "How do I help?" she asked. "Is there anything a simple birch spirit can do?" It suddenly occurred to her that she might be intruding where she was not wanted. Surely united, the Powers could fight off the army of woodcutters.

The Holly Queen smiled. "We knew someone would come. We thought it might be you."

Vyiliish had not even realized that the Powers knew her from any elm or ash in the forest. She gazed at the Power, her eyes wide and searching. "Me?"

"You." The Holly Queen laughed in a whisper of leaf on leaf. "You see what few others see. You knew our need, and you came."

"But..." Vyiliish felt even more confused. "Why are the humans acting in this way? Why are they felling Wystwood? Why kill the animals? I have even heard some of them speak of setting fire to whatever is left, and sowing the earth of Wystwood with salt once everything living has been destroyed. Why would they do such a thing?" Her voice rose to a high pitch like the screech of a falcon.

The Summerchild's long, twiggy fingers reached out for Vyiliish's arm, growing extra joints as it did so. "They blame us for what is our nature, and what is theirs." It giggled. "Most humans cannot understand the magics of Wystwood. They come to play, but they want to stop too soon." A loop of vine spiraled upward from its arms, small tendrils twining around each other. "We don't force them to come, and we don't force them to go, but they blame us anyway. They're very foolish."

"I don't understand." Entirely confused, Vyiliish looked to the Holly Queen for an explanation. "These men come to destroy, not to play." Though perhaps she did understand. The Summerchild held no malice, but its play was occasionally dangerous; its careless joy took little heed of consequences to its playmates. But that did not explain so many men, and so much hatred.

The Oak Youth caught her gaze; a hint of green flickered through his eyes. "The woodcutters and the soldiers serve the prince of this country." Before Vyiliish could manage to ask what that meant, he continued, "The country is a place, as Wystwood is a place, but not held together by Powers and the Earth Stone. It is a place where many men dwell; as many as the ants in their hills."

Vyiliish opened her eyes wide. "That many?"

"Yes." The Oak Youth's voice rumbled through his bole, as if the thought was distasteful. "More than you can imagine, little sister mine. They breed quickly, but they are predators, and dangerous ones. Over the years it has been hard to hold the border against them, and it grows harder as their numbers increase."

"For a long time," said the Holly Queen, her tone liquid honey, "they simply feared us. But because fear breeds anger and hatred, we have let them come, in ones or twos or threes. Some of them — "

"Some of them," interrupted the Summerchild, giggling again, "are wonderfully fun. Those with supple minds: children, poets, dreamers." It turned a cartwheel, scattering flowers of red and blue into the air. The flowers had not been there a moment earlier.

The Oak Youth ran a hand through his hair, acorns ripening at his touch. "Most do not have such supple minds. Those are the ones who come to Wystwood to challenge us, to try their strength against the Powers."

"Oh!" Suddenly it began to come clear. "Like boars trying their strength against each other, so that they may mate." That made sense. If men were as ferocious as the great boars, they would not care for rivals near their territory.

"Somewhat." The Holly Queen turned her palms upward. In them was the tusk of a boar. As Vyiliish watched, it shrank and turned into a wolf's claw. "Say rather, Vyiliish, like the wolves, who try their strength, but who hunt together. These men are hunters, and now all of Wystwood is their prey." She passed her hand over the claw; it became a feather, and wafted into the air, dissolving into the sun-shadows of the heartwood.

"You see," said the Oak Youth, "the prince – their pack leader – had a foster brother who rode into the trees, calling challenge to us and seeking to master our magics."

That was something Vyiliish did understand. "Was it something the Summerchild did?" she asked, wondering why the Oak Youth or the Wolflord had not intervened.

The Summerchild laughed scornfully. "It wasn't *that*!" Its ears grew long and pointed, and perked forward. Hunching down, it wrapped its arms around its legs, and wiggled its head into the space in the center of all four limbs. "I *said* they didn't understand Wystwood's magic. It's not what I do, it's what they see." Its upside-down triangle of a face pouted at her.

"And this man," said the Oak Youth, "left after three days, raving of sights no one should see. Not a strong mind, nor a wise one, and not one that could bear defeat of the senses."

"I see," said Vyiliish, for she finally did. "His brother loves him, and bears malice toward the forest which took his mind from him. And so, as pack leader to his people, he leads them in an effort of destruction to what he also now sees as a danger to all of his folk."

"Very good, Vyiliish!" said the Holly Queen, clapping her hands delightedly. "I knew you were one of our clever ones. Now, can you think what needs to be done?"

This was a much harder question, and one which Vyiliish had not thought to answer. "Why do you need me? Is there something I can do which you cannot?"

"Think, Vyiliish," said the Oak Youth softly. "Against the

Wolflord, they bring weapons. Against myself and the Holly Queen, axes, against the Summerchild they will bring fire, and against us all, they will bring salt. There are always more of them. What do we bring that is more powerful?"

Was it a trick question? Vyiliish was only a simple birch spirit, and did not possess the wisdom of the greater trees, but it seemed an obvious answer. "The Earth Stone. But how do we wake it?"

"We are buying time." The Holly Queen looked down from her great height, more imposing than ever.

Vyiliish could only think of how much she adored them all, these Powers of the forest. She waited, dumbly, for their wisdom, for she still could think of nothing at all.

"We hold the border as strongly as we may; if we leave the heartwood, we weaken all." The Oak Youth's wood resonated so loudly that it hurt Vyiliish to be near it. "Our magics here tie us to every living thing within Wystwood's bounds, but not beyond. Humans are not part of the forest; they have never truly belonged here. We need two things; time to wake the Earth Stone, and for one human to bind himself to Wystwood so that we may bring our magics to bear against all who share that blood."

"How?" asked Vyiliish in an almost inaudible rustle.

The Holly Queen took Vyiliish's hands and looked at her green-white skin intently.

"Powers, trees, and animals, all here have given their sap to the Earth Stone. Not so of the men who attack us, and the Earth Stone's power over them is limited. Bring a human to the heartwood, let him offer his sap willingly, and the Earth Stone will be able to act."

Vyiliish realized that this was no mere manner of speaking; the Holly Queen meant that Vyiliish herself must bring the man to the heartwood. But how could she accomplish such a task? She looked at the Holly Queen in bewilderment. "I don't know how. I am willing, but I don't know how."

"We will give you the gifts to accomplish our task." The Holly Queen let go of Vyiliish's hands, and caught her gaze in a stare so intense that Vyiliish felt like a rabbit kitten fascinated by an owl. Her eyes began to hurt, but still she could not look away. She felt a pressure grow inside her head like a sprouting seed, its unfurling roots and branches pushing against her mind with tremendous force. Her vision dimmed with pain. Then, as if it had broken through the earth, the growing gift inside her mind burst through the pain and unfolded to the sunlight.

"The gift of discernment," said the Holly Queen.

Vyiliish looked around at the heartwood. Somehow, the colors had not only deepened, but blossomed into shades and tones that Vyiliish had never known existed, but which seemed illuminated by their own internal light. It was not so much that she saw new colors, but that the interstitial space between the colors she knew had split into new and clearly differentiated hues. She still stared, but now in wonder.

Then she looked at the three Powers, and every other thought fell away.

There were three vortices of whirling light and shadow,

interconnected in all Vyiliish's senses. Threads of light touched and wove like a spider's net. The scent of damp leaves and pine resin mingled with the compelling sweet-acrid smell of autumn flowers. She could hear the breeze, barely wisping through the branches, brush the wings of ladybugs. And below everything else was the pulse of sap whose rhythm precisely matched the Earth Stone's slow, deep somnolence.

Somehow, as if two images lay in one space, she could still see what she had always seen: the Powers as they presented themselves to the denizens of Wystwood. Focusing on their physicality helped Vyiliish to dampen her sudden perceptions and to understand how to interpret what she saw.

"You will know," said the Holly Queen, "which man to choose."

The wind suddenly gusted, blowing Vyiliish's hair into tangles and knots. Smiling, the Oak Youth spread his arms wide. "The gift of persuasion," he told her. An influx of warmth, like the buffeting of summer wind, hit her squarely. She felt her bark swallow it, and the warmth ran through the rings of her wood and into her core.

That was harder to test out; the Powers would not be vulnerable to their own gifts, and there was no one else to try it on. Perhaps she should speak to Amashi later, and see if it worked on him.

"You haven't my gifts yet!" The Summerchild grinned, and sprang at Vyiliish, clinging to her like a baby opossum. Almost immediately, Vyiliish began to feel weak and faint as the Summerchild's limbs lengthened into strangling vines and its hot breath instilled the sensation of burrowing termites drilling Vyiliish's wood from the inside out. Alarm shot through her as she fought for breath. Then she felt a wrench and a painful twist, as if she had been broken and reassembled by a ferocious wind. The Summerchild gave her a kiss and slid from her bole, its limbs retracting to a shorter length. Vyiliish stepped back, terrified.

"The gifts of glamour and beguilement!" the Summerchild said triumphantly. "Now you may seem what you will — at least to the humans. You may appear as a human woman, or a hawk, or a doe, anything you imagine to any man as you choose, as long as your roots remain in Wystwood's soil. And when you call to a man, he will come, and think it his own will. Though be careful not to use it on the one you choose: it must be a willing choice."

Vyiliish was still frightened, but everything in the forest knew of the Summerchild's capriciousness, and the limits of that capriciousness. It would not act contrary to the needs of Wystwood. She nodded and lowered her head.

"Go quickly," said the Holly Queen, "and return soon. We have little time, all of us. We will strive to hold Wystwood while you work, but it must be soon."

There were more questions Vyiliish wanted to ask, but she knew she had been dismissed. Feeling herself felled and re-grown, she hurried away from the heartwood.

She was joined partway through the forest by Amashi, who followed her silently as she stepped through its quiet population of creatures and growing things. There was so much life here that it was hard to imagine what it might become if she did not succeed. With her new discernment, she could feel it all, tangling like roots below the forest floor, rising into towers of great trees, and webbing all into the heartwood and the dreams of the Earth Stone. Amashi's strength was like a mass of deep green roots, holding him firmly to the earth.

Amashi's silence was troubling; he was always one for a joke and a smile. Finally, Vyiliish turned and faced him. "What's wrong?"

His response was subdued. "I was right. Standing before the Powers is dangerous. You're changed, Vyiliish. That day you spent in the heartwood — "

"Day?" Vyiliish simply stared. "I was only there for a turn of shadows!"

Amashi shook his head. "You were there past the setting sun and through the night. What did they do to you?"

"Set me a task." Vyiliish absently ran a hand through her cascading hair. "If it's been another day, more trees have fallen, more animals have died. I have little time. Too many are gone already."

"Brave like an oak spirit, I said." Amashi looked sad. "I was wrong. You're braver. I hope this won't cost you more than you're willing to give."

Vyiliish stopped and turned to stare at Amashi. "What do you mean?"

Amashi put his hands on either side of her face and looked into her eyes. "The Powers aren't like us. They care about Wystwood, and they are concerned with our wellbeing, but each one of us only matters as part of the whole. We're losing our brothers and sisters;

they're losing a piece of the forest."

"But they know us." Vyiliish shook her head, softly so that she did not jar Amashi's hands. "Each of us. They know our names."

"And they will remember our names through eternity. But that doesn't mean that they will spare us — any of us — if we stand between them and the welfare of Wystwood."

"We won't." But Vyiliish knew what he meant. She could still feel the Summerchild's strangling hold, and the pain of the Holly Queen forcing her mind into a larger understanding of truth. Yes, she had asked what she could do, but they had not in turn asked her if she would accept their gifts.

It was too late now to worry. "I have a task," she repeated, to remind herself as well as Amashi. She gently lifted his hands from her face and turned toward the outskirts of the forest. "Don't hinder me, Amashi."

He continued to follow her, his silence more troubling than words. Vyiliish did not look back, but was nonetheless aware of him, with that strange new sense that had been instilled in her by the Holly Queen.

The edge of Wystwood was closer than she had realized; the men had felled dozens of trees since the previous day. Vyiliish looked out on a barren plain of trunks and stumps, leaves withered, and fruits spoiled. Dead animals lay everywhere, left where they had fallen instead of being returned to the forest earth as was natural.

She began to have a deep ache, as if woodpeckers had riddled her bark. The ache intensified, become a sucking sense of absence, and a drain of sap into sand. Wystwood's border had not contracted — the Powers still held it fast — but it was like rotten wood, and felt as if it could crumble with a touch.

The men had moved on, leaving a wasteland behind them; this was not where Vyiliish needed to be. Far from avoiding them, she needed to be in the midst of the humans, to select and persuade the one who would help them. But they hated Wystwood enough that she wondered how she could find any to come with her to the heartwood. Vyiliish hoped that the Oak Youth's gift would prove strong enough for the purpose.

Still followed by Amashi, she turned from the broken bodies of her brothers and sisters and retreated back into the wood, following the ache until she found the human source. Here, metal and wood met in dull thunks, hawks screamed, and a tremendous bear roared a challenge from its bloodstained and foam-fleck maw. A deep red cedar spirit wailed in terror and flickered out like a firefly. The Wolflord lowered his head and speared his sharply honed antlers into the flesh of a large, muscular swordsman, goring him in the intestines. Those closest to the man shouted in horror; Vyiliish remembered that they could not see the Powers. The man must have seemed to explode from the inside.

She centered herself in the soil and thought of the Holly Queen, asking her gift to reveal what was needed. Agony washed in and out of her body. Then she felt strong hands grasp her from behind and hold her tight; Amashi's touch grounded her. Gratefully, she reached back and gave his hand a squeeze. Opening her eyes as wide as she could, she *looked* at the mass of men, who seemed to her as indistinguishable as flies on carrion.

Her gaze was drawn almost immediately to one of the woodcutters. He was small; her perceptions told her that he was young, perhaps a sapling, or an older cub. A cub, she decided. The green light of Wystwood flickered on his face and glimmered in his blue eyes. He seemed unhappy, and reminded her of a young walnut spirit, lean, browned, and strong.

"That's the one," she murmured to Amashi.

She was not sure how to use the gift of the Summerchild, but she must use a seeming if she was to talk to the cub. She could not speak with him among other humans, however. She must lure him away to a safer place, then use the Oak Youth's gift of persuasion.

As if the Summerchild itself sat in her mind, the image of a woodland hare formed in her mind. Without completely understanding what she did, Vyiliish concentrated on two things: the glamour of the hare, and the need to prevent other men from seeing her at all. She felt herself into the hare, thinking of its powerful hind legs, its long ears, the speed of its running. This was a creature a predator would chase, and these men were clearly predators. She wanted the lure of the chase to be irresistible. She felt Wystwood's power feed the illusion, strengthening it not only with sensory potency, but with the Summerchild's compelling beguilement.

The human cub gave a startled cry, then dropped his axe. None seemed to notice as he bolted off after Vyiliish; Amashi followed them both. She led the cub deeper into the forest, instinctively seeking out a deep grove where it was impossible to see the sun, and from where he was unlikely to find his way. She darted under a bush, and transformed her appearance to that of a human woman with autumn-gold hair and snow-pale skin. She did not know what he might find beautiful; for that, she would have to rely on the glamour.

His eyes were mazed with light and Wystwood's magics. Vyiliish reached out one hand and touched each of his eyes in turn, willing him to see her new seeming. As she did so, his eyes grew wider and wider, till they seemed to stretch painfully.

"Lady!" he said, and dropped to his knees. "Forgive me!"

Now that she had him here, Vyiliish did not know what words to say to convince him to help her. Still, she must try. She smiled and reached down to touch his hair. It was very like any animal's, a soft brown the color of ash bark.

"Why was I drawn to you?" she asked, half to herself.

The cub's eyes filled with dew. "Will you forgive me, lady?"

Across the grove, Vyiliish could see Amashi frowning at her. She ignored him, keeping her attention on the cub. "Forgive you?" she asked. "For what?"

"For cutting your trees," he said. "I did not want to join, but my uncle said if I did not, the others would say I was like my father, a tree-lover, and they might do me harm. I didn't know that the goddess of the wood might come to me. Forgive me, lady!"

His words made little sense to Vyiliish; the only ones she truly understood were 'tree lover'. Clearly she had chosen the right one. "You love the trees?" she asked. "Truly love them?"

The cub's gaze was guileless. "Your trees? Yes, lady. I love them. What the prince is doing is wrong. What may I do to atone for my part in this?"

She felt a sudden, brief warmth at his words; he might be just a cub, but he was wiser than the angry, hate-filled army of woodcutters. As she opened her mouth to use the Oak Youth's gift of persuasion, Vyiliish felt a pang of shame and reluctance. If she led this cub to the heartwood, what happened to him would be her fault. She was not so young that she thought the Powers would care about what happened to a single human cub when they would let their own fight and die for the safety of Wystwood. But she was a birch spirit who bent with the wind, and neither a fighter nor a killer.

She looked across at Amashi. To her senses, his concern framed his spirit much as his needles framed his face, and his expression was grim. He should go back to his tree, she thought, and wait for her. Back to his tree —

That was when she realized. The destruction of the forest's edge had changed her landmarks so thoroughly that she had not understood how far the men had encroached. Amashi's pine was not so close to the heartwood as her birch; perhaps two days away at the pace their axes moved. Perhaps less.

He knew it, and had not told her. Terror at the thought of losing Amashi flooded her. She could do nothing to stand between his tree and the woodcutters; she had not enough substance. There was only one way she could fight: by bringing this cub to the heartwood.

"You wish to atone?" she asked, the sweetness of honey in her words. "What are you willing to give?" Her accents promised forgiveness and reward. She hated the implicit lie.

"Anything," he answered, innocently as any larva in the spring of life. "Whatever you ask of me."

"Then come with me." Vyiliish reached out her hand. "Come with me to the heartwood, and offer your sap there to the Earth Stone." Again, her tones suggested that everything would be well, if he would only come.

The cub's brows rose into questions, but he only nodded. "I will follow you, lady. I trust you."

Better you trusted the wolves and bears, she thought. Outwardly, she nodded. Inwardly, she wondered whether she was becoming as damaged as the Wystwood border. She held out her hand for him to take; though she still had no substance, the beguilement bridged the difference between them. His hand felt unexpectedly warm and alive, like the paw of a squirrel, or the shallow heartbeat of a mouse.

"Come," she said, and led him to the heartwood.

The cub looked back and forth in obvious wonder at the grove of oak, holly, and clinging vines. He showed no fear; clearly he trusted Vyiliish. Amashi had dropped back before reaching it. Vyiliish was not sure if that was because he did not want to face the Powers, or because he was unhappy at her actions. Either was plausible.

When the Oak Youth stepped forward, the cub did not see him. Vyiliish turned her gaze toward the Oak Youth, hoping that he would tell her that this cub was not acceptable, and to take him away. But the Oak Youth instead put a hand on Vyiliish's head, sending a quivering down her entire bole. "You chose well, sweet birch," he told her. "Take the boy to the Earth Stone."

Vyiliish nodded, understanding that she must follow this through to its end. "Cub," she said, "follow."

As she approached the Earth Stone, she could feel a difference in the grove. A singing buzz thrummed through the soil beneath her feet, setting the trees, the stones, and even the air moving in its rhythm. The Oak Youth strode beside them, shedding acorns which fell softly into the silence. Soon the Holly Queen joined them, and the Summerchild, half-seen, but rustling among the vines and brambles.

The cub heard something, clearly; his head swiveled from side to side, and his eyes were opened wide in apparent fright. But his set, determined expression told Vyiliish that he would not turn and run, but would do what she asked of him. Her own expression, she guessed, was much the same. She felt a bond with him; as he obeyed her, thinking perhaps that she was one of the Powers, so did she obey the true Powers of Wystwood.

The Wolflord darted in just before they reached the Earth Stone; his muzzle was matted with blood, and his golden eyes were fierce. He gave Vyiliish an approving glance, then turned his predatory attention toward the human cub, watching each movement intently.

The Earth Stone loomed before them as soon as they parted the vines. Immediately, Vyiliish could tell that this was the source of the dynamic hum within the grove. The Earth Stone was awake, and its intentions were far stronger than its dreams.

Whether it was Vyiliish's enhanced senses or a change in the Earth Stone itself, it did not look the same to her. It still had a rough, mottled surface, but the colors had deepened from gray and gray-brown to much deeper browns, blues, and greens. A veining of red gleamed brightly even though it was barely a thread in the rock. Though it had no eyes, she could feel it watching her with a keen interest; she had no doubt it knew exactly who she was, and why she was there.

"What do I do now?" she whispered, hoping that one of the Powers would simply take over.

She looked at the cub; he was shaking hard. "What must I do, lady?" he asked, still in the same trusting tones.

A tingle ran through the earth underneath Vyiliish, took root in her feet, and infused her with the surety of what she must do. Around her were the other four Powers: to the east, the Oak Youth, to the south, the Summerchild, to the west, the Wolflord, and to the north, the Holly Queen. Vyiliish could feel their configuration, the Earth Stone in the center, as part of a great web of power which was waiting for the last spark to fire the magics that would defeat the human army.

Vyiliish hesitated. *For Amashi*, she told herself, and put her will into the keeping of the Earth Stone.

She reached out and snapped off one of the thorns from the dense but dormant vegetation. "Give me your arms," she told the cub. He held them backs up; she turned them so the palms were uppermost. For a moment she looked at the veins of red threading his wrists. Taking the thorn, she scored both wrists hard, ignoring the gasp of pain that the cub gave. He flinched only a little, and kept his arms steady.

"Now," she said, "place your arms on the stone, and heal the harm your people have done to this forest."

He met her glance just once, and Vyiliish realized with startlement that, young as he was, this cub understood intuitively what she was asking, just as if he had been an owlet, or a fox kit. He loved Wystwood, too, and that was what the Powers had wanted her to find.

He placed both wrists down on the Earth Stone.

The surge of magic almost knocked Vyiliish off her roots. The human cub stood, transfixed, as the heartwood pulsed with power, sweeping Vyiliish and the cub both into its eddies. She could feel the Earth Stone drawing the cub's sap out through the open veins in his wrists; it spread across the mottled surface like a sheen of red dew, draining his body.

Vyiliish felt her own sap turn to a stream of stone, running through her so slowly that it made the speed of winter-slowed sap seem impossibly quick. And yet, stone could change in an instant, avalanching down a steep hill, cascading through a tumbling stream, cracking from an assault of ice. Now the Earth Stone was moving swiftly, gaining momentum as it chose its path.

The other Powers were the roots that held the soil of Wystwood together, made of so many connections it would be impossible to untangle them. Through them, and through the earth itself, Vyiliish perceived what was happening.

As the cub's sap flowed through the Earth Stone, the Earth Stone drew the blood deep into itself, and into the roots of Wystwood, where it became part of the life that fed and connected everything in the forest. That infusion made a firm and strong connection with all the humans attacking Wystwood, where before there had been nothing. There was no wish on the part of the Earth Stone for retribution: only for restitution. And since the humans were both within Wystwood's borders, and now connected by human sap, they were beneath the Earth Stone's power.

Comprehension was beginning to come to Vyiliish. To the Earth Stone, balance was simple. With sap and blood, root and soil, branch and limb, it reached out, sending tendrils of magic through the soil and into the body of each man who wielded axe, sword, or spear against Wystwood. Vyiliish was held, transfixed, in the web of magic as the Earth Stone's awareness crept into bone and muscle and flesh, comprehending what they were, and what they might become.

In a mighty swell, the enchantments of all five Powers funneled through the tunnel of the cub's human self, and every human in Wystwood was transformed. Bones stretched into wood, blood thinned into sap, skin roughened into bark. Their feet spread, dug into the ground, split into roots. The few who seemed quick to understand what was happening cried out in horror; most were caught before that understanding could reach them. Faster than a squirrel could scale a trunk, the humans became an army of trees, replacing those they had felled.

Then the Earth Stone hummed a softer song, one of the

forgetfulness of winter and of long sleep. When they awoke there might be questions, but it was clear that the Earth Stone meant them to learn through sleep what they had not learned in their human lives.

The Powers finally released Vyiliish. The Earth Stone's hum softened to the sound of bees in their hives, and to the rush of breeze in the leaves. She could feel it subsiding, resuming its eons-long slumber. Its colors returned to muted grays and browns. The other Powers, in perfect step, moved more closely to Vyiliish and the Earth Stone.

Suddenly remembering the human cub, she looked again at where he had been standing. Instead of a cub, a fire-crowned ash sapling stood beside the Earth Stone, its arms raised in joyful salute. Before Vyiliish's startled eyes, a tall young ash spirit stepped from the tree, looking at himself with wonder.

It was done. Vyiliish gave the ash spirit a rueful grin, then turned and sped out of the heartwood. The gifts given by the Powers were still with her, she could tell, but they were less burdensome now that her task was done. There was only one thing she still wanted. She ran as fast as she could toward Amashi's tree.

He was waiting. For now, it was enough.

air Trade

Mari dodged Gawter's fist, which missed by a hand-span and hit the wall beside her head. Cursing, he swung again, grazing Mari's cheek and knocking her off balance. She cringed, but hoped that her husband would continue to attack her rather than to harm the baby, who lay in his cradle unaware of the fight. She could take Gawter's blows; Anwel could not.

Eight-year-old Bea stood against the far wall, her fist at her mouth, her pale hair in disarray. At Gawter's second strike, she wailed, "Don't hurt Ma!" and rushed to Mari's side to wrap her arms around her mother. Enfolding their daughter in a tight embrace, Mari stuck out her chin and stared defiantly at Gawter, more angry that he was frightening the girl than at his attack on her. Mari's cheek throbbed, and she guessed that a bruise was settling there.

Gawter was a big man with the heavy muscle of a woodcutter, but he seemed to deflate as he regarded them. He turned away, his shoulders slumping, and sat down on the long bench which flanked the room's heavy, weathered table.

Mari cautiously relaxed, guessing from long experience that this bout of temper had run its course. There was little room to escape each other in the small, neat cottage where Mari worked so hard to make a comfortable home for her husband and children. The table took up nearly half the room, and the stone fireplace and hearth most of the rest; Anwel's cradle occupied a small space next to the hearth, under rafters laden with herbs, vegetables, and cured meat.

"How can I believe you, Mari?" Gawter's voice was plaintive, and Mari's own temper immediately evaporated in a cloud of sympathy. Her husband, not a patient man, had tried to trust Mari in the long two months since Anwel was born, but town gossip and speculation had finally driven him to question her word explosively.

"Isn't nine years enough?" She smoothed Bea's hair and moved to where her husband sat. "Haven't I been a good wife? Haven't I been faithful? Lands, Gawter, between caring for your children and keeping your house, when would I have time to lie with another man?" She gave the baby a quick glance over her shoulder, to reassure herself that he was still all right.

"You and me, Mari. The children. Everyone in my family. We've all got bark-brown eyes and hair like dandelions gone to seed." Gawter stared at her helplessly, as if willing her to understand. "Anwel's eyes are blue, and his hair is crow's wing black. How can that be?"

Mari did not know either, but she was sure of her own innocence. "Children are sometimes born with dark hair, and it lightens. And all of the children were born with blue eyes."

"Dark blue. Not that sky shade. Not clear."

A wind blew through the window, fluttering the blue and white curtains over the table. Mari put a tentative hand on her husband's shoulder, and wondered whether to send Bea outside. Probably not; her presence would help Gawter to stay calm. "I told you the truth. Anwel is your child, and no other man's. What else is possible?"

Gawter let out a long, shaken breath. Turning toward the table, he crossed his arms and leaned his head onto them. "I don't want to think of you with anyone else," he told her in a long exhalation of breath.

Mari knew the signs that Gawter's temper was subsiding. "His features are a bit like your mother's. She had some dark kin, isn't that right?" She did not know any more than her husband where Anwel had gotten his looks, but they must have come from somewhere. Sensibly, the baby's appearance must hearken back to some ancestor or another.

Gawter nodded his head where it lay pillowed on his arms. "Perhaps." He sounded unconvinced.

The two younger children peeked their heads warily through the door. Mari looked at Bea, and saw that her daughter was crying quietly. She bit her lip and scowled at Gawter's back. She did not like her children to witness these fights. It frightened them, and they could not possibly understand why their father was so angry.

She went to the crib and picked up Anwel. He was a placid and happy baby, the easiest of the four. Anwel never cried. She picked him up and put her finger to his mouth. If he sucked at it, she would know that he was hungry. It was the only way she could tell he needed to be fed; unlike many children, he did not suck unless he wished to eat. She would have preferred him to be fussy and fretful.

Gawter sat up and turned toward Mari. "You're a good woman," he said to her. "I know that. Perhaps Anwel does look like my mother." He patted Mari's thigh, and smiled at her with the lightning-quick change of mood that could transform him from a frightening and violent stranger to the gentle man Mari had married nine years ago this summer.

Mari relaxed and returned her attention to Anwel, who was now sucking at her finger. "Look, he's hungry." She shifted the baby into one arm and opened her bodice to expose a breast, at which she positioned Anwel. He latched on strongly and Mari relaxed against the mutual comfort of feeding.

Gawter frowned again. "Mari, it's not natural for him to be that silent. What's wrong with the child?"

Mari wanted to know the answer herself. It had taken her three weeks to realize that Anwel was not waking her at night with his cry; three weeks during which the baby had not eaten enough.

"I don't know," she responded. A pang of worry tugged at her throat. "I've been meaning to take him to the midwife. If you can spare me for an afternoon, that is."

Sighing, Gawter nodded. "I'm not fond of the old hen, but Libby knows about babies. You may go, but try to keep to the point, and don't let her gossip half the day away. Bea can watch her little brother and sister, can't you, little one?"

Bea nodded, her dark eyes wide. She took her responsibilities as the eldest very seriously. Mari smiled at her, and gestured at the door with one elbow. "Bea, go make your brother and sister wash in the pump, and when they get hungry, you may give them the heel of the loaf from the breadbox. And feed the chickens." She hoped fervently that Libby could give her some answer to the mystery of Anwel's nature.

Outside Widow Libby's cottage door, Mari waited with Anwel in her arms. She hesitated before knocking, fearing the midwife would find something deeply wrong with her child that no one could fix. Still, she had to know; ignorance would not help her child. Taking a deep breath, she rapped sharply on the stout oaken door.

Libby answered almost immediately, ushering Mari in with a gesture and a warm smile. The midwife was plump and neat, the apron which covered her skirt spotless, and her gray-streaked hair gathered tightly in a bun. As always, her presence made Mari feel unkempt and disorganized. Mari was only too aware of the wisps of blonde hair escaping from her own untidy coif, and of the milk stain spotting the bodice of her dress.

"Sit down, dear," Libby said, gesturing to a rocker which sat before the window. She herself sat on a long bench, similar to the one in Mari's cottage. "What's the matter, Mari?"

Weak sun, struggling through an overcast sky, lanced into the room past cheerful but faded curtains which sported a bright pattern of daisies. The day was warm, and no fire smoldered on the hearth.

"I want you to examine Anwel," Mari said, deciding that it was easiest to simply launch into the problem, rather than to equivocate. "I think something is wrong with him, and I want to know what."

"Oh, my dear!" Libby said in a startled tone. "Is he ill? He was healthy enough at birth; I looked him over head to toe, and every part of him was perfect. What makes you think something is wrong?"

Mari looked down at her infant. Anwel was beautiful. His large eyes held an extraordinary fringe of dark lashes, and his features, though fine, would settle one day into manly strength. A mop of unusually thick dark hair covered the top of his head, but he had none of the soft down that mantled the skin of many infants. He certainly looked perfect. But Mari knew better.

"He doesn't cry," she said flatly. Her older three children had howled when hungry, when wet or soiled, and occasionally for no apparent reason. Mari knew all the cries, from the catlike newborn mew to the older children's bawling explosions of distress. But little Anwel was different. All he ever did was to smile his infant smile, showing no discomfort or desire. As Gawter had said, it was unnatural.

"He cried when he was born," Libby replied. "Remember that I said he was strong and healthy? He bawled like a soldier giving orders. Howled, even." She drew her brows together in a concerned expression. "Every child cries, Mari. Some children cry more, some less, some never seem to stop. But the only tearless child is a lifeless one."

Anwel blinked up at Mari with clear blue eyes, as if she were the sun, and the day cloudless. The look flooded Mari with overwhelming love; she kissed the top of his soft head, and tucked him closer to her body. "I know," she said unhappily. "But he doesn't cry, Libby. I mean it. Not ever."

Libby frowned. "You're right; I need to look at him." She rose and took the baby from Mari's arms. Anwel blew a contented bubble as the midwife unswaddled him and began to manipulate his legs and feet. The infant kicked out, but not strongly: Libby's frown deepened.

Mari waited, almost afraid to breathe as she waited for Libby to finish. Five years ago she had lost one child in infancy, and she did not think she could bear to lose another. She watched anxiously as the midwife looked inside Anwel's mouth, ears, and nose, scrutinized his fingernails, and carefully checked his genitals.

"He's very thin," Libby muttered. "You're not having trouble with your milk, are you?"

Mari shook her head; her milk was more than ample. "And he does eat a lot." As if answering the thought, her milk let down. "I don't know how he can eat so much and still be thin."

Libby frowned. "What does Gawter think about all of this? I see he's been at you again." She gestured toward Mari's bruised cheek. "Doesn't he think you're taking good enough care of his child?"

"That's another thing," Mari told her, exasperated. "Gawter doesn't like Anwel's hair and eyes. He wonders why they aren't like the others."

Libby snorted. "That man is a fool. I've heard the rumors too, but no one with sense should listen to them. He should know that he'll be felling trees of pure gold before you are ever unfaithful." She wrinkled her forehead thoughtfully. "Mari, There's something that's troubling me about all of this. Something I've heard about but never seen." She pulled a bronze hairpin from her bun. "You won't like this, but I must test something. I hope I'm wrong."

She unwrapped Anwel's foot and turned the sole toward herself. Before Mari could stop her, Libby took the hairpin and stuck it firmly in Anwel's heel.

Mari found herself snatching Anwel out of Libby's hands before she even realized she was moving. A spot of blood formed on Anwel's heel, slowly beading and trickling down his sole.

Rage suffused her. "How could you do that, Libby? He's only a baby!"

Long lines formed down the sides of the midwife's nose. "He's not crying."

Mari's anger stopped cold. She looked at Anwel, and realized that Libby was right. Anwel's features were pinched and drawn, but no tears came from his eyes. She looked up at Libby, hoping the widow could make sense of what had happened. But Libby's face was somber, and her lips were pursed.

"What is it?" Mari asked, fearing the answer. "What you did — that told you what was wrong, didn't it?"

Libby nodded. "I'm sorry, dear. I never thought I'd see anything like this. But I know the lore, and I'm afraid I know what this means." She closed her eyes, then opened them again. "Mari, this child is a changeling."

At first Mari could not understand the words. "A changeling?" She too knew the tales, but they made no sense when speaking of Anwel. Then suddenly the words sorted themselves out in her head, and she realized what Libby was saying.

Horrified, she remembered the stories told to her as a child. There was a race of magical people, the Hillfolk; they were said to be beautiful and soulless, and were known to wreak havoc on mortals.

Sometimes they carried off newborn children and left wooden effigies in their stead, or strange, weak creatures who were only superficially like the children they replaced.

Dismay flooded her; Anwel was no changeling! She had labored to birth him, had held him night after night, suckled him, cleaned him, loved him. He was her own true child; how could anyone doubt that?

"Remembering," Libby said, sorrow in her voice, "I can see it. He was so strong when he was born, and he had that hair, but it lightened as soon as it dried. I thought perhaps it would fall out — it often does. And now he is overly thin, his hair is black, and his eyes watch everything we do. And he doesn't cry, which means he has no soul." She sighed. "Mari, you have to accept it."

Mari looked hard at Anwel; the baby smiled a sweet, toothless smile that she could feel all the way into her heart. She kissed his forehead, and he cooed. Then she looked down and saw where his blood had trickled onto his swaddling blanket. Fear drummed through her veins, as she wondered if Libby were right.

"If you're right..." She did not want to say the words, but she needed to know. It made sense. If this baby were indeed a changeling, it meant that her true child was somewhere with the Hillfolk. The thought shivered down her skin and lodged icily in the pit of her stomach. "What do I do? How do I get the real Anwel back?" Behind this thought lay the terror that Gawter would find out. He would certainly blame her.

Libby stood and walked to the window, where she looked out silently. Mari waited, hoping that Libby would reconsider and give her another explanation for Anwel's strange behavior.

Finally, Libby said, without turning around, "There are two ways of which I have heard. The safer of the two is to torment the child; to scratch him and burn him and squeeze him, and to make him suffer enough so that he will call to his mother and compel her to return. The Hillfolk have a code; they must trade one child for another. If the mother takes hers, she must return yours."

Mari's breath almost stopped. The thought of harming a helpless infant, even one of the Hillfolk, horrified her. She shook her head.

"I don't like it either," said Libby, "but neither do I like leaving your true human child with a soulless phantom. Consider it, Mari. Please consider it."

"And the second way?" Mari was not sure she wanted to hear any more, but she needed to know.

Libby finally turned and faced Mari. Mari could see that her jaw was set. "It's far more dangerous, dear. It's not something you want to do."

"It's not something I can do if you won't tell me," Mari responded tartly. "You're not the only one who can tell me. Widow Grisha knows the stories, as does Old Lagh. If you don't tell me, I'll ask them."

The midwife frowned, then strode to her chair and sat back down crisply. "I have little choice, it seems." She shook her head. "The second way is to bring the changeling to Crown Hill under a full moon, and to lave him with water from the spring which has its source there." She cleared her throat. "Or so I have been told. The water has a property — it will strip away any glamor that has been laid on the child. Once the glamor is gone, the Hillfolk must take him back, because he will be exposed as one of them to the eyes of decent people."

She hesitated and tucked a single strand of hair into her bun. "In addition to that property, if you bathe your eyes in that spring, they will never again be deceived." She shuddered. "You know how steep Crown Hill is. If you took a wrong step, you could fall to your death." She twisted her hands in her apron. "Because the water is so potent, the Hillfolk guard it, and they will defend it against good human folk. If you succeed in climbing to the top, you will face their anger."

"But the water won't hurt Anwel — the baby?" Mari shifted the infant onto her shoulder and smoothed his back.

"I think not," said Libby. "But the attempt might hurt *you*."

Mari moved the baby back down to where she could see his face, and was rewarded with another of the sweet smiles that said she was the most important being in creation. In that moment, she made her decision: she would go to Crown Hill.

"I must try," she said.

Libby did not answer, but turned silently back to the window.

A few nights later, Mari stood with the baby at the foot of Crown Hill, under the streaming light of the full moon. The hill was an old, weathered tor which jutted up from a sheep pasture like the unassailable walls of some ancient fortress. It was not impossible to climb, but it was extremely dangerous, as its rocks were jagged and split, and the path was littered with thistles, sharp grass, and scree.

She had crept out of the house after Gawter was abed, hoping that he would not hear her leave; for the first time, she was glad that the baby did not cry. Wrapping the infant in a warm blanket, she had walked carefully from the house, taking as much care as she could that the door did not squeak or slam behind her.

Now, looking up, she was uncertain of her decision. It would be hard enough to scramble up the path in her everyday skirts, but with the baby in her arms she was not sure how she would manage. Still, if she did not, her own child was in danger.

"Waiting won't mend clothes," she said aloud, and took a deep breath. She put the baby across her shoulder, holding him firmly with her left arm, and set her foot on the bottom of the path. Already the loose rock beneath her boots threw her off-balance, and caused her ankles to wobble.

She intended to go slowly and carefully, but almost at once she slid, barely managing to keep her balance without dropping the child. Setting her teeth, she determined that she would reach the hilltop even if she was forced to climb on her hands and knees.

After that, she moved even more slowly, making sure each foot was firmly seated before moving the other. It took an agonizingly long time to get even a short way; soon her feet began to cramp, and her left arm to ache. Mari started to wonder if she would even make it to the top before moonset. She looked back the way she had come, and drew a sharp, frightened breath; she was higher than she had realized. Quickly she swallowed against dizziness, and turned her head back to the slope in front of her. A stone behind her loosened and bounced back in the direction she had come.

In two places, the slope was so steep that she could reach out and touch the path with her free hand. The arm which held the baby was locked in place, and throbbed wildly. Her breath hoarsened in the night air, and rasped in her throat and chest as she panted harder and harder.

Finally, as the moon climbed over the hill, she reached the crest. Dragging herself onto the relatively flat summit, she rolled onto her back and laid the baby on her stomach. Beyond, she could hear the spring, a soft plinking splash that flowed down the other side of the hill to become a steep-walled stream. Slowly she turned her head to look. The baby gurgled and kicked his heels.

The spring was a bright glint at the edge of a dark vortex. Mari inhaled deeply, put the baby on the ground beside her, and sat up.

She could smell the tang of rock-borne water. The wind sang a wild tune in her ears as it gusted over the hilltop. Mari knew she would be terribly stiff in the morning; but in the morning she would have her child back. Anwel.

Picking the infant up, she brought him to the lip of the spring. The stone here was smooth, not jagged and splintered; instead of gray, it had become a crystal-flecked brown and black. As she turned her head, Mari thought she could see streaks of light, but when she looked straight at them, they were gone.

She took a deep breath and gazed into the spring. The stone seemed darker where the water spilled, welling slowly out of the rock like tears from sorrowful eyes. Wisps of vapor formed and dispersed again as the water eddied, giving the illusion that Mari was looking at minute clouds against a miniature night sky.

She checked the baby's blanket, then laid him on the ground, careful that only the cloth would touch the damp stone. Cupping her hands, she reached down to scoop up some of the water.

"Mari, no!" Gawter's voice behind her startled Mari into falling forward. She caught herself on the edge of the spring. Water splashed into her eyes and ran down her chin.

Startled and frightened, she glanced down at the baby. With shock, she realized that he looked different; though he was still a beautiful child, with blue eyes and dark hair, his looked less like Anwel. His features were finer, his fingers longer, and his ears curled back like unfolding leaf buds. She stared, even Gawter's presence forgotten.

Then Gawter spun her around and slapped her hard on the cheek. Mari's gaze snapped back to her husband. Gawter's face was flushed with dark red and his eyes were shadowed with fatigue; he was breathing hard. He slapped Mari again, harder.

"What are you doing?" he shouted, his voice distorted with anger. "Are you mad? What are you doing with the baby on this hilltop, at this spring? Don't you know this is a haunt of the Hillfolk?" He took her by the shoulders and began to shake her so hard that Mari's head was jolted painfully back and forth. She tried to jerk away, but was afraid that she would fall into the spring. She could not think how to answer Gawter's questions.

Gawter turned her around and shoved her to the ground. Mari's vision went briefly white with pain, as her hip hit the hard, rocky ground. As Gawter lifted his foot, she braced for a kick, knowing that any attempt to evade or to fight back would result in a more severe beating. Something flickered at the corner of her sight, but she was more concerned with Gawter's anger. She shut her eyes.

The kick did not come; Mari opened her eyes. Gawter stood with lids closed in a serene face. He breathed evenly, as if he were asleep, though he still stood. Mari gaped. Then, turning her head, she saw the woman who stood behind her.

The woman was tall and slender, with dark hair that hung loose to her knees. Her face was angular and delicate, her skin a milk-pale that had a blue cast under the flooding moonlight. She wore an azure gown, made of a shimmering fabric that Mari could not identify. Then Mari saw her eyes — a clear, pale blue, fringed with the longest lashes she had ever seen — and realized who she must be. This was the baby's mother.

The woman stepped forward and scooped up the infant from where he lay on the ground. Turning back to Mari, she smiled a sweet, winsome smile. She kissed the baby's forehead. "He looks well," she said.

Mari's pulse began to drum through her temples. "What did you do to my husband?" Her breath scraped in and out of her throat. Gawter might be difficult, but she did not want him hurt. Then her confused thoughts converged, and she stood up, despite a sharp pain in her hip. "Where is my child?"

If a stream could have laughed, it would have sounded like this woman's mirth. "Your husband sleeps. Your child is safe. I would never let any harm come to such a precious nursling."

Mari could barely breathe. She was terrified that this woman could harm her as easily as she had put Gawter to sleep. At the same time, she desperately hoped that somehow she could convince the Hillfolk woman to return Anwel to her. But unexpectedly, she felt a twinge in her chest at the thought that she must give up the beautiful child she had loved and nursed for the last two months. Even knowing that he was a child of the Hillfolk did not ease the loss she was already feeling.

"Why?" she asked softly. "Why take my Anwel? Why leave your own child?"

The woman bent her head over the baby. She put out a forefinger, and the infant grasped it, cooing happily. A spasm of jealousy shivered through Mari.

The woman turned her gaze on Mari, catching her with a fascination that Mari could not even wish to break. "You are a good mother, and have strong milk," she said simply. "And our infants resemble each other. That will be important as my little one grows older."

Mari stared at her. "I don't understand."

The Hillfolk woman sighed. "It's hard for us to have children, and sometimes their blood is weak." She smoothed her hand over the baby's head. "Those children usually die if they stay with us." Her eyes seemed to look past Mari into the realm of memory. "Our milk is thin, and our constitutions delicate. We are not like you mortals, who give birth many times, and whose abilities to feed all your children stretch with necessity." She took a deep breath. "You are a mother. Would you watch your child die if you could do anything to prevent it?"

A surge of sympathy took Mari by surprise. She shook her head, not sure if she should be agreeing or not, but beginning to understand. What mother would not do anything in her power to protect her child? In response, her caution rose; this might be part of some deadly snare into which she meant to pull Mari. Still, the baby's condition spoke to the Hillfolk mother's honesty. "He's so thin," she said.

The woman flashed a beautiful smile, a mirror of her infant's expression. "Not so much as he was when he came to you, my Brascêt." She examined his little fingernails, stroking each finger one by one. "He is a full moon older than your son, for all he looks younger. With your strong milk, he grows bigger."

It had not occurred to Mari that the child had his own name. "Brascêt?" she asked slowly. She shook her head. "Where is Anwel?" Disquiet was growing in her mind, and she was afraid the woman was casting some subtle glamor over her. "Why did you have to take him?"

"He is fine." The Hillfolk woman looked at her kindly. "Unlike our children, your mortal children thrive on very little." She sighed. "Your infant is well, and is cared for not only by me, but by my mother and sisters and maidservants. He will be loved and educated, taught letters and philosophy, music, and the skills of the hunt. He will have fine things no mortal noble can even imagine. He will live a long, healthy life, free of pain and disease. And he will be happy."

It sounded wonderful, but Mari was still confused and uncertain if the woman spoke the truth. She took a step forward. "Why did you take him? If this child — Brascêt — needs only to be nursed by a mortal, why did you not ask? Why exchange the two children?"

The woman lifted a sharp gaze to Mari. "Would you have nursed the soulless child of a Hillfolk woman if you did not think he was your own?"

It was true; there was not much Mari could answer to that. She dropped her own gaze to the stones at her feet. "What now?" she asked, fearing the answer.

The woman turned her face aside; it shone palely in the moonlight. "I must find another mortal woman with whom to trade, though it is not easy to find suitable mothers. But Brascêt will die if I do not."

"And us?"

For the first time, the woman turned toward Gawter. "Why are mortals so angry?"

It was not what Mari expected her to say. She gaped. "What do you mean?"

"You say we have no souls," said the Hillfolk woman, almost as if she spoke to herself. "Yet this man, who claims to love you, is so angry with you that he hurts you constantly. You are angry with him for hurting you, yet you allow him to touch you with violence, and do not defend yourself. I have always wanted to know — why?"

The sudden change of subject gave Mari the same sense of disorientation she might have felt in a dream. She seized on the one thing that made sense. "Is it true that you have no souls?"

The woman regarded her with a grave demeanor. "We love; we mourn; we hope. What do you believe?"

Mari did not know. The woman was so beautiful and so sad, but how could Mari trust her? Perhaps she was a Hillfolk sorceress, trying to convince her to accept a child who would be a serpent in the sparrow's nest. Or perhaps she wanted Mari to give up all claim to Anwel, making him, in some arcane way, no longer human. Beauty might hide a dark spirit, like poison in the enticing berries of a yew.

Another solution tugged at Mari's mind. "Give me back my Anwel," she said, "and perhaps I will help you nurse this one. I have enough milk." She was not sure this was a good idea either. Gawter would be terribly angry, and might prove dangerous to the Hillfolk baby. Still, it was hard to think of the sweet child dying for lack of something Mari could give.

"The problem is deeper than that." The Hillfolk woman blinked; Mari thought the woman's lashes glittered a little in the moonlight. "The rules of magic are different when children are involved." She gave a deep sigh. "Grown folk, ours or yours, are anchored to one of the world's halves; no matter in which half they dwell, they retain their essence and their interaction with the world. But because children are so mutable, they may take on characteristics with which they were not born, though their essences remain the same. This unbalances nature, and we must do our best to keep its harmony. For children, there must be an exchange. I cannot give you Brascêt, even if you would take him, without keeping your own son."

Mari was not sure she understood the explanation, but what she did understand was that the other woman would not give her both children. Determined to have Anwel back, she closed her eyes and tried to harden her heart against the blue-eyed stranger she knew as her son. It was not her responsibility to help the Hillfolk. She was responsible only to her own. She took a deep breath to say as much to the mother.

The baby cooed.

Mari's eyes snapped open. The baby was sucking at the Hillfolk woman's finger; Mari felt her milk let down, and her defenses began to crumble. How could she abandon any child, let alone one she had loved and raised, kissed and changed and swaddled? Deciding what to do was wrenching. The child's fate weighed on Mari's heart like a stone in her chest.

Suspended together were thoughts of Gawter and his anger, and of the years of her acquiescence to his whims. Helping the other woman would mean brooking Gawter. But now, looking at the Hillfolk woman as simply another mother, Mari realized that the world was suddenly less simple than she had ever been taught to believe. With startlement, she realized that the glitter on the woman's lashes were true tears.

Like a key in a lock, her entire perspective turned. She stared at Gawter, wondering why she let him beat her, when she did nothing wrong for which to be punished. It was Gawter who acted as if he had no soul. This mother before her had given up her child to a woman she did not know, hoping that it would save the child's life.

The moon's luminescence waned as a cloud passed overhead; Mari swallowed, realizing for the first time that she had the power to change the course of her own life. She lifted her gaze to the Hillfolk lady's, and asked, "Will you be able to find another to nurse your child?"

For the first time the woman seemed uncertain. "Perhaps. It is easiest to substitute the babies at birth; the parents are still learning about their children. The glamor will only last so long, and when it fades — the futures of some children are bleak." The budding tears finally bloomed, and spilled down both pale cheeks.

Remembering what Libby had told her, Mari was horrified. She stepped forward and looked at the baby she had called Anwel. Brasĉet. She reached out a hand and touched the baby's soft head, feeling the thick baby hair against her fingers. Now that the glamor was gone from her eyes, he looked a little different, his features finer, his eyes clearer, his skin paler. But he still looked like himself. A wave of love inundated her as she contemplated Brasĉet. No — Anwel.

"I will take him back," she said softly. "As long as my son will be happy, I will raise this one as if he were indeed my dear Anwel."

The Hillfolk lady drew a sharp breath. "Are you certain, Mari?"

Mari nodded, her entire body relaxing, though she had not been aware of how hard she had been tensing her muscles. "I am certain."

She reached out and took Anwel from the lady's arms; he burbled at her. "Lady, I love him. If I must give him a poor life and a poor father, I can still keep him alive, and give him the affection of a mother, brothers and sisters." Relief rushed over her in torrents. She had not known how terrified she was of losing him.

The lady smiled her sweet smile yet again, though silent tears still seeped from the corners of her eyes. "In my years dealing with this world, I have never met a mortal so generous. And in truth, I did not want to give up your son. I have grown to love him. Meeting you, I begin to understand why." She walked over to stand by the spring and to stare into its shining depths. "My blessing is upon you and yours, Mari, and that is a potent magic. You will find that your fortunes will rise; you will have enough to feed your children, and their health will never wane. You have a loving heart, and your reward will be great."

She knelt, cupped one hand, and drew a draught of spring water, which did not trickle out as it would have from Mari's. Rising, the lady went to Gawter and stood contemplating him. "That anger will harm all of you, and it is not easily altered." She wetted one finger with the spring water and drew a pattern on Gawter's forehead. "I will take him with me, and perhaps he will learn better than to visit his pain on another." Opening her fingers, she let the rest of the water drip onto the ground.

Mari swallowed. The thought of living without Gawter was appallingly pleasant, but she had promised to be a good wife to him. Should she let him go, or should she try to continue their life, that had grown so painful? The answer was clear: she must let him go, for herself, and for the children.

Nodding, she faced the lady. "He will come to no harm?"

"He will come to good," the lady replied.

Mari walked to Gawter, stood on tiptoe, and kissed him on the forehead. Her lips tingled for a brief moment. Stepping back, she said, "Take him, but be good to him. That anger was not always so strong in him."

"Bless you, Mari." The woman placed a hand on Gawter's arm. Their forms began to shimmer, as if another flood of moonlight illumined them from the inside. The air around them kindled with color, then started to coruscate, its hues running from reds and purples to brighter colors until they seemed to converge in a white blaze of magic. Mari blinked against so much light. When she could see again, they were gone.

Anwel grasped her finger with his tiny hand. His mouth made sucking noises; her milk let down as she noticed. Mari looked at him, knowing that he was her child in every way that counted, and would be for life. "Mama loves you, Anwel," she said her heart full of laughter. She would find some way to appease Widow Libby.

Shifting him onto one arm, she opened her bodice and helped him to latch onto her breast. "Drink well, little one," she told him. "You are going to grow up big and strong."

raining Ground

Spring never came so early to the mountain city of Tolin. Vandeyr Atenel removed and shouldered her wool cloak, pretending that here in the Aelin Plains she had expected the day to turn warm. The little things, they warned her, drew greater notice than the large. But whoever would have expected a full thaw midway through the year's third month?

No mistakes, she warned herself. She was here for a purpose and nothing must distract her. She must appear completely at ease, as if she crossed the Aelin Plains routinely on business. Any hint of what that business was must remain unthought. Vandeyr threw back her shoulders and marched forward along the road with all appearances of a cheerful confidence.

There was the inn, a half-timbered structure badly thatched and painted a garish shade of salmon pink which reminded Vandeyr of a creeping fungus. A muscle twitched in her jaw, but she retained tight control as she hauled open the heavy front door and passed under the lintel into the inn's common room.

The room smelled of rancid smoke and mildew, and was populated with a half dozen men and women who appeared to be lunching. "Ho!" the barkeep greeted her. "Will it be a room you're wanting, or just a good meal and some ale? Best ale in six towns hereabouts, and we put some squirrel in the stew just two days ago." He grinned, showing a sizeable gap in his upper teeth. "Pretty girl like you might even be able to pick up a few sweets, if she cozies up to the right man." He rubbed the beard stubble on his chin and chuckled as if he had said something clever.

Vandeyr was not intimidated; the day she could not gut any ordinary village oaf was the day she would turn in her assassin's dagger. She was aware of its weight in her boot sheath, the triangular black blade unmistakable to anyone in the four countries that comprised this section of the world. Here, in the country of Telardur, its possession would spell her death. This did not worry her, as she did not intend anyone to find it.

"A room," she said in a pert but amused tone. She might need the goodwill of these people later. "And a meal. But save your sweets for the kind of woman you can buy for that cheap a price."

The other patrons of the inn, who had been listening intently, burst into riotous laughter. "She's got you there," bellowed a woman who from the look of her muscles and scar-spattered skin was the village blacksmith. The woman patted the unoccupied seat next to hers and her two male companions. "Come sit with us. We're good company, and we're not interested in robbing the cradle, unlike Maric over there."

Vandeyr looked at them and decided that it made sense to make provisional friends of the village folk, despite the fact that they seemed determined to embarrass her if they could manage it. She slid into the seat next to the blacksmith, gratefully hanging her cloak from the back of the chair.

"Thank you." She pulled out the first part of the carefully

rehearsed story she had decided upon. "I was on my way through the plains, but I've had a bit of trouble – first my horse shed a shoe, then went lame, and I decided I was going to have to sell it. Well one thing led to another, and there wasn't a single horse there fit to ride for any distance, so I found myself on foot, and gods, these boots pinch! I'm about done in, and my blisters have blisters."

One of the woman's companions, a deftly tailored man of middle age, looked at her kindly. "How old are you, dear?" he asked. "Pretty young for a girl traveling by herself, aren't you? Don't you worry about wild animals or bandits?"

"I'm seventeen," Vandeyr told him, aware that she did in fact look younger than her years, a fact not helped by a slight figure, delicately molded features, flaxen hair and eyes as open and blue as an autumn sky. Before her exceptional competence had silenced her rivals, Vandeyr's classmates had often taunted her that instead of a real assassin, she should become a 'satin assassin': a lovely killer whose entire mission centered upon the bedchamber. But Vandeyr was better than that, and before long she would prove it. This was her first mission, and she intended to make her family and city proud of her.

"Where are you to?" the blacksmith asked, maternal concern evident in her voice. "Is there anything we can do to help? We don't have many good beasts to spare, but maybe we can find somebody willing to cart you over a town next firstday or two. Do you have enough money, sweetie? We're not rich here, but we haven't forgotten that hospitality is our duty to the gods."

Vandeyr found herself oddly touched by the woman's solicitude. Catching herself, she took a deep breath and set the feeling aside to deal with later; it was not to be ignored, for it could rise up later with crippling force, but it must not play a significant role in her actions. *A good assassin*, she heard in the voice of her uncle and teacher, *knows himself and does not lose sight of his goals.*

"I have a little money," she said with a smile. She relaxed her posture and patted the pouch at her belt. "It should tide me over if I'm careful."

In fact, Vandeyr had more than a little money. Stashed about her person was a valuable gem she could sell should she fall upon desperate times. But it would be foolish for an assassin to be robbed by a thief. Besides, she wished to draw no undue attention to herself. Some notice was inevitable in a town this small, but the less the better. Placing herself in the public eye as a harmless traveler was her best strategy, so that no one should come to suspect her true purpose.

The third companion at the table, a small dour man with bulgy eyes, finished his beer with a slurp. "Back to work," he grumbled, as if he hoarded every word. "Earth's not going anywhere 'less I till it." He plunked down the tankard and threw a copper royal onto the table where it spun on edge for a moment before clattering to a stop on the portrait of the faldren King Dwinhir.

The blacksmith pushed her seat back. "Don't forget what I said, dearie. You need help you come to me. I'm the blacksmith, my name's Gracilla. I'll make sure you get what you need. We're a friendly town. Fruit of Coran's womb, this town, the best. I couldn't ask for better neighbors." She rose and dropped two copper royals on the table. "One of those is for your lunch. Don't argue, now. Just humor an old mother and let me do for you what I hope anyone would do for one of my girls." With a parting swoosh of air she was gone, followed closely by the dapper middle-aged man.

Having settled in, Vandeyr now prepared to go to work.

The day was bright, and most of it still remained to her; in the mountains she would have had less time before the sun dipped below their stony fingers.

Vandeyr made a quick job of scouting the town, noting where each building sat, where each man and woman plied their trade. Especially she examined the mill where her target lived and worked; the town miller. He seemed inoffensive, a stout, cheerful young man, and Vandeyr had no idea who would want him dead – or for that matter, who in this tiny town could afford to hire the City's services. It was none of Vandeyr's affair; she was only the hand, neither a Council member nor a contract lawyer.

Retreating to her room at the inn, Vandeyr considered what to do next. The stipulations of the contract were that the miller was to die within two weeks, he was to die of obvious violence, and the black dagger was to be left on the body. Other than that, Vandeyr had a free hand with her work. In order to hasten her out of danger she had a small stone which possessed the magic to gate her from this town back to the environs of the City in an eyeblink. Most assassins would not have benefit of such magic, but Vandeyr was a valuable trainee, and they did not wish to risk losing her.

Her room was small and dingy, which Vandeyr hated even though she had expected as much. Though a child of privilege, Vandeyr had been well-trained, and understood the privations of the outside world. Now she would be evaluated on how well she had received her training. She did not know who would evaluate her, or on what criteria, and she did not expect to find out. She would learn exactly as much as she was told, and no more. That was the lot of a soldier.

A spider threaded down from the thatch directly in front of Vandeyr's eyes. She knocked it to the floor and crushed it beneath her boot. Pacing quickly back and forth, she considered what she had learned of the town.

She must find the miller alone, a task more daunting than she would have thought before assessing the situation in person. The miller seemed to have many friends and was the apparent father of a swarming family of eight or so children. In addition, the mill nestled close to three other riverfront structures, all within easy earshot and plain view of the mill.

A creeping relief that the warm-hearted blacksmith was not her target left Vandeyr with a faint sense of guilt. Such considerations should not affect her. *You must understand your target*, Uncle Cordelayne's voice sounded in her memory, *but sympathy is dangerous. It makes you forget your purpose, and that purpose is greater than any one person*. Vandeyr knew that was true. Tolin, known in Telardur only as "The City of Assassins", made order out of what would otherwise be the chaos of murder, amateur spycraft, and other such activities. The City's professionalism kept its missions clean and focused, keeping the danger to innocent parties to a minimum and providing a much needed service. Though the outside world did not properly appreciate Tolin's mandate, fearing and hating the City instead, Vandeyr was proud to be even an ordinary citizen, and especially proud to have been chosen for the elite corps of assassins whose work kept the City functioning. She could not expect her job to be easy.

Deciding to retrace her steps in case she had missed something vital, she left her room, stopping briefly in the inn's common room for a friendly ale so that the barkeep did not become suspicious of her comings and goings. The ale was friendlier than she would have preferred, as the barkeep attempted to talk her into bed with him once more, but Vandeyr found no difficulty remaining firm and polite at once. She was used to this game; though cruder, it was the same one that her suitors practiced at home when she was allowed a carefully chaperoned date with a young man of quality. At least those young men, however annoying, had teeth.

Returning to the mill, Vandeyr took careful notice of all the trees and shrubs she could see in the vicinity. Unfortunately, there was not much. Scraggly bushes no higher than her waist and as yet unleaved from winter trailed a thin line from the back chimney to the water's edge; these might provide cover in an emergency, but Vandeyr doubted they would prove sufficient. Two evergreens, standing like soldiers between the mill and the tanner's on the right, held their branches so stiffly at their sides that Vandeyr doubted she could even insert herself among them, much less use them as a safe base for an attack.

The most likely spot was a patch of reeds and cattails which poked a mixture of green and last year's gold through a spongy bit of bank on the far side of the mill, past the paddle wheel. Unfortunately, there were two problems with this location. The first, manageable but tricky, was that these plants grew from a marshy patch of ground close to the river's edge, obviously at least ankle-deep in mud and perhaps more since the spring thaw had already broken up the river ice and brought it level with the high water marks. This boded poorly for the speed of Vandeyr's attack.

The other problem was simply that no one broached the river in that area. The miller's wife took her washing to the near side of the mill wheel between the mill and the tanner's home. The tiny shack on the far side seemed to contain one housebound occupant whose house door faced away from the river. It would do Vandeyr no good to hide in the rushes if she could not approach her target more closely than the lengths of several mill wheels.

She shook her head slowly. She wanted to do this job thoroughly and right, passing her initiation into the fellowship of assassins with skill and flair. She wished to impress Uncle Cordelayne and prove Mother's faith in her, but more than anything she hoped to make Father shine with pride. He had so many troubles; he was on the Council of Tolin and even at an ordinary time must deal with many difficulties and disappointments. But now demons involved themselves in the City's affairs; the esch, manlike but filthy creatures of earth, gray-skinned and heavily muscled, who were occasionally useful but just as often vicious nuisances, spoke quietly of future war with Telardur; the political climate in Tolin did not favor the Atenels at the present time; and were that not enough, Vandeyr had a troubled younger sister whose behavior no one could seem to control. Father needed Vandeyr to succeed.

During the next few days Vandeyr decided that she must strike somewhere besides the area of the mill. But it was almost impossible to find the miller by himself. He seemed a popular fellow, with drinking and gaming companions in plenty. He was generous with aid to his neighbors, and when not working at the mill could almost always be found lending his donkey to help a farmer with the spring plowing or shoring up a makeshift dike against the spring floods. What little spare time he had, he spent playing with his children; and Vandeyr was very loath to kill him in front of them. If she must, she would, but she would do everything she could to find another way first.

In fact, Vandeyr was beginning to have a sense of disquiet about her mission. Though she was not truly blooded, she had sat through sessions of interrogation and torture; the City would not send her if they were not sure she was capable of killing. But this man did not deserve to die, and though it was her responsibility to end his life, she did not like it.

She took refuge in Uncle Cordelayne's words: *A good assassin does not love killing. We do not want the sort of man who glories in the deed. An assassin knows his responsibility to the City and is prepared to do hard things, even when they are distasteful.*

As days slipped into a week Vandeyr found excuses to stay in the town for longer than she had planned. She feigned exhaustion and lack of funds; she found fault with riding beasts offered to her; she wrote a false letter and sent it to a City drop point to cover her inaction and provide a reason for her to wait for an answer.

While she waited she integrated herself into the life of the town, accepting Gracilla's motherly concern, fending off Maric, the barkeep, flirting with the regular crowd at the inn, and generally attempting her best to appear the least suspicious she could manage. The responses she garnered from the townsfolk suggested she was succeeding well.

She continued, frustrated, to search for ways to catch the miller alone. After the first two days she even began to creep silently out of her room's window, stalking the mill in the dark and considering whether she should invade his home at night and kill him quietly in his sleep. The problem with this tactic was that he and his wife slept in one large room with all eight of their children, one or the other of who always seemed awake no matter what the hour.

Vandeyr's frustration level rose as time ticked closer to the end of her mission. She must find some way or the City would forfeit the contract, and the City had never forfeited a contract in all the two thousand years of its history. Desire to make her family and City proud subsided into a gnawing fear that she would in fact disgrace them unutterably.

It was almost with relief that, ten days into the mission, she was approached by another assassin she knew slightly from advanced training sessions. Vandeyr stood in the shade of a pin oak, half hidden by the draping branches, trying to figure out how to near the miller who was fishing with three large friends on a bony spur of rock some ways downstream from the mill. The black dagger in her boot seemed to weigh heavily against her ankle.

The assassin, Laepez, slipped into the shade behind her, taking care that none but Vandeyr should see him. He was perhaps ten years older than she, and Vandeyr knew he was a seasoned agent, reliable and well regarded. He immediately gave Vandeyr her personal password for this mission so that she would know that he was sent officially by the City. She waited for what he would say, her heart beating a slow rhythm of defeat.

"You've taken far too long for this simple a mission," Laepez told her. His tone was not angry or accusatory, but Vandeyr knew she had failed this test. "The City is recalling you. I'm to do your job."

Vandeyr was very glad that her training had covered not only control over her expressions but also over things that most people thought of as involuntary; facial color, respiration rate, tears. She did not want Laepez to know how deeply she felt the dishonor.

Laepez however, was more experienced than she, and did not seem to be fooled. "Your evaluator seemed to think that your technique was mostly sound. However, you've made things too complicated. It's something many first timers do. Don't get overly upset; learn from it. And watch what I do." He drew an assassin's dagger from his belt.

With a fluid movement Laepez emerged from the shadows and walked to the edge of the river where the four men fished. All of the men faced the river, and Laepez made no sound. Without fanfare or apparent unease, the assassin approached the miller, slid the knife into his back, and walked away. The miller fell forward silently. His companions turned to him in confusion, unsure of what had happened until they saw the dagger protruding from his ribs. But by the time they grasped the situation and looked for the assailant, Laepez was out of sight, back under the pin oak with Vandeyr.

Vandeyr was not sure what she felt. Pity for the miller seemed to have shattered with the sharp relief she felt that she would not be the cause of the City's ultimate disgrace. She felt empty, as if her own hand had wielded the knife.

"There," said Laepez, without particular satisfaction or pride. "The job's done. Let's get out of here." He reached into a pouch at his belt and simultaneously took Vandeyr's arm. She felt the stomach-wrenching of a gate spell and the world spun from trees and river into the gray stone of Tolin's inner walls.

Uncle Cordelayne stood waiting, a thoughtful frown on his face, framed by the same pale hair as crowned Vandeyr's head. "You could have done better," he told her. "But you could have done worse. I think you're ready to try again." His voice sharpened. "Are you?"

Vandeyr thought of the past few days; her doubts; her fears; and most of all her foolish delays which had cost her in the City's eyes. For the first time she thought she truly understood what Uncle

Cordelayne meant when he told her that sometimes she would be called upon to do hard things. Next time she would not fail.

She raised her blue gaze to meet her uncle's brilliant green one. "The City calls," she told him firmly. "I am ready."

A Trip to Moonpark

"Your turn to guess! Where do you think we're going this summer?" Mr. Yeager asked the children, as he turned off their high definition holographic show. Madden and Mark looked at each other, then at their father. Every year they went somewhere different and both were overflowing with excitement.

Madden flung herself on the living room couch, pulled at her long brown ponytail, and tucked the end in her mouth. She was twelve and believed she was very grown up, but she could not seem to break herself of the habit. "Skiing on Mount Everest?" she asked indistinctly.

"Maybe scuba diving in the Marianas Trench!" Mark piped up enthusiastically. At eleven, he was ready for adventure. "I want to swim with the giant squids!" He knew that even with the ocean tourist vessels, diving so deep was impossible, but he liked the idea anyway.

Both children felt very lucky to be going on vacation this year. Mr. Yeager had lost his job programming personalities into artificial intelligence within the last year. And though their mother had a good job working at the Large Hadron Collider in Switzerland she was often gone for months at a time, and money was tight.

"Wrong and wrong." Mr. Yeager grinned at them and tossed the remote at Mark, who caught it one-handed. "How do you feel about — Moonpark?"

Mark thumped the back of the couch so hard that the hair fell from Madden's mouth. She shrieked and jumped up. "Really, Dad? Really?" she screamed, as if she were six instead of nearly thirteen.

Moonpark was where every kid wanted to go. When the United States had stopped manned space flights, big companies had taken over. Those companies had built on the moon after developing cheap, efficient shuttle fuel and gravity cushions. The moon was now a tourist attraction where you could eat moon-grown food or shop at department stores that had the latest lunar styles. But Moonpark was the best.

Madden and Mark knew it was too expensive for their family. They could hardly believe they were really going.

"We leave tomorrow." Mr. Yeager grinned. "Better start packing!"

When the shuttle-bus took off from Earth, Mark could hardly breathe because of the excitement swirling in his stomach. He watched eagerly as the moon swelled in the window, its face dimpled with hundreds of impact craters from an impossibly long time ago. Staring with wide eyes, he watched distant stars drop below the moon's bright globe. Near the surface he could see the spindly towers of Copernicus Industrial Park and the smooth pavement of Mare Imbrium Speedway, where pilots raced special cars that skimmed over the low-gravity track. His heart thumped so hard he could feel it in his throat.

Madden pretended she was not excited but she could not keep her gaze on the e-reader she held. When the shuttle-bus docked at

Luna Central Station, she could not stop herself from making a thrilled squeak. When they got on the ferry to Moonpark, she grabbed the seat in front of her so hard it made her hands hurt. Still, she could not help being a little worried. Could they really afford this trip? It must, Madden thought, cost a fortune.

Was this one of those trips that parents gave their children before they told them bad news? Maybe, "*We're going to lose our house*," or even, "*Your Mother and I are getting divorced*." The more she thought about it, the more likely it seemed. But Madden wanted to enjoy her time here, so she pushed the thought into the back of her mind, trying with determination to think about having fun instead.

It seemed like hours before they got through the credit and security scans and exited into a long, low building at the park's edge. The moon's low gravity, a sixth of that on earth, made Mark's stomach flutter. To experiment he jumped, and found himself in the air near the ceiling before coming down very slowly. Laughing, Madden jumped too, and both of them bounced up and down until Mr. Yeager signaled for them to stop.

"Here," said Mr. Yeager, giving them each a wristband with a long piece of plastic embedded on the top. "Your credit strips and ID passes are both encoded on these. Don't let them out of your hands!"

Mark's was blue, and Madden's was green, but the plastic was an identical beige. They would have to run the passes every time they went to a ride or an exhibit, and they would not be able to play games or buy anything without them.

Mr. Yeager grinned. "I've got something I need to do while we're here," he said. "I think you two are old enough to go off on your own. Remember, park security are in the chrome vests with the crescents on them. *Stay together*! Give me a call if you need anything, and I'll meet you back here in four hours." He walked off in the opposite direction, leaving Mark and Madden together in a crowd of other families drifting in and out of the building.

"Come on!" said Mark, and darted out of the building, followed closely by Madden. A transparent dome arched over the entire park, letting in earthshine with just a little sun. Mark stared in wonder at the half-globe of the earth, which hung in the sky like a blue and white Chinese lantern. He bounced a little, enjoying how high he could jump from the shiny walkway beneath his feet.

"Where do we go first?" Madden looked around to see which way to go. Many of the laughing, chattering crowd around them had gone to look at a bright display ahead of them. It might be a map. She grabbed Mark's hand and pulled him along, making the display in a few leaps.

It was an interactive map of the whole park. Madden could see that if she touched her location and where she wanted to go, it would tell her how to get to any ride or attraction.

"Pirates of the Jovian Moons!" shouted Mark. He quickly touched the right places on the display, and a line of light showed them how to get there. Mark sped off, not even waiting for Madden to follow him.

"Pirates of the Jovian Moons" was a famous attraction, based on the holographic movie series of the same title. As they walked into the building that housed it, they were greeted by rakish pirates in silver spacesuits, who carried lasers covered in buttons and dials. Soon, two actors dressed as the movies' main characters challenged each other to a duel. Mark and Madden watched as the two began to fight, before the actors launched themselves into a full-fledged brawl. It was not something the children could have seen on earth, because the pirates could jump so high and so far. It was both funny and exciting. Madden loved it.

That was wonderful, but Mark knew where he wanted to go. He rushed toward a door which said only "Space Battles" and opened it eagerly. Inside were several copies of small fighting spaceships used in the movies. Mark went to the nearest and climbed inside. He was just about to shut the door when Madden joined him. She followed, and the two of them strapped themselves into their seats.

The ship moved back and forth while in front of them, holographic stars and asteroids appeared on a glass window. Mark and Madden used the touch-screen controls to make the ship seem to fly through space. Soon, the images of other ships appeared, and they joined in the virtual space battle against the Pirates of the Jovian Moons.

As soon as their turn was over and they exited the ride, Madden grabbed Mark's elbow. She knew where she wanted to go. "We're going to look at the Space Hangar," she told him. Moonpark's attraction on the history of space flight was famous. She might even learn a thing or two she could use in school next fall.

The Space Hangar was a gigantic geodome, and was part hands-on exhibit and part museum. Madden walked through the museum part, enchanted, as interactive audio-video displays told of the great pioneers of space travel: Yuri Gagarin, the first man in space; Neil Armstrong, the first man on the moon; Valentina Tereshkova, the first woman in space; and Pablo Martinez, the first to set foot on Mars. With glee, she watched the display on Chuck Yeager, the first pilot to break the sound barrier. Madden felt like she was living through all the history: Apollo and Sputnik, Skylab, Voyager, and the international space station. The last was still in use today, though it had gone through many changes since it was first built.

At the same time, Mark checked out the insides of a rocket, space capsule and a shuttle; strapped himself into a spacesuit; and looked through cameras which showed views of unmanned probes on the surfaces of Venus and Mercury. *Maybe I'll be a space explorer one day, he told himself. This even beats the Marianas Trench! I could be the first person to land on the moons of Jupiter*!

Excited and happy, Mark and Madden bounded out of the geodome back into the main area of the park. Here, Mark found a game which involved hitting a virtual moon from the Sea of Tranquility with a laserscope. To his surprise, Mark managed three hits in a row. Dumb luck, he supposed, but it did not stop him from choosing as his prize, a small robotic cosmonaut which he intended to put in his room at home.

Madden looked at the prices for playing the games, and decided that she was more likely to get something for a reasonable price if she bought it, rather than trying to win it. "Let's get some drinks," she said to Mark. "And there's someone selling meteor rings that I wanted to look at."

But when Madden put her wristband into the scanner to pay for their drinks, she was shocked to see the large amount of credit their father had given them. Deciding to share her worries with her brother, she turned to Mark. "We can't afford this vacation," she told him. "Not any little bit of it. I'm scared that there's something really wrong at home, and that Dad is trying to do something to make us happy before he tells us what it is."

Mark turned a shocked, scared face toward her. "Do you really think so?" he asked her. "I mean, maybe they had money saved."

"But Dad just lost his job." Madden frowned and took a sip of her drink. "They wouldn't spend it all on a vacation. You know how they're always telling us not to spend too much when we go places. But I've got two hundred units on my wristband, and I bet you do, too. Where is the money going to come from?"

"I don't know." Mark glared at her. "I don't want to talk about it now. Let's just go have fun, okay?" He slurped his own drink and turned away. "I want to go on the Zero-G coaster."

Though Madden tried to forget her fears, she worried all the way through that wonderful day. When she and Mark finally met Mr. Yeager for supper, he took them to a restaurant perched high on a narrow spire overlooking the entire park. A combination of holographic images and carefully placed lights made it seem like every table floated among the stars. A virtual meteor streaked across the darkened room to Mark's left just as the waiter delivered their meals on trays designed to look like the ones used in the international space station.

Mark scowled, and Madden picked at her food, but Mr. Yeager was more cheerful than usual. "Are you having fun?" he asked them. "We've still got three days left here. I hope you're enjoying yourselves, because I have something important to tell both of you."

Madden dropped her fork. Mark bit his tongue. "What is it?" Even to his own ears he sounded angry.

"It's about my job," Mr. Yeager said.

I knew it! thought Madden. *We're going to lose our home*! She pouted at Mr. Yeager. "What about it?"

Mr. Yeager beamed at her. "I had a job interview this afternoon. The owners of Moonpark think my skills would be just right for continuing work that they're doing on a lot of the exhibits and attractions, and I'd earn a lot more money than I did before. I do program personalities into artificial intelligences, you know." He stopped and grinned at them before continuing. "How would you two like to move to the Moon? You'd even get free all-year passes to Moonpark."

Mark's whoop was only a little louder than Madden's shriek. "Really?" he yelled. "We're going to live at *Moonpark*?" In his opinion, this was the most exciting thing that had ever happened to him. They could even go to the park any time.

"Well, not in the park itself." Mr. Yeager smiled. "I think we can find somewhere close by, though. They've also offered your mom a job. She'll be joining us in a few weeks, as soon as she wraps up the project she's working on in Switzerland. So we'll have a chance to be a family again."

Madden breathed an enormous sigh of relief. A feeling of happiness filled her from the top of her head to the soles of her feet. Nothing at all was wrong. Instead, everything was right. "Oh, Dad," she whispered. "Really? Really truly?"

"Really truly." Mr. Yeager reached out a hand to Madden and Mark both, and squeezed. "We'll all get a new start. And about time!" He let go of his children and reached for his fork.

"Now," he said, examining the tray. "What do you suppose their 'moon pot pie' tastes like?"

wan Song

She could remember being alive. Even now, Eala could feel warm breezes on her cheeks, savor the crisp of a windfall apple, see the swirl of wild swans on the river at sunset. She and Anza had watched the swans many times, until their laughter rang across the water, startling the birds. The two were inseparable then, fair and dark twins with the same blue eyes and echoing features. Then, Eala could not imagine a future when her sister would betray her.

Vision was strange now, since she had become all carven bone and strung hair. But she could still see without eyes, and hear, and feel in some degree where her breastbone lay as a bleached inset in the harp's soundboard. Her twisted strands of hair caught the wind, humming even when no one played, and her finger pegs cradled the harp's willow frame in a perpetual caress. Yet weeping was denied her.

Eala did not truly understand how Anza could have changed so much from the loving sister she had once been. Only since they had grown to a marriageable age had any real rivalry come between them. Eala tried to make sense of the gyrating chaos of memory, to pull events into coherency. Her remembered heart still ached with love for her sister, and with the pain of Anza's treachery.

It was a sunny morning in early spring, just after snowmelt: the time both of floods and the infancy of budding leaves. Cloaked against the wind, Eala walked in the side garden beside the squat, rectangular body of Corydon Hall, searching for the few flowers that were already blooming. Crocuses and white hyacinths speared through the soil, heralds of the wild growth to come.

She heard the commotion while she was still out of sight in the garden. Hooves clattered over the flagstones of the front courtyard, followed by the sound of a man's voice speaking. Curious, Eala raced toward the house, wondering who had braved the wind's bite to visit them.

As she rounded the corner, a stranger came into view. He dismounted and tossed his horse's reins into the hands of a stable hand, turning toward the front entrance. Eala could not see him well, silhouetted against the morning light. All she could tell was that it was a man, tall but not overly broad, who walked with pride and grace.

He vanished into Corydon Hall's entrance. Eala smoothed her skirt, pulled some windblown tangles from her hair, and went after him, walking quickly. By the time she made her way in through the front, he was gone. Looking around to make sure no one saw her acting like a hoyden, Eala lifted her skirts and sprinted up the broad staircase that rose in a graceful curve to the second floor of the hall.

Anza sat in their room, combing her luxuriant black hair before the large mirror they jointly possessed. Eala grabbed her own comb and began to sort out her tangles while she told Anza the news.

"You've another suitor, I think," said Eala. As the eldest, Anza would be married first. "I didn't see him well, but I think he's young.

He certainly sat his horse well!"

Anza arched a brow. "Is he handsome?"

"I'm not sure." Eala yanked at a persistent elflock and frowned. "I didn't get a good look at him."

"Well, let's go!" Anza tossed her comb onto the bed, caught hold of Eala's wrist, and pulled her toward the door. Eala pocketed her own comb and followed her sister downstairs to their father's parlor.

Before they got there, a servant directed them instead to the smaller dining room. Anza pushed the door open, and they entered.

Lord Arcill smiled as they approached. He sat at the head of a long table, a dented goblet before him. Beside him sat the stranger; young, as Eala had guessed. His features were clean and well sculpted, his tousled hair like pooled sunshine. Large, dark-fringed eyes shone an astonishing cornflower blue, eyes any woman would envy. He was lean, but muscled, with a manly breadth of chest and shoulder.

Anza breathed in, a half-gasp which Eala understood to mean that her sister was delighted. Eala frowned in mild envy, though she did not really begrudge Anza a handsome suitor. Not really.

Lord Arcill nodded to his daughters. "Girls, this is young Wilgem of Greenlake, where his elder brother rules. Wilgem, these are my daughters, Anza and Eala. Manners, my daughters. Someday you both will be chatelaines of your own household."

Eala hid a grin. Their father seldom stood on ceremony, though he would have denied any impropriety with vehemence. She dipped a curtsey, a bit deeper than strictly required. Anza followed suit, looking as if she were about to swallow her tongue.

Wilgem stood and bowed to them both, his expression caught midway between amusement and admiration. "A fair daughter and a dark one, beautiful as day and night," he said. "Lord Arcill, you are truly blessed." He smiled, and Eala felt her breath catch in her throat; Wilgem's beautiful smile sent a quick shiver all the way from her chest to her belly. She threw Anza a half-glance, and saw that her sister breathed quickly, and that Anza's cheeks were tinged with pink.

"Girls," said Lord Arcill, "Go and inform the steward that Master Wilgem will be staying. And tell the cooks to make a sumptuous dinner; we at Corydon must not fail in hospitality." To Wilgem, he said, "They are obedient and capable girls, both of them. Anza is the elder by an hour, but I have reserved lands for Eala as well. I wish to provide for both my daughters, though Anza will inherit Corydon Hall and the greater share of its properties. He who marries her will be lord here one day."

Wilgem began to speak as Eala and Anza left the room, but they did not dare stay to listen at the door. They went instead to carry out their father's orders, then retired to their chamber, where they could dress themselves for dinner and discuss handsome Wilgem without interruption.

Anza hopped onto the large goosefeather bed the two had shared since birth, and tucked her feet neatly beneath her. Sun dripped into the room through imperfectly shuttered windows, painting her face with streaks of light. She began to giggle as if she had been drinking wine, or some of Lord Arcill's carefully hoarded brandy.

"He's so beautiful!" Anza said, small spurts of excited laughter bursting out between every few words. "Handsome enough to be a *prince*! I'm going to be his wife!" She looked Eala directly in the face, and her smile softened. "But we won't leave you out. Perhaps he has a younger brother. We could all live here, and never have to part."

Eala felt a flash of irritation with Anza, though she was not truly jealous. It was sometimes hard to be the younger; Anza accepted firstborn privilege as her due. Then a stab of guilt lanced through Eala, and she leaned forward to take Anza's hands in a sort of penance.

"Perhaps," said Eala. "I never want to leave you. I want us to be together always." A cold breeze shivered over her, like a memory of the future.

Anza rolled over and burrowed into the blue quilt that warmed the bed, pulling it up to her chin. Becoming suddenly serious, she said, "Don't worry. Father won't make you marry anyone you despise. It's not as if you had no prospects."

"No," Eala said, wondering why she did not feel easier about Anza's suitor. "Not as if I had no prospects."

Wilgem proved a charming guest, and rapidly won Lord Arcill over; Anza was already won. Eala's feelings were mixed. She wanted to be happy for Anza, but the needle of envy that bored into her heart seemed to strengthen each day.

It did not help that Wilgem was attentive to both girls, or that the three of them were constantly together, for it would have been inappropriate for Wilgem and Anza to be alone with each other. As Corydon's lands woke from winter sleep, the three rode out frequently; to hawk; to a dance at a nearby manor; to watch the swans on the river, which stretched its sleek green-brown curve from the northern hills through Corydon Wood to the south.

On a morning in the late spring, they took the nearest path to the river so that Anza could gather wildflowers. Eala knew her duty, both to her father and to her sister; she must oversee the two, while giving them as much freedom to be together as she could. It was hard to feel her way through the snarl of loyalties to father and sister both.

Engorged with snowmelt, the river roiled over wave-smoothed stones with a loud rush, then slapped a low bank matted with tangled reeds and grass. The slope contained black willows, woven together as if holding hands against the water's power. Farther from the river's shoulders, other trees sprouted, both in clumps and separately. In the grassy stretch between, early wildflowers spilled in tumbles of yellow, white, and blue.

Anza jumped lightly down from her horse and began to gather some of the spring blooms. Eala dismounted more slowly, watching her sister laugh. Anza's dark hair glinted red in the sunshine, and her face glowed with happiness, as if sun shone from inside her as well as without.

Wilgem remained astride his horse until it became clear that Anza would not immediately leave the riverbank. But when Anza disappeared into a copse of silver birch, he too dismounted.

Eala waded through white clover after Anza. The small blooms clung to the hem of her dress, leaving a faint scent in their wake. She did not glance back at Wilgem, but she could hear him follow, his footsteps soft in the flower-drenched field. Then his hand touched her shoulder and she startled; she had not realized he was so near. Stopping, Eala turned to face her sister's suitor.

Wilgem lifted a few strands of Eala's hair and held it out to catch the sun. "Spun gold," he marveled. "The sun should envy you, since it is not so bright as your beauty."

Eala stared at him, shocked out of words. This was not the touch of a brother. Wilgem's beautiful eyes gazed at her tenderly, and for several long moments, Eala forgot he was Anza's. It was enough time for Wilgem to bend down and kiss her softly. His lips tasted of salt and honey. Eala responded to the kiss with a passion that surprised her, grasping his face in her hands and pulling his face down to a level with hers. Blood thudded in her veins, leaving a teasing echo of fire to trickle throughout her body.

A choked cry sounded from behind Eala. Immediately she wrenched away from Wilgem, her mouth still tingling with the imprint of his lips. She turned to face Anza, who had reappeared and was clutching a bunch of jonquils so hard their stems had broken. Anza's face was whiter than the heads of clover beneath her feet.

"Anza, I – " Eala could not find the words. How could she explain the unforgivable? It was not even Wilgem's fault. Eala had not only let him kiss her, she had encouraged him. Apologies would not mend that rift.

"How could you?" Anza's words were almost inaudible, as if she spoke to herself.

Eala had no answer for her. She knew why she had let Wilgem kiss her; it had been a combination of envy and longing, neither of which were Anza's fault. But telling this to Anza would only worsen matters. She remained dumb before her sister's scrutiny.

Anza dropped her flowers on the grass and headed for her horse, which was contently munching the grass, oblivious of human conflict. Without waiting for Wilgem to help her, she swung herself up, anger and hurt radiating from every sharp movement. She did not look back to see who was following her.

Eala shook her head at Wilgem as he moved forward to help her, and mounted by herself, following Anza without a word. She was no longer sure that she trusted herself, and after what had happened, she trusted Wilgem not at all. But propriety required that she remain with them until they reached Corydon. Wilgem rode a prudent distance behind.

At the hall, Anza dismounted, her expression rigid. She made her way through the door without speaking a word to anyone. Eala had never seen her behave like this. Anza was casually generous, and always willing to forgive her sister. Eala trailed her to their chamber, hoping that she might find some way to apologize and reconcile with her twin. Wilgem stayed in the courtyard.

When they were alone, Anza turned toward Eala, her gaze icy. "Why?" she asked, speaking the word as if she had swallowed a shard of glass. She stepped before one of the long windows, the sun at her back obscuring everything but her silhouette.

Eala found that her voice did not wish to obey her. "I didn't..." she managed, then swallowed and tried again. "I didn't think."

"Do you hate me for being the firstborn?" Anza's tone remained sharp and brittle. "How long have you planned to steal him from me?"

Eala felt heat rise to her cheeks. "I never planned to steal him! The one kiss is all, and that was foolish, thoughtless, cruel. I don't hate you, Anza. I love you." Her voice threatened to die again. "I never wanted anything to come between us." A tendril of cloud softened the sun, but Eala still could not see Anza's expression.

"It's too late," Anza said bitterly. "Something has."

Anza would not speak to Eala for days. Instead, she sought out Wilgem, spending most of her time in his company, servants playing chaperone instead of Eala.

Eala spent this time quietly mending clothes, as if with her needle she could mend the rift with Anza. At times, she vacillated between anger, remorse, and confusion. Why did Anza not blame Wilgem for the same betrayal? Anza always forgave Eala, no matter what the offense. What made this so different? But Eala knew that she had crossed a line that made forgiveness an adult matter, rather than a child's misadventure. Despite the warm spring days, the atmosphere in the sisters' room remained frozen.

As the days turned toward summer, Anza finally began to melt. Though her words to Eala were still tight, Anza again asked her sister to comb her dark hair, or to help her lace the stays of a dress. In turn,

Eala was careful to avoid the subject of Wilgem. At dinner, she spoke to him only enough for bare courtesy, addressing most of her remarks to Anza and Lord Arcill. Gradually the strained feeling lifted, and Eala began to feel as if life might settle back into the placid unfolding of days.

It was Midsummer morning when Anza woke her before dawn, a riding skirt in her hands, and an eager smile on her face. "Eala? Eala? Come riding down to the river with me! We'll watch the swans and see if any summer roses are blooming."

A surge of gladness rose in Eala's chest, pushing its way into her throat where it lumped into a block that words could not pass. Since they had been old enough to leave their nurse's skirts, they had made this annual trek on Midsummer morning. She nodded and jumped out of bed. Even Wilgem was forgotten in the relief that rushed through her like the river itself.

They helped each other to dress as they had from childhood, and tiptoed out of the house in soft-soled boots that alerted nothing but mice. They let the stable boy sleep; the sisters were not faint town girls with no skills but embroidery and helplessness. As they rode into predawn mist, the sound of hooves echoed like an entire troop of fairy steeds.

At first, the river was merely a greater mist within a lesser, but as they dismounted, the first rays of sun knifed through the clouds around them and lit the river with rosy light. Eala felt a great joy and closeness with Anza that she had missed desperately while they quarreled.

"We'll never see the swans like this," Anza said briskly. "Let's go down to the edge, and maybe the fog will lift." She lifted her skirts and picked her way down to the water's brink. Eala followed her, cautiously feeling for snags still veiled by morning. The bank was slick with dew; she slowed as she attempted to keep her footing on wet grass and earth.

The fog was thickest in the river's center. Eala squinted, looking for white wings that might shine from the misty water, reflecting the sunlight that was just now breaking through the haze. Beside her, Anza breathed hard, as if she were trying to store up breath for some great effort. Eala turned to her, questions unspoken on her lips.

Anza pushed her into the river.

Eala fell backward into the chilly water. Instantly sodden, her skirts seemed a leaden weight. She gasped at the cold, inhaling a mixture of water and wet air. Coughing, she flailed at the shifting surface. Panic and disbelief mingled as she realized her strength was failing rapidly. Somehow, she managed to croak, "Help me, Anza!" But when Eala saw her Anza's face, it was as unyielding as a cairn of stone.

"You'll never have him," said Anza. No expression marred her voice.

Then the river pulled Eala down into a turmoil of tumbling water and darkness.

A clear light shone in Eala's sight. She tried to open her eyes, but could not force them to move. Gradually she realized that she felt nothing: no breath, no touch, no warmth or cold. Once, such lack of sensation would have terrified her. Now, she felt a deep, enveloping peace. Only she and the light remained.

"He's a bad one," someone said, so faintly it was like the memory of a whisper. "Wilgem of Greenlake. Ambitious, ruthless, and a cruel hunter."

Eala had no voice to respond. Memories spilled in random fashion across her mind, but none of them identified this speaker. And, wondered Eala, where was she anyway?

A touch brushed her, and suddenly Eala wore skin. She still could not move, but her body enfolded her, heavy and dense. The light came from somewhere in front of her closed eyes.

"Ssh," said the voice, stronger now. It seemed to belong to a woman. "Don't fret, Eala. I cannot right what's been done, but I can give you a chance to amend it."

Who are you? Eala tried to ask, but her mouth was unresponsive.

A hand stroked her eyes, and though they remained closed, suddenly Eala could see. She seemed suspended in brightly lit white-churned water. Before her floated a woman unlike any Eala had ever seen. Her pale skin matched the water's tone, and white-plumed feathers streamed from her hair and tufted from the outer edges of her brows. The arch of her neck seemed too long for a mortal. She looked, Eala realized, like a swan in woman's form.

Why help me? Again, Eala's words stopped before reaching her lips.

The woman smiled. "You have fed my children, and they have

never come to harm. Wilgem hunts them to adorn his table and to ornament his hats with their feathers. Sometimes he kills them for naught but practice with his restless bow. It is the same way he treats the deer among the trees and the hare in the field. And now, you. He hunts things that cannot fight back."

Confusion flooded Eala's thoughts. *But it was Anza who pushed me, not Wilgem.*

The woman shook her head. "Your sister was the weapon, Wilgem's bow. The game he hunts is all of your father's lands. Do you still not see how he used you both? He has worked on your sister all the weeks since he came to your father's hall." Her voice softened, as if in thought. "I am minded to give you your chance at vengeance against both. Will you take it?"

Sorrow colder than the river in winter streamed over Eala, hardening into the ice of anger, pain, and loss. *How?*

"I will give you your eyes, your ears, and your voice," the swan woman answered. "What you do with them is your decision. Will you accept?"

Eala did not understand, but it did not matter. *I will.*

She felt nothing more for what seemed a very long time. She drifted on a dark wave of emptiness, her only anchor the promise that the swan woman had given her. If she could have nothing else, she could have vengeance.

Gradually, light grew, beginning as a faint haze and growing stronger until it turned Eala's darkness to a morning of forgotten sensation. Eala found that she could see in all directions, though her eyes remained closed and her body still retained the numbness of the icy, drowning water.

She lay beside the river, at a shallow bend washed with pebbles and mud. Above her hung willows laden with summer green, their shaggy heads draping down to their roots, which disappeared beneath the water's edge. Beside her knelt a young man, cradling her head in his hands. His clothes were threadbare, and beside him on the ground lay a small harp. Tears brimmed in his eyes, though his expression seemed less sad than thoughtful. He stroked her, brushing hair from her face. Eala could feel the touch distantly, much like she had once felt the pulse in her veins.

"I didn't know," the man said softly, as if he thought Eala could hear him. "She told me I would find a swan here, and its bones would make my harp the wonder of every kingdom from one ocean shore to the other. I should have known better than to believe it was as simple as she said."

If Eala's voice was to be returned, it was not yet. She wanted to speak to him, to tell him her story, to ask why he was here, but her body's silence was absolute. Eala guessed 'she' to mean the swan woman, but she could not ask even that.

"Do I dare?" the young man asked himself, looking at the sky. "If I do not..." His words trailed off, and he took a deep breath of resolve. "Those who do not dare are forgotten by time and history. Fortune's gifts favor the bold." He stroked Eala's face. "Maiden, your voice will live on. Forgive me if I do violence to the rest."

It did not hurt. Eala was glad of that. The young minstrel was deft with his knife, and prized out her breastbone easily; her blood had long since congealed. He treated her with a strange reverence as he skinned her fingers for pegs and sheared her pale hair. And though most of her body still lay on the riverbank, Eala's sight and hearing moved with her bones to the willow harp that seemed to be his only possession.

As the minstrel twisted and braided her hair into strings for her new frame, Eala realized that her voice had indeed been returned. She whispered, and the sound woke harmonies on the wind. The minstrel started, then smiled a sad smile.

"Swan maiden," he said, "she spoke true. You are a harp with which to make legends. I hope that I am worthy of you." He picked her up by the strap and slung her across one shoulder. Then he stopped and set her back down.

"It is not right to leave your body here like a cast-off gown," he said, speaking more to her new body than to her old. "I have no spade to bury you, but I can give you back to the river. Perhaps you will travel down to the sea. Forgive me, maiden."

Eala watched, unmoved, as the minstrel knelt beside her form. Still wet from the river's wash, her shortened hair looked darker; she looked like Anza. The minstrel pulled Eala's bodice over the opening in her chest, and tucked it carefully under her chin. Then he picked her up as if she were no heavier than a swan, and walked out, knee high, into the water. He smoothed her hair back from her forehead, and placed her gently into the river's deeper channel. Eala saw her shed form bob and float, carried away by the current.

Now, her soul encased in wood, Eala had time to look back over her life, and to wonder how the bond between herself and Anza had shattered. On nights when the wind accompanied the minstrel's fingers on her strings, she remembered, and her voice cried out in exquisite melody the pain she could not shed.

The minstrel had indeed gained Fortune's gift, Eala thought wryly. He was skilled, but it was Eala's tones, her pure, high notes, and the whisper in her strings, that captivated all who heard her. She grew to like the young man; his voice was clear and tuneful; he knew how to follow her lead and to match her tones while allowing the magic in her to enthrall his audience. Sometimes her voice darkened as she waited and sang; the swan woman had promised vengeance, and she meant to have it in full measure.

Soon the minstrel was summoned to the halls of mighty lords for their feasts, their balls, their ceremonies. Gold flowed into his purse, and his name was spoken on the lips of the great, as was that of his harp: Swan Maiden. He always remembered to give Eala her due, and spoke to her as if she were his friend and companion.

The following spring, Eala's wait ended: the minstrel was summoned to Corydon Hall for the wedding of Anza and Wilgem. Eala watched the familiar fields and trees come into view as the young man journeyed into the lands of her youth. She sighed out tears made of crystal notes, remembering when she and Anza had played in these fields and dreamed of their futures together. Now Eala had no future beyond that of a voice and a shadow.

Lord Arcill's face was lined with grief and sorrow, and his smile was sad as he greeted the minstrel in the great hall that was used only for important occasions. Flowers and banners adorned the hall, and tables striped its confines, linen cloth and greenery decking their wooden leaves with festive color. Around each of the eight pillars that supported the room were long garlands of woven swan feathers.

That was not what caught Eala's notice. At the first table, which Lord Arcill headed in a lavishly carved chair, were nobles dressed in fine clothing, their expressions cheerful with excitement and wine. To Lord Arcill's right sat Wilgem, in blue and gold satin, swan feathers fringing his collar and sleeves. But even that was not enough to hold Eala's attention.

Anza sat to her father's left, clothed in a glorious red and gold brocade gown that teased out the red in her hair and brought color to her cheeks. She did not look happy, as should a maiden at her wedding feast, but a trace of lingering sadness seemed to darken the air around her. The minstrel startled, staring most impolitely at her features before remembering his manners and his position.

Eala breathed rainbow melodies in the air, wanting both to comfort her father, and to be enfolded once more in his strong arms. He looked much older than a year's span should have aged him.

"It is a happy occasion," Lord Arcill told the minstrel, his voice more subdued than Eala remembered. "We in Corydon need happiness. My younger daughter, my Eala, drowned in the river last summer, and was washed out to sea. We have spent much of the past year mourning, but it is finally time for my other daughter to have her own happiness. She is to marry Wilgem of Greenlake this night."

The minstrel looked hard at Lord Arcill, then at Anza. "Your daughter drowned last summer?" he asked, a hidden quaver in his voice. Eala knew him well enough by now to realize he had guessed her secret.

Lord Arcill nodded briefly. "But now is not the time to discuss sorrow. You are renowned for your mastery of music. Play something sweet for my daughter Anza, so that she may be gladdened on her wedding day." He turned toward his seat at the high table.

The minstrel nodded and took Eala from his shoulder. It was only then that Eala realized what her voice could do now, to Anza and to Wilgem. Before the minstrel put fingers to her strings, she began to sing in wordless melodies, as she explored the limits of the swan woman's gift. Desperately anxious to reach them all, and especially to comfort Lord Arcill, her wordless voice suddenly coalesced into one single cry: "Father!"

Lord Arcill stopped in mid-turn, and all color drained from his face. "Eala?"

Much as she loved him, Eala was not here to comfort her father. She watched Wilgem and Anza as she resumed her song. Wilgem seemed confused, but happiness unfolded on Anza's face, like a rose opening petals to the sun. Eala had not expected that.

She sang on. It was as if she had transcended her harp's body, and was formed of air and music. In a voice purer than a mortal woman's, she told the assembled guests what had happened on that morning; of Wilgem's manipulations and of Anza's treachery; of how Eala had died alone in the river's turbulent waters.

Wilgem wore an expression of horror and fear. He worked his mouth, but Eala sang over him, drowning his explanations and excuses. But on Anza's face, tears answered, though a glimmer of joy shone through them.

Suddenly the last answer came clear. Eala knew, with the certainty of the bond between the sisters, that Anza did not wish to marry Wilgem. She also knew that Anza had never regretted anything more in her life than pushing Eala into the river. Eala's frozen anger melted, and finally tears spilled, coursing from her breastbone down the harp's frame in salty streams. Her strings finally fell silent.

His face darkened with wrath, Lord Arcill glanced briefly at Wilgem. "Guards," he said, "take this monster and lock him up until he can stand trial for the murder of my daughter."

Then he turned to Anza, his features tight and controlled. "Daughter I will not name you. Traitor to your own kin, to your own sister!" He spat on the floor. "Leave, now. You are not my daughter. I do not want ever to lay eyes on you again."

Eala whispered to the minstrel, in tones only he could hear. "Go. I must not stay."

For once, her minstrel chose prudence over boldness. While Lord Arcill's attention, and that of the wedding guests, lay on Wilgem and Anza, the minstrel slipped like a shadow out of the great room and through the door into the spring sunshine. But Eala had one more task for him. "Wait," she murmured. "Wait."

The minstrel halted, obedient to her commands. Perhaps, thought Eala, he had also learned to know her during these last few months. It was a strange half-life for one who had begun her days as a maiden, but there was a certain contentment in it. There was only one more thing for Eala to wish.

The doors opened and Anza stumbled, a bundle on her back. She looked around, blind in the light, wisps of stray hair trailing around her neck and forehead. She had changed her dress, but tears still streaked her face.

"Now," Eala said. The minstrel nodded, then approached Anza. She stared at him as if she had never seen a minstrel before. Or perhaps it was Eala at whom she stared.

"My lady," said the minstrel. "Do you wish to come with me?" He stopped, and considered his words. "Do you wish to come with us?"

Anza looked at Eala, at the minstrel, then back at Eala. Wordlessly, she nodded.

The minstrel took her hand, and they walked off into the growing fields.

The Seal King

Horsch walked along the shoreline at nightfall. Scattered pebbles, as yet unrounded by the ocean, cut his feet, but he scarcely noticed; like the pebbles, his grief was still sharp. A half-moon gleamed down upon still salt water, and somewhere close to shore a fish jumped, breaking the quiet with its splash.

He stopped at last and looked around. He had come far from the bay where he had given his mother to the sea, leaving her to its final mercy. He felt strange, as if waves leapt in his blood. His mother had never allowed him within sight of the ocean, though they lived near the sound of its breakers, and she had enforced her prohibition with tales of dread which stifled his youthful curiosity. Now he wondered how he could have lived so long without a glimpse of its waters. He felt as if he belonged there, among the strange shells and tiny creatures washed up by the tides. He looked around at scattered rocks and driftwood, blackly silhouetted against moon glimmer reflected from the waters.

The sound of Horsch's own name caught his attention. "Horsch!" he heard, and then again, "Horsch!"

A chorus of "Horsches" followed it. He looked around and saw no one. He listened carefully, but the sound seemed to come from the waves themselves. He shivered, wondering how anyone here could know his name. Memories of his mother's tales came to him, stories of mermaids who lured sailors to their deaths, and of cold things with human voices.

The chorus grew louder, and Horsch held his breath, afraid to move or speak. Suddenly white waves foamed in front of him, and he found himself staring into a face which seemed startlingly human, and yet not human at all.

Horsch swallowed hard and reached for a weapon, anything with which he could defend himself. Then tension drained from him and he laughed, as dozens of seals began to clamber onto the beach. His mother had also told him about the natural ocean dwellers.

"Horsch!" they called in sea-loud voices. "Horsch!"

The face which Horsch confronted was that of a large seal, brown, whiskered, and full of human expression. Horsch felt foolish for imagining danger. His legs trembled with relief. He reached out a hand and gently touched the seal's sleek head.

"I am unfamiliar with your world, though I have lived near you for sixteen years," he told it. "I mistook your song for my name." He laughed again with relief. The seals seemed friendlier, now that he knew what they were. *I have much to learn about the world my mother would not let me experience.*

The seal shook its head and looked at him with moist eyes. "Horsch," it said. "You have come."

Horsch's head spun in wonder and disbelief. His breath whistled in his throat. "What creature are you?" he asked. "And how do you know me?"

Seals crowded around Horsch, brown seals, gray seals, mothers, and white spotted pups. Their singing was mournful and eerie.

"Horsch!" some sang, but other words blended into their song. "We are Selkies," they sang, "keepers of the deep. Horsch!" Horsch's name seemed to take on strange significance in their deep voices.

The brown seal who had spoken before pushed a pup out of his way and confronted Horsch again. "We are the Selkies, keepers of the deep," he said. "We sing for the Sea Lady. Tonight you gave your mother to the sea."

An odd sense of recognition came to Horsch. "Tell me why you have come to me," he said quietly. "But tell me without this song you sing, in which my name takes central place." He sat back on a slimy rock and waited for the brown seal to speak.

"We are the Selkies, the keepers of the deep," said the brown seal.

"You said that before," said Horsch. "Continue."

The brown seal looked at him with an inquisitively cocked head. "The tale is an old one to us, but new to you, I think. Years ago, the Sea Lady, goddess of the sea, mated with our king, the Great Bull Seal, who took human form for their mating. She bore a daughter, half seal, half goddess.

"The Sea Lady told her daughter that she could only survive if she remained near the sound, the scent, the sight of the sea. We raised her; she was beautiful and sleek and had the power of our people to take human shape. She was the best swimmer, the finest diver, and the pride of her father. But she was always curious, and that was how we lost her."

Horsch suspected where the tale led, but he waited for the story to continue, while his pulse sounded, like the sea, in his ears.

"Soon," continued the brown seal, "she learned that what her mother had told her was not entirely true. She could not go beyond the sound of the sea or beyond its salt taste; she could not go inland. She could, however, go beyond its sight. It made her weak, to go that far, but she did not die. Once she went to a village and saw young men playing with their nets. She would not mate with one of us. She would have only a young man. So she left us for a mortal man."

Horsch nodded, sure now that the seal spoke of his mother. It explained why she never traveled away from the ocean that she taught him to fear; but not why she feared it. "What happened to them? The seal lady and the mortal man?"

"The Seal King, her father, was greatly angered. He drove her off, hoping that she would die on the shore where she had chosen another over himself. Then her mother, the Sea Lady, cursed her so that she could not return to the sea. The daughter grew weak, and died away from the waves, as her father had hoped, though it took many years. Tonight you gave her body back to her mother—your grandmother."

Horsch felt the tides pulsing onto the shore, sweeping over sharp broken logs, driftwood, and the masts of sunken ships. *If that is true,* he thought, *then I am very little human, and much part of the ocean. But to believe the Selkie, I must believe that my mother's mother was a goddess, and my mother's father was a seal.* Horsch looked at his hand. It was brown and muscular and had scars from fishhooks he had fashioned for his father, dead these past three years. It did not look like a divine hand.

Part of Horsch doubted the Selkie's tale, yet it filled him with a strange sense of wholeness, as if a part of him long missing had been returned. He remembered his father trying to calm his mother when she told Horsch tales of the sea. A good fisherman, his father had drowned one night while alone in his boat.

"How can all this be?" he asked the brown seal.

The seal looked up at him in disgust. "Half human, like your father, one of the earth people's own," he said. "Though you are my half-sister's son. It is like a human to ask, 'How can this be?' It is, that is all. There is no 'how' about it."

Horsch breathed in the scent of salt and fish and rotten wood. "If this is so, why am I allowed here, now? Why not drive me away as you did my mother?" He felt anger stirring at the tale, that his mother was so cruelly treated by these less than human beasts, who claimed kinship with him.

"You are here," said the brown seal, "because, whatever you are, the fault is not your own. The prohibition banned only your mother. You were free of it, had she only known. You are the only living kin of the Sea Lady, in spite of your mortal blood."

"And the Great Bull Seal?" asked Horsch. "My grandfather?"

"He is here," said the seal.

The sea's surface heaved, and a great black head rose from it. The form which came forth was larger than a brace of oxen and blacker than moonless night. Horsch knew this must be his grandfather, the Great Bull Seal, whom the Sea Lady loved.

Horsch studied his own reflection on the waters. Only sleek black hair betrayed his Selkie blood. His form was long and wiry, not powerful like a bull seal. His eyes were the gray of the sea on a stormy day, and his reflection in the water was streaked with sea-plant green and the woody hue of submerged logs. His skin was the smooth brown of his mortal father.

The seals made sounds of obeisance to the great one rising. Horsch did not.

Horsch watched as the Great Bull Seal heaved himself upon the land, pulling himself forward with corpulent but strong flippers. The sight revolted Horsch; he felt more kin to the brown seal than to this monstrosity. The Seal King was black and slimy and exuded a scent of rotting fish and stagnant water that caused Horsch to wrinkle his nose and turn away.

"Welcome, daughter's son," said the Seal King in a voice harsh as rock grating against bone.

"I will give you no welcome in return," said Horsch quietly. "You drove my mother off to die, never able to approach the sea she loved. You are not worthy even of my contempt." His voice shook on the last word. The Seal King's presence caused his stomach to tighten and his muscles to clench with anger.

The air took on a chill beyond the nighttime coolness. The Seal King made a sound of disapproval deep within his chest. He hit a boat-sized rock with his powerful flipper, shattering it with a sound like lightning striking. "Your mother did not teach you respect for the great ones of the ocean deep," he growled.

"My mother had no reason to respect you," Horsch returned. "I do not respect you, either. You are cruel, and incapable of understanding the love she had for my father. He died years ago, but he was a good provider." Horsch reached carefully for a sharp shell that he had spied at his feet, and slipped it between his fingers.

"You are young," said the Seal King. "You do not understand these things. Your mother was half a goddess, and she gave up her birthright to become the woman of a greasy, string-haired mortal who pulled fish from the water so gracelessly that every sea creature groaned to watch. You have something of your mother's grace and beauty. Do you not understand? Will you not claim your birthright?"

Feeling strangled, Horsch faced the Seal King. "I will claim my birthright when you join her," he said. "I defy you, and I defy the Sea Lady, who is also cruel. I lost, too. I lost my mother, whom I loved, and my father who taught me to be a man. I lost sixteen years away from the realm for which I yearn. Nothing but your death can satisfy me."

The seals loosed a chorus of alarmed "Horsches". They backed into the sea, leaving a path for Horsch to follow. The Seal King headed toward the water.

"A challenge has been raised," said the brown seal in a loud voice. "The Great Bull Seal against Horsch, Anemone's son, daughter of the Sea Lady!" He met Horsch's gaze and said, "No one has ever won the challenge against the Great Bull Seal. He is one of the first of the Sea Lady's creatures and one of the greatest."

"I am not afraid," said Horsch, though he was.

Horsch took his sharpened shell and waded into the water. It swirled cold around his hips. The smell of salt made his eyes water and his vision blur. His heart pounded. The shell sliced into his palm with the force of his grasp, and he let the blood fall into the water, salt and red mingling. The sea-water stung the wound.

Suddenly Horsch no longer felt afraid. "Come, my mother's father," Horsch said. "Let us do battle."

The water heaved before Horsch, and the monstrous head of his grandfather broke the surface. The Seal King opened his mouth. Horsch could see rows of teeth, sharp as a shark's and yellowed from the many years the Seal King had lived in these waters. Each tooth was as long as Horsch's forearm. Horsch floundered, and narrowly avoided impaling himself upon them. His head hit the water. Immediately, he fell beneath the waves, seeing the bulk of the Great Bull Seal and the world below.

Horsch's eyes adjusted without difficulty. The Seal King dived beneath the surface, moving with incredible speed through the waters. Horsch dodged, feeling as natural swimming as running, though he had never been taught to swim. He felt no urge to breathe and wondered briefly why not. Then the Seal King lunged at him again. Teeth sliced into his shoulder. Blood spiraled upwards in a crazy pattern. Pain made his vision spin, and he swallowed salt water. He coughed, and fear touched him again.

Horsch could not move his arm because of the lancing pain. He kicked backwards, seeking anything he could use as a weapon. He found only the shell which he held, loosely, in his injured hand.

Taking it in the other hand, he slashed at the Seal King. The Seal King's hide split, and dark seal blood poured out. The seal's hide ripped the shell from Horsch's grip, where it spun downward into darker water.

A great watery impact smashed Horsch deeper into the water. The Seal King's tail swished by. Horsch knew that he could not take much of this watery battle with a leviathan. He could not run or swim far enough to escape. His muscles already ached from the strain of unfamiliar movement. He tried to think of some way to move this fight onto some ground where he could hold his own.

The thought struck him with hysterical force. Why was he fighting in the Seal King's own territory? *Ground! I could fight this on the shore, where this monster, no matter what his size, is clumsy and slow*! He stroked backwards through numbing pain, trying to feel his way to shore and comparative safety. The Seal King dived at him, and Horsch lunged out of the way. Then Horsch felt slimy things and rocks under his feet, and he backed up out of the water.

His hands and feet bled, trailing red through the rough sand and stones. He gritted his teeth, picked up a rock and threw it at the Seal King, aware of the futility of the gesture. The stone arced through the air and bounced off the Seal King's thick hide. The Seal King dragged his ponderous weight onto the rocky beach behind Horsch. The great creature was swift, even on the land. Horsch did not know how anything so big and awkward could move so fast. He had not expected that.

Slipping on the wet rocks, Horsch dropped to one knee before the Great Bull Seal. He groped for something to throw. The Seal King bore down upon him as Horsch thought of how foolish his challenge had been. Blindly, he pulled another sharp rock from the ground and threw it.

The Great Bull Seal bellowed in agony, a sound like waves roaring. Horsch glanced up. The rock had struck the Seal King's eye, and blood streamed from the wound. Air filled Horsch's lungs, and he realized he had not breathed since he first entered the water. Desperate, he launched himself at the Seal King.

Diving into the water, he found one of the submerged logs that lay beneath the tide line. Grasping it like a spear, he rose and held it steady against the Seal King's advance. The Seal King wavered, but it was too late to stop his charge. The sharpened log pierced the Great Bull Seal's chest, driving into his body. He fell with no sound but a tremendous splash, bobbed for a short time, then floated out to sea.

Horsch looked at his hands. The skin was scraped and galled where he had held the makeshift spear. He lowered his hands slowly to the salt water, and let the sting of the sea wash them clean.

The brown seal greeted Horsch first. Horsch looked at the seal warily, uncertain if he would be attacked by yet another of the tribe. But the brown seal raised his eyes and said, "Horsch. You are the Seal King now."

Horsch stood without comprehending until the other Selkies chanted his name. "Horsch," they said. "Horsch. Horsch."

"I did not fight him to become the Seal King!" Horsch said angrily.

"That is the price of the battle," the brown seal said.

Horsch stared at them. "If I refuse to be your king? What then?"

The seals hummed a mournful chorus. "Then," said the brown seal, "you may never come back to the sea. Rule us or lose your birthright forever. There are no other choices."

Horsch stood mutely before them. A gull cried, lonely, overhead. The waves lapped at the rocks as the tide made its slow way up the shoreline. Clouds gathered.

"My birthright. As you knew I would choose."

Sea Lady, he thought. *Mother of my mother. You are cruel. I am only a slave to your creatures. I am not as strong as my mother; I cannot refuse the salt in my veins. But beware – I will not serve you well.*

He waded out until the water reached his hips, and beckoned to the seals. "Come," Horsch said. "Show me the sea."

Then the water was all about him, and he swam into his new world.

The Smallest Spark

Blue sparks cascaded over the Players, skittering around the stage like demented fireflies before merging into a glow which haloed the actors with faint luminescence. The audience of townsfolk gasped, then applauded in almost perfect unison. *A good start!* thought Arlyth from her place in the wings, knowing these traders and fisherfolk were already snared in the net of magic and story which her family presented. This would be a good evening; pray the gods it would also be a lucrative one.

The play began, and Arlyth forgot about the crowd. Adapted by her father from an old ballad, the story was one of her favorites: a tale of the dragons and their defeat of an evil mage who wielded power stolen from the lives of innocents. Behind the set, their own mage cast illusions, adorning the stage with a myriad of intangible people and exotic places.

On cue, Arlyth slipped onto stage as the young queen whose early death had drawn the dragons' attention. She loved this part, since it gave her scope to act the transformation of a healthy woman into a wasted, dying wraith. She was just now, at the age of thirteen, old enough to portray the ruler effectively, and it was challenging to make the role convincing within the short span of the play. Tamisal, their mage, could make Arlyth's body appear emaciated, but only she could make the audience believe it.

Arlyth had always loved tales of the dragons. The first created beings, their gods-given task was to set right the wrongs of the world, and to prevent the misuse of power and magic. Their own magic was legendary, their wisdom supernal. Guardians, shapechangers, and immortals, their deeds were threaded into the tales of every intelligent race that walked, swam, or flew. Arlyth cherished a secret hope that someday she might see a dragon, even if only as a brief speck in the clouds above.

The actors, all family by blood or by name, spun the story into a living dream, sweeping the rapt audience along by their words and the resonant magic of legend and narrative. Arlyth spoke her dying speech, expired, and was carried out by the tumblers, Messaise and Kip. A black dragon made of cloth, wire, magic, and Arlyth's two brothers, battled the evil mage and destroyed him in a shower of blinding light and small fireworks.

She watched the rest of the play from the wings. As the last act wove together the final strands of plot, Arlyth sneaked a quick glance at the crowd. Amid the townsfolk, she could barely glimpse her five-year-old sister Merla carrying the money bowl around for donations. Merla's golden curls and brilliant smile usually added several royals to the take.

The actors froze in their places and waited for the epilogue. "And so," her father Gamidyn declaimed, "the evil was cleansed, and the kingdom freed from the tyranny of magic that oppressed it. And the dragons watched over them, and the gods were pleased. May we all have such guidance, and may the dragons always guard us from those who would use magic for evil purposes." He bowed, and a rainbow arced over the stage, the ends anchored on each side.

The townsfolk exploded into wild applause. Arlyth could hear the chink of coins as they landed in the bowl. She let out a deep sigh; they were welcome here, and the monies would repair the loose wagon axle and replenish their depleted supplies.

She joined the others onstage and curtsied gracefully, still in the character of the queen. Messaise, Kip, and Tamisal also came out to receive their accolades, as did Arlyth's brothers, divesting themselves of the dragon's framework so the audience could see their faces.

They would stay here several days, hoping their welcome would hold. This was a large town, and they could entertain many more people while gaining a brief respite from the wandering life of a Player family.

The crowd dispersed, and Arlyth began the business of helping to pack up the stage from the open field on the edge of the town and load it onto one of their three wagons. They would simply have to unpack it again tomorrow, but it was safest to have all their gear stored and ready to leave in an instant. Though the entertainment Players brought was usually well received, this was not always true of the Players themselves. Their mostly unearned reputation as thieves and beggars often chilled their welcome in settled communities.

She found herself working with Messaise and Tamisal. The contrast could not have been greater between the two men. Tamisal had pale hair, sky blue eyes, and a fine-featured, almost beautiful, face. He wore a blue costume of loose pants, long coat, and an improbable sky-blue turban which gave him a mysterious wizardly air, belied only by his mischievous expression. Messaise was a human man, lean and taciturn, with skin the color of maple sap. A seamed scar ran down one cheek, and he seldom smiled.

Arlyth knew that Messaise, in addition to being a tumbler, was also a skilled mage: his talents ran to protecting the troupe from animals and bandits, lighting fires in wet wood, and finding the right path to take through the wilderness. He and Tamisal had formed an improbable friendship, possibly based on their shared position in the troupe; Gamidyn had signed them on after their previous mage had died of the pox. Neither Messaise nor Tamisal spoke about their past, except that both had worked in a troupe before. She did not know if either were Players by birth.

"Arlyth, catch!" Tamisal tossed her a copper royal which someone from the audience had thrown past the money bowl. Arlyth picked it easily out of the air, and grinned.

Answering her grin, Tamisal opened his hands to show them empty. "Wait," he said. "I think there might be another." He closed his hands, then opened them again, revealing two more royals. "Missed those the first time. Do you want them?"

"Do I want them?" Arlyth tried unsuccessfully to scowl at Tamisal, but it was impossible in the face of his good humor, and her expression came out as a lopsided conglomeration of frown and laughter. "Might as well ask if I want dinner while you're at it. Do I want them. Hah."

Messaise looked at the field, rapidly fading to gray in the evening's dying light. "Better go scavenge before it's too dark to see.

Shame if we missed a royal for darkness." He turned and slowly walked into the field, scanning the ground for missed coins or other useful items which might have been dropped.

On the far side of the stage wagon, Gamidyn had lit a fire and was busy re-heating a delicious-smelling stew. "We'll be there in a moment!" Arlyth shouted, tucking a wooden crown into the box of stage props. "Just have to get a few things finished!"

Arlyth and Tamisal made short work of their part in the cleanup. They joined the cookfire right before Messaise finished his check of the field, and before Arlyth's brothers and little sister, who were beginning a heated argument. The other four troupe members, two aunts, an uncle, and a cousin, took seats and warmed their hands; night was still cool in these parts, despite the warmth of mid-spring.

Kip brought the dishes and held them as Gamidyn ladled out the stew, passing them to each of the family in turn. Arlyth's brothers and sister stopped fighting abruptly, dropped their last props, and rushed to get their own dinner; a savory blend of rabbit and onions. They demolished the meal quickly, and Merla, having done an excellent job collecting money, was allowed to scrape out the pot.

As night's shadows dusted the field, everyone began the nighttime routine. Arlyth's oldest brother drew water for washing, Arlyth unpacked the bedding, and Messaise went to ward their camp from wild animals or townsfolk who saw them as easy prey. Tamisal entered the third wagon to clear sleeping space for anyone who preferred not to sleep outside.

Kip disappeared into the town, and Arlyth knew that he would return with a chicken or a pie, or whatever else he could scavenge from someone's yard or windowsill. Perhaps, she thought wryly, their reputation was not *entirely* undeserved.

Just as Arlyth readied her father's bedroll, dizziness flooded over her, assailing her senses with a smothering fog of hopelessness and despair. She reached out blindly for support, and finding none, toppled onto the blankets, bumping her nose on the cold ground. For long moments she lay there, seeing no reason to rise unless the ground refused to accept her.

The dizziness ebbed slowly, leaving behind it a profound lassitude that was almost as bad as the choking despair; almost, but not quite. Arlyth's nose suddenly began to hurt. She touched it with her forefinger and felt the wetness of blood.

Lifting her head to look around, she saw that she was not the only one who had felt the suffocating sensation. Her father sat on his haunches, his expression one of exhausted horror. By the dishes, Merla whimpered quietly. No one else Arlyth could see made even the smallest sound. Even the crickets were still.

Then Tamisal exited the third wagon. His usually cheerful face was full of worry, his mouth firmed into a thin line. He did not seem as drained as Arlyth felt, but anger compressed his motions into the fluidity of someone hunting for an assailant. He looked over the campsite, apparently taking in everyone's position and condition.

Arlyth sat up and Tamisal joined her quickly. Arlyth's nose was beginning to hurt a great deal. With grim countenance, Tamisal dropped down beside her, crossed his legs, and took her head in his hands, examining her face minutely. His blue gaze full of concern, he lifted one hand to Arlyth's nose. Arlyth felt a sharp stab of pain which subsided almost immediately.

"Not as bad as it might be," Tamisal told her. He smiled a small but real smile, which Arlyth returned with heartfelt relief.

Tamisal stood and began to walk around the camp, helping people up with a proffered hand and a strong back. Arlyth found that her weariness had vanished, and she rose to help him. Gamidyn stood and began to swear steadily, using some words that Arlyth could only glean from context.

Kneeling in front of Merla, Tamisal suddenly froze. Worried, Arlyth ran to his side, followed closely by Gamidyn. Arlyth dropped down beside her little sister, hoping Merla was not hurt. She was having the uncomfortable memory that she might have experienced the terrible feeling before, though not with the same strength that had hit the Players tonight.

Merla was worse than Arlyth expected. The only color in her face was a pale tinge of blue, darker around the lips. Even Merla's curls seemed darker, and drooped around her face. Though her eyes were open, they were dull, and did not focus. Arlyth had never seen her sister so limp, even when she lay ill with the same pox that had killed their previous mage. Shivering, Arlyth looked toward Tamisal, hoping that he knew how to revive the little girl.

"What's wrong with her?" Gamidyn asked abruptly, making Arlyth jump. His tone was harsher than Arlyth had ever heard it, even when they had been chased out of one town by farmers with sickles.

"Shouldn't she feel better by now? The rest of us do. What happened, in the name of the Four?"

"She was hit harder, and she's smaller." Tamisal gathered Merla into his arms, where she lay without resistance. "I hope it hasn't done too much damage."

Before anyone else could say a thing, Kip's cheerful voice sounded from the near edge of camp. "Got a piglet this time! And with luck, the owners won't notice until we're long gone – the place is a pigsty!" He chuckled, a low, warm sound which usually elicited answering laughs from the troupe. Only silence answered.

"Is something wrong?" Kip stepped into the circle of firelight, light limning his hair with a golden nimbus. The piglet, a rabbit-sized patchwork of black and pink, squirmed slightly in his arms, but seemed content to remain. A crease appeared in the space between Kip's eyebrows. "What's wrong? What's the matter with Merla?"

The corners of Gamidyn's mouth turned down. "Some sort of magic, I think. It hit everyone here. Ask Tamisal – he seems to understand it." Gamidyn fixed his firm attention – the uncomfortable regard which always caused the troupe to work doubly hard — on the blue-clad mage. "What *did* happen, Tamisal?"

Arlyth's oldest brother said, "If someone's hurt Merla, I want to know who it is."

Gamidyn nodded. "So do we all. Tamisal?"

Tamisal bent over Merla and laid a hand on her forehead before answering. "She looks a little better." Arlyth noted with relief that color was creeping back into her sister's face. Merla moaned.

"That's not an answer," Gamidyn said. His brows drew together.

"No, it's not." Tamisal eased Merla carefully onto his shoulder. She lifted her arms and clutched them around his neck. Arlyth thought for a moment that she saw a blue glow coalesce around her sister's form, but as soon as she focused her eyes, she lost the vision. She wondered if her sight was still reacting to the fall she had taken.

"Do something with that pig before it starts squealing," Gamidyn told Kip. He turned his attention back to Tamisal. "I'm waiting."

Instead of answering, Tamisal met Gamidyn's gaze and said, "Have you felt anything like this attack before?"

"No," Gamidyn replied at the same time as Arlyth said, "Yes." Tamisal looked from one to the other, eyebrows slightly raised.

"My daughter seems to know more than I," said Gamidyn. "Arlyth, are you sure?"

Arlyth's wisps of memory suddenly consolidated into a single recollection. "Three nights ago," she said. "We played in – what's that town's name? – Eddiba. I was scrounging for lost coins, and Messaise was setting the wards, when I suddenly felt weak and a little sick to my stomach. I thought I'd just got one of the bad pasties, you remember, there were several we had to throw out. I sat down for a while, and it passed." She paused, thinking of how to explain the similarity. "I wouldn't think anything more about it, but it was the same feeling. Not my stomach, the exhaustion. As if I'd been crying for hours and was too tired to care what happened anymore." She shuddered as the moment solidified with the telling. Simply the thought of that abyss of emotion and energy terrified her.

Gamidyn swore.

Arlyth touched Merla's curls, guilt knotting her midsection. "If I'd only told someone..."

"You know what this means?" Gamidyn said. "It means it's not a townsperson. It's either one of us or something we're carrying."

Arlyth took a deep breath, which she held, distantly, until dizziness forced her to empty her lungs.

"Is everyone here?" Tamisal looked around, but the troupe, gathering about Gamidyn, returned him blank looks. From the second wagon, Arlyth could hear the piglet screech as Kip tucked it out of sight.

One of us? Arlyth thought. *Why? What's to be gained?* She could think of no reason for one of them to harm the others, and Players kept faith with other Players. It made more sense that someone had found a cursed coin, or that some magic had been cast on them by a disgruntled village mage, and had followed them as they toured.

"Messaise is still out," Arlyth's oldest brother said. "Should we go looking for him? He might be hurt."

"Don't go alone." Gamidyn spun on his heel. "Go in twos or threes. Whatever this magic is, it's powerful." He sighed. "Tamisal, I'm *still* waiting."

Tamisal adjusted his turban. "I know. If you wait a little longer, I may have an answer for you."

Before they had a chance to look for him, Messaise appeared at the edge of the firelight, apparently unharmed. "Wards are set," he said in his usual abrupt way. "Anything else before I turn in?"

The entire troupe turned to look at him. Arlyth felt an unpleasant sensation in the back of her throat, as if she were gagging on a moldy piece of bread. *Messaise?* she wondered. *He's new, and he's a mage. But why? What reason would he have for harming any of us?*

Tamisal's cool blue gaze assessed the other man. "Messaise, would you mind coming with me first, so I can talk to you?"

Messaise's features drew together into a scowl. "Can this wait?"

"No," Tamisal told him.

The scarred mage hesitated a moment, then nodded curtly. "Very well. I hope it's important."

"Oh, it is," Tamisal said softly. He put his hand on the other man's shoulder. Messaise did not shrug it off, but sighed as if Tamisal's hand were a heavy burden. The two walked off toward an arc of trees that cupped the green in a semicircle of darkness.

Gamidyn exhaled in a long breath, and frowned at the troupe. "Everyone sleeps together tonight, and we post a watch, just like we would in the Southern Forest. No one is to go off by themselves."

"Even them?" Arlyth's Aunt Laish muttered, gesturing at the place in the trees where Tamisal and Messaise now sat, talking quietly. "What do we know about either one of them?"

Arlyth looked at the mages, then at her father. "I'll go," she said, knowing that someone must listen to the conversation. It had suddenly become desperately important to know more about both men.

Gamidyn started to shake his head, but stopped suddenly. "All right. But be careful, Arlyth. I don't have any spare daughters." He smiled tightly, as if it cost him great effort.

Arlyth did not wait, but sped silently over to the tree line, a little distance from Tamisal and Messaise. It was dark outside the firelit circle, but Arlyth averted her eyes from the light, and gradually the wood's edge swam into the gray focus which starlight allowed. She entered the wood almost noiselessly, knowing how best to avoid the sound of cracking twigs and the flutter of last autumn's leaves. Much of a Player's life was spent on the road, and Arlyth had traveled in woods and forests in her earliest memories.

She wriggled into a bank of bushes which angled across the center curve of the trees, hiding herself in their large, glossy leaves. Crawling noiselessly beneath their cover, she managed to position herself within earshot of the mages, though she could barely see them, silhouetted now against the troupe's campfire.

"...and then?" Tamisal asked, both gentleness and curiosity in his tone. "What did you do?"

Messaise's voice, harsh as a crow's contrasted sharply with Tamisal's. "What could I do? Myself, against twenty bandits? I hid. I hid and watched as they slaughtered my family and my friends, down to my sister's seven month old baby." His voice roughened still more, until Arlyth found it difficult to understand his words. "I walked north after that, trying to find a troupe to take me in. Worked on my wards. Still can't get the pictures out of my head."

Tamisal laid a gentle hand on the other man's shoulder. "You say you worked on your wards. How did you work on them?"

Messaise frowned. "What do you mean? I practiced them."

A white moth landed on Arlyth's nose, tickling it. She blew lightly, trying to dislodge it without breaking her silence. But despite her care, Tamisal's head whipped around, centering on the bushes where she lay.

Tamisal said, "Arlyth? Is that you?"

Chastened by her quick discovery, Arlyth wormed from beneath the bushes and stood, brushing off dirt and leaf mold. She felt ashamed, as if she had looked into the heart of Messaise's private memories. Messaise lost all trace of expression, and simply stared at her as if she were a woodland insect instead of the girl he knew.

Tamisal sighed. "Arlyth, this was a private conversation."

Arlyth scowled, unwilling to be scolded, no matter how chastened she felt. "You're both mages. We've had a magical attack on the troupe, and we haven't known either of you all that long. What do you expect?"

Tamisal held her gaze for a long moment, before nodding his acknowledgement. "I didn't do it. Messaise didn't do it, either." Tamisal seemed troubled. "At first I thought it was he, but he has managed to reassure me. All he did was set the wards, with his own birthfire, not life stolen from others." He frowned, an expression which aged his usually cheerful face. "Too much life. In Eddiba it wasn't that strong, and the time before, it was hardly noticeable. Whoever is using the birthfire is becoming less cautious, or perhaps is acquiring a taste for it. And that's serious."

"Life stolen from others?" Arlyth knew from the tales that the gods expressly forbade theft of life's energy, or birthfire, to fuel one's magic. Dragons had died fighting workers of such magic. She knew it was the first warning given to all beginning mages.

Tamisal stood, followed by Messaise, who unfolded his long body with tumbler's ease. "Let's get back to camp," the blue-clad mage said. "I've got to talk to your father about that illusion he wants me to do on Laish's character. I don't think it will work very well, but Gamidyn knows what he wants better than I do." He grinned, seeming to Arlyth as if he became lit from within by a joyful heart, despite his obvious worry over possible evil magic in the troupe's midst.

They walked the short distance back across the field in silence. Arlyth blinked her eyes as the firelight strengthened, blinding her to the night. All three wagon doors stood open as the troupe finished preparations for bedding down in the cool night. Only Gamidyn still sat by the fire, continuing to feed it sticks to keep it bright. Arlyth did not blame him – given what she had felt tonight, she would have preferred daylight.

A frantic screeching from the second wagon was joined by a set of crashes and Merla's shriek. "Pig!" Kip yelled, as a small black and white form darted through the door and headed straight for the field. It streaked over the edge of the fire, sending sparks and coals flying. Gamidyn grabbed for it and lost his balance, sitting down heavily on the empty stew pot. Kip ran after it, easily avoiding Gamidyn, the fire, and the confusion of bedrolls which littered the campsite.

Arlyth felt a painful jolt, like the sharp blow she had once taken from a wagon's crossbar. Her legs went limp and gave out under her as if they were made of fabric instead of flesh, and a miasma of black despondency choked her mind and spirit. In the corner of her vision, she saw Messaise stumble and also fall. The piglet gave one terrified squeal and crumpled to the ground. Even the fire seemed to burn less brightly.

Beside her, Tamisal's form seemed to glow with sudden blue flame. Despite the soup of misery which inundated the camp, Arlyth felt her heart lighten. With effort, she turned her head to look at the blue-clad mage.

Tamisal's form blazed with light the color of a morning sky. "Kip," he said, in a tone that thrummed through Arlyth's bones and tickled her veins. "Stop." Though he spoke quietly, it was impossible not to hear him.

Arlyth immediately felt less weighty. Bee sting tingles threaded down her extremities. She sat up, still staring at Tamisal. Light was a simple illusion spell, but this glow was somehow different. She would ask him about it later, but she did not wish to place herself in the middle of an argument where mages were involved.

Her attention turned to Kip, who wore a mulish expression that he usually kept only for offensive villagers. His muscles were taut, and he shook with either fear or exertion. "Stop what? I'm not doing anything." The words were more defiant than his stance.

Messaise pushed himself from the ground and struggled to his feet. His eyes were wide and dark. He looked at Kip as if the other tumbler had grown wings.

Tamisal's cheerful friendliness was gone, replaced by a somber mien and inexorable tone. "The magic you are using does not belong to you. It's hurting everyone around you."

Kip shook his head. "I haven't taken much. Just a little, here and there. For the good of the troupe."

Arlyth blinked several times, confused. Kip was no mage; she had known him all her life as the cheerful tumbler with a facility for craftwork, and a penchant for making off with villagers' pigs, chickens, spare clothes, and occasional loaf of bread.

Messaise spoke for the first time since returning to camp. "Haven't taken much?" he asked in a voice like the scrape of a knife against a whetstone. "You nearly killed Merla."

Kip's face paled. "That was an accident. I didn't mean to take so much. I just wanted to get a good, stout piglet without causing us any trouble during our stay. So that no one would notice. What's wrong with that?"

"Look at the pig," Tamisal told him.

Kip gingerly approached the piglet's prone form. It did not move as he prodded it with the toe of his boot. Arlyth could tell even from where she sat that it was dead.

"Was that what you meant to do?" Tamisal asked softly, his eyes catching the light like glittering sapphires. "Kill?"

Kip's breathing quickened. "I was just trying to stop it from running. I just took a little power, from the troupe, from the pig – this can't have happened." Sweat began to collect on his forehead in tiny droplets.

"How did you learn this skill?" asked Tamisal, gently, but inflexibly. "Did someone teach you?"

A little prudent fear touched Arlyth's mind. Tamisal's tone was not friendly. This was not the same man she knew from weeks of working together in the troupe. This was the voice of a judge passing sentence, with the certainty that he had such a right.

Kip shook his head. "I've learned a few tricks from the mages over the years, but I'm no mage. Fire starting, lights; still, I always wanted to be on the stage, not behind it." His voice roughened, and a groove creased the skin between his eyes. "But people throw away power on all sorts of things that don't matter. Why shouldn't I use that power to help the troupe? There's plenty of it, and no one ever wields it. I used what I knew to call out that power before it was wasted."

"Look around you," said Tamisal in even, measured tones. "You took the life of that piglet. You nearly took Merla's. You've taken life and power and strength from everyone you care about. And you're taking more all the time."

Kip merely shook his head, whether in denial or disbelief, Arlyth could not tell.

Tamisal continued, inexorably. "You want more, don't you? It feels like you could do anything, as if you had an endless store of magic. That's the danger. You're not the one who pays the price; it's paid in birthfire by the ones you love. It gets easier and easier to take, until those unfortunate enough to know you lose everything."

Messaise stepped forward with a menacing fluidity that chilled Arlyth. Kip held his ground, whether from a reserve of courage or simply defiance she could not tell.

"And that," Messaise said, "is why the gods forbid the working of another's magic. You're taking something to which you have no right." His muscles tensed, as if he readied himself for a fight. "Haven't you ever heard the first law taught to mages?" His voice dropped to a hiss. "The birthfire of others is sacred, and no mage has the right to turn it to his use."

"Well, that's good," Kip said, almost spitting in Messaise's face. "Because I'm no mage. And what I and the troupe do are none of your business, *peasant*." He stepped closer to Messaise, fighting distance. Arlyth cringed, both at the insult and at the incipient violence.

The entire troupe was awake by this time, and they all stared at the three men. No one seemed willing to intervene in their argument. Arlyth considered it, and immediately dropped the idea as far too dangerous. She knew little about what Messaise and Tamisal might do, and even Kip had become a sudden stranger.

Swifter than Arlyth's eyes could follow, Messaise reached out and grabbed Kip's arm, pinning it behind him. Kip immediately collapsed, throwing Messaise off balance. Kicking out, Kip swept his legs into Messaise, and the two men fell.

They were well matched. Messaise was quicker, but Kip had the advantage of solid strength. Kip tried using his weight to pin the other man, but Messaise eeled from his grasp and rolled to one side.

Arlyth looked around, hoping that someone could halt the fight before either man was injured. "Stop, please!" she called. "We'll talk about it! We'll work it out! Just stop!"

"You're both acting like fools," said Gamidyn, disgust in his voice. He stood and strode forward toward the pair.

Tamisal got there first. He grabbed Kip's collar and Messaise's sleeve, forcibly separating them with more strength than Arlyth would have ever guessed he owned. "Stop!" he said, in a voice which demanded compliance, and reverberated through the camp like a river in flood.

Kip, caught in the motion of standing, squatted there like a rising toad. Not until Tamisal dropped his hold on both combatants did he get to his feet, slowly. He glared at Tamisal, who met Kip's gaze with a level stare of his own.

Kip rolled his eyes. "I don't recognize your right to command me," he snapped at the mage. "I don't know what magic that was, but keep it and your hands off me if you value your fingers."

Messaise made a small gesture with his hand. Kip seemed to freeze, unable to do anything but breathe. Arlyth wondered what they would do, now that Kip seemed to be under Messaise's control. She knew that she could forgive Kip – he was one of her family – but she was not sure she could ever again trust him not to use his draining magic.

Then Arlyth felt a pull of something trying to suck her spirit from her body. With all the life and strength she had, she pulled back. There was a moment of perfect tension as Kip's limbs moved and straightened. He shook himself, like a dog shedding water, and turned angrily toward Messaise. Arlyth began to feel the weakness of life flowing from her to Kip.

Tamisal made a small sound of disgust. "That's enough," he said firmly. Strength rebounded into Arlyth, as Kip's hold snapped. Tamisal backed up until he was at the edge of camp, against the green.

Then he began to change. His form lengthened, stretching and stretching out behind him into ropy coils of muscle and tail. Smooth skin scaled over, and fine features melted into a long-snouted, narrow face which confronted the Players with enormous blue eyes. Arlyth found herself looking at a slender sky-blue dragon, huge enough to fill the entire field.

Arlyth could not believe it. Each of Tamisal's blue eyes alone was larger than her head. Even in the dark, his scales shimmered with an iridescent blue glow, like a rainbow in an evening sky. He was hornless, but a feathery crest flowed from his head and down his neck, where it ended at the shoulders. Behind this, massive wings folded into compact pleats of lightweight skin; Arlyth guessed that unfolded, they might span the village. On each of his four feet were five flexible toes, capped with talons of cobalt blue. When he opened his mouth, Arlyth could see rapier teeth which she uncomfortably guessed could bite through a demon's hide.

Awe suffused her; this was her deepest wish, to meet a dragon and not simply to glimpse one. Tamisal was the most beautiful creature she had ever seen.

A quick glance showed everyone staring at the immense dragon confronting them. No one spoke, or even breathed hard. It was one thing, Arlyth thought, to tell tales of dragons, and quite another to have such a tale come to life in their own camp. Her heart pounded with excitement and a profound joy that such creatures existed in their own small world of plays and travel.

Kip looked at him in shock, finally dropping his gaze to the ground. "I never meant to harm anyone," he said, his voice shaking.

Tamisal nodded his head just enough for the gesture to be recognizable. "It's why you're still alive. But you must stop. Right now."

Kip lifted a scared face to Tamisal. "I'm not fool enough to think I can fight you. What must I do?"

Tamisal drew a deep breath that created a breeze strong enough to pull the fire in his direction. "Swear that you will never again take the birthfire of another. I will bind your power so that you cannot use it; and if you try, I will know. If I am forced to return because you are working such magic, I will kill you. You have only one chance, Kip. Take it."

Kip straightened his back and dropped his arms to his side. "I so swear," he said in a trembling voice, barely audible to Arlyth. "I will never again take the magic of another. If I do, the dragons may do with me what they will."

As soon as he stopped speaking, Kip's figure was suffused with an intense blue flame that seemed to wrap around him and pour through him like ink through water. He gasped, but the flame faded almost as soon as it appeared. Kip staggered back a step, then caught his balance and steadied. He drew a breath as if to speak, then ran from the circle of firelight to the shelter of the second wagon. The dragon did not move to stop him.

Blue sparks seemed to explode from Tamisal's dragon body, which suddenly winked out, to be replaced by the blue-clad mage Arlyth had learned to love. Lines of care smoothed from his skin as he contemplated Kip's trail. The sparks glittered, fountained, and vanished.

Arlyth finally felt safe enough to step forward and speak. "Tamisal? You're a *dragon*?" She stared at him in fascination, trying to see traces of the majestic creature in the blue-turbaned mage. The eyes, she thought, were the same.

"So it would seem," Tamisal said dryly, but his mouth quirked with characteristic good humor.

"But why?" asked Arlyth, confused more now than when he had appeared as a dragon. Dragons in stories were lofty creatures who commanded kings, not laughing people who took orders from mere Players. "Why ride with us and play at stage magic when you're one of the world's guardians? What's so important about us?"

Tamisal's expression became solemn. "Everyone is important, Arlyth. Don't tell yourself that Players are beneath notice." He looked over at the second wagon, where Kip hid. "It's much easier to keep a problem small than to confront it when it becomes big enough to topple kingdoms." He grinned, his countenance so impish that Arlyth could not help but grin back.

Gamidyn said, "Lord Tamisal – what next? Are you going to leave us? Now that we know you're a dragon? Surely you can't mean to ride with us any longer."

Tamisal snapped his fingers, and blue sparks sprinkled his hands like tiny stars. "I'd like to stay; I've enjoyed traveling with you. But other matters are pressing." He gestured toward Messaise. "Here's the only mage you really need. He's a good man, and he'll do well for you."

Merla, the only member of the troupe who did not seem intimidated by the truth of Tamisal's nature, looked up at him with her eyes wide. "Are you going away? I don't want you to go!"

Tamisal leaned over and picked her up, placing one hand on her head. "I have something for you." He held one hand palm up where she could see. Into it popped a blue glass hawk, the size of an apple, and brilliantly styled so that it seemed almost ready to move and take wing. "Take this and keep it safe. It won't break, I promise. And you can think about me when you look at it."

Merla put both arms around Tamisal's neck and hugged him tightly. Then she took the bird and looked at it. Tamisal set her on the ground, and smiled a little sadly.

"Farewell," he said. "All of you. Care for Kip, and try to forgive him. And take the blessings of a dragon with you."

He winked at them. Then, in a rain of blue sparks, he vanished.

Following Seas

Black tresses drifted in waves to Noémie's booted feet as her knife severed the last strands of long hair. She brushed dark threads from the arms of her leather jacket, smoothed them from her breeches, and picked them from the collar of her canvas shirt. No regret lingered behind the fall of hair; she had already sacrificed her honor and her maidenhead to Jandith's urgent courtship.

Luck had made her slender, boyish. Love and witchery would conceal her from the ship's crew, and from Jandith's clever eyes. Noémie patted the pouch next to her heart which contained the witchwife's charm of wax, etched with her name, then melted together with secret herbs and a drop of Noémie's blood. Even those who had known her from birth would see only a young boy, eager to seek his fortune upon the high seas.

She cast a last look around the cottage where she had lived all her life: she would never see it again. Even if her father did not discover the truth of her tryst with Jandith, he would never allow her to return after she had disgraced herself by running off to sea with a ship full of sailors. 'Whore' might not be the worst thing he would call her.

Bidding farewell to the pots and pans, the toothless old broom, the meager furniture, Noémie hefted the pack containing her few provisions and a small amount of money. She would not take much. Those who sought work on the great trading ships were often desperate or destitute. An unskilled sailor was a potential liability for the crew, and need not expect good treatment at the hands of his shipmates – at least, until he learned his ropes and knots.

Jandith was no native of Noémie's town. The *Sea Crow* had blown into harbor two months ago, with an eastern squall and the spring tide. Gathering on the shore, Noémie's friends and neighbors had waited, ready to save lives or salvage cargo. But the captain, experienced and calm, had steered his ship over jutting rocks, through the shallows, and into the harbor without loss of life. He had spent much of the last two months arranging repairs for the rock-damaged hull and disposing of cargo to make way for a new voyage and new profit.

A weatherwitch's warding had been one of the most expensive items to replace, but also one of the most important. Weatherwitches could protect a ship from dangerous gales and high seas, but they were rare, and few would do such exhausting work without sufficient pay. Only one lived in this town, and his fees were high. Still, a merchant's cargo was well worth the price.

Noémie had met Jandith a few days after the *Sea Crow* faltered into port. He had entered the market square intent on purchasing fresh baked bread and a bone-handled knife, his words quiet and hoarse. She did not learn until later that he was the ship's boatswain; she noticed him first for his nimbus of gold-touched hair, then his large frame and work-roughened hands which held the market wares with a delicacy at odds with their appearance. Noémie loved those hands, which had come to cherish every part of her body with a lover's skill and gentleness.

Despite living among seafarers all her life, she did not know how to swim, nor did she possess the most rudimentary seamanship. But she was stronger than she looked, and willing to work. She shrugged the pack onto her shoulder and slipped out the door, letting it swing back into the frame with a clap of wood against wood. Outside the sun scoured shadows from her vision, winking and scintillating on the sloping waterfront only a few houses away. The odors of salt and fish, wood, ropes and sailcloth assailed her nose.

Jandith had sworn his faithfulness each time they made love, his words honest and tender. Noémie believed him; tears stood in his eyes when he spoke of leaving her alone and unwed. "When I return, I will bring you a ring," he whispered into the hollow of her throat the last time they lay together. Her own eyes stinging, she wondered then if the *Sea Crow* would return. Her body ached for him, but the pain in her heart was worse. It was after their last liaison that she had conceived the idea of joining him upon the seas, even if he would not know her.

She picked her way downhill over coarse grass and stones, trying to look as confident as she wished to appear. A neighbor woman hung her washing on a line strung between a ramshackle cottage and the remains of a weathered pine, but did not even glance at Noémie as she passed. Two men who had known her since babyhood ignored Noémie as well. The baker's tot looked at her in interest, but she thought that more likely to be curiosity than recognition; strange sailors and merchants frequented the town whenever a ship docked, and there were almost always two or three ships in port. Nonetheless, Noémie sighed in relief at this first successful test of her amulet's efficacy.

She looked toward the *Sea Crow*: the largest ship anchored in the semicircular harbor, with bare masts that would raise wings of rope and sailcloth when the tide rose that afternoon. On the bow, the wooden form of a perched cormorant lifted its gaze of faded paint toward the hills. These slanted steeply from the shoreline, protecting the vessels from the worst gales which engulfed the inland beyond the hills during the winter months.

As Noémie passed, she saw sailors lading cargo, food, and water onto the *Sea Crow*. Most of the deckhands would be busy with this task, but the captain would occupy himself with other business; keeping the books; studying his charts; bargaining with the weatherwitches; hiring crew. If her timing were correct, she would find this captain, not aboard ship, but in the filthier of the two waterfront inns that strove for clientele among the temporarily beached seamen.

Down the narrow lane, irregularly spread with cobblestones and horse manure, rose the *Mermaid*, a squat structure built of driftwood and salvaged ship's planking. The chinks were crudely stuffed with pitch-sodden grass, which did nothing to keep out the wind in winter. Noémie yanked at the door where it stuck against its sill, and entered. Inside, men looked up from their tankards with eyes red-rimmed from the previous night's carousing. Three dock whores, their bosoms almost fully exposed, gazed at her intently before dismissing Noémie as inexperienced and penniless.

Jandith's captain, Signy, sat alone on the end of a long table behind a plate of potatoes and kelp greens. He was a tall, lean man, his hair iron-gray, his matching gray gaze bright and clever. Pushing her way past the common sailors, Noémie presented herself at the captain's seat, ready to argue if he found an excuse to turn her away.

His eyebrows frowned, and he barked out a mirthless laugh. "To sea, then, lad? It's a hard life, and more work than pleasure. If you ship out with the *Sea Crow*, you'll soon find that there's no toil you've ever done can compare to what you'll find aboard. Let me see your hands." She held them out for him to examine her palms and fingers, covered with calluses from a lifetime of maintaining her father's house. "Hmm, at least you're used to work. Don't know as you'll be strong enough for the sails, but a limber cabin boy, there's uses for those." He released her hands and stared at her in what seemed a sort of friendly challenge.

"Yes sir," Noémie answered. "Work I'm willing to do, the harder the better. My family's gone, I've no home. You'll never hear complaint from me, Captain. It's the sea for me, if you'll take me on."

"I'd better hear no complaints," Captain Signy responded. He looked her critically up and down; Noémie held her breath as waited to see if his perception would pierce her amulet's illusion. A wave of ice seemed to wash through her, and she barely held back a shudder of excitement and apprehension. This would not be the only time she must trust wholly to the charm she wore and let it arbitrate her destiny.

After moments which stretched longer than they ought, Captain Signy nodded. "We sail with the tide. Go to my boatswain, and tell him I said you're our new cabin boy. If you're not there, we'll leave without you. If you can't keep pace with the crew we'll toss you overboard." He laughed.

Noémie was not sure if the captain's last comment was meant seriously, but she grinned back. "I'll be there, Captain. And you see if I don't make the best cabin boy ever sailed on the *Sea Crow*."

"Save your words," said the Captain Signy. "Before long you'll need the breath."

Noémie went immediately to present herself at the *Sea Crow*. The length of two tall trees laid end to end, its three bare masts loomed over all the other ships in the harbor like the arms of an enormous wooden monster. Two long and narrow boards served as a gangplank, stretching from shore to upper deck in uneasy alliance with the water's edge. Noémie scrambled up, looking around for Jandith.

Of the twenty crew members, several worked on deck. Two crewmen directed her to wait while they sent for the boatswain. Noémie gazed around her in fascination, at the ropes and the rigging bound tightly to the masts. The upper deck was divided in two parts. The masts impaled the deck where Noémie stood; a higher tier, a third the ship's length, rose to meet the bow. This section was capped by a sheltered enclosure from which the ship's wheel peeked hesitantly. The cormorant figurehead stared outward, its wings half-spread.

On the mainmast, an iron charm hung, the weatherwitch's amulet which would fend off the worst storms and keep the ship sailing through rough seas.

Though Noémie had always lived by the harbor, this was her first time aboard ship. She felt motion beneath her feet, though the deck was more stable than she expected. Her imagination had envisioned the vessel bucking and leaping like a horse with saddle sores.

Jandith's head emerged from a hatch across the deck's width, followed by his strong, muscular body. Noémie felt her breath catch and hold with the wonder that such a fine man would love her and wish to spend his life with her. A pulse beat wildly in her throat, and she forced herself to take a deep, even breath as she remembered her deception. If anyone would see through her disguise, it would be Jandith.

Jandith approached, looking at her dubiously. "New cabin boy?" He frowned. "Last one took half the crew's money in cards and lit out as soon as we dropped anchor. You'd best not follow that example."

"Captain Signy took me on." Noémie lifted her chin defiantly. "What do I need to do?"

Jandith nodded. "Got mettle, I see. Captain Signy's the best. You needn't fear the crew while he's your master. None of that aboard the *Sea Crow*."

His words confused Noémie, but she nodded as if she understood. "What are my duties?" she asked. "And what do I call you?"

"Sir," answered Jandith. "You call everyone sir while you're green. Your duties are to care for the captain's cabin, to bring him food and drink, to run errands for him. When he's got no need of you, come to me or to the quartermaster and we'll set you other chores." He frowned again. "We've twenty-one crew aboard, twenty-two, if you're to be counted. Then there's the captain, the quartermaster, and me." He snorted. "You look none too likely, lad, but I'll wait to try you. The captain must've liked your look, however girlish you seem. What's your name?"

A single hammer stroke pounded Noémie's heart before she realized that the comment was merely chance, and Jandith had not recognized her. "Nim, sir," she squeaked out, realizing that she had succeeded. "What do I do now?"

"Nim, eh? Stow your pack in the captain's cabin, and meet back here before we cast off." Jandith gestured to a crewman. "You! Take young Nim to the cabin, show him the galley, and keep him out of the way until we're at sea."

The crewman, twice as big around as Noémie, with an exaggerated definition of muscle, spat onto the deck and gestured with a crooked finger for her to follow him through the hatch where Jandith had emerged. A ladder, wooden and polished with the traffic of years, led to the lower deck. Noémie waited a moment for her vision to adjust to the faint light coming from above and from the sprinkle of portholes in the hull. She wrinkled her nose; here it smelled strongly of tar, fish, and standing water. The floor lurched beneath her feet, and she grabbed the ladder to keep her balance.

The crewman turned and laughed in derision. "Green as they come. Listen to me, boy. You're the novice on this ship. You do what anyone tells you, no questions, no fuss. You do that, you earn your place. You give anyone trouble, the voyage won't be short enough. Hear me?"

"I hear," said Noémie, then added a hasty, "Sir."

"You're learning. Good. Cabin's this way."

Noémie would not have thought to call the enclosed space below the bow a cabin; 'closet' might have been closer to the mark. Two ledges jutted from the wall, one which spread into a narrow bunk, and another covered with charts and papers. The entire space had perhaps a length and width equal to the height of a tall man. A trunk with rotten leather straps was wedged into the space between the bed's foot and the door. If the ship had been bigger, she might have thought the crewman was jesting with her.

"Where am I to sleep?" she asked, her arm describing the cramped room. "There's nowhere even to leave my pack." She cleared her throat. Sir."

The crewman folded his arms and laughed even more derisively than before. "There's floor, isn't there? You need satin sheets and velvet pillows? You're so fancy, go sail on some lord's ship, not on the *Sea Crow*. We're plain men here. Be glad you don't sleep above decks like the rest of us."

Repulsed, Noémie hesitated, and wondered if she had made a mistake. Then she remembered Jandith's gentle hands, her severed hair, and her father's inflexibility. She was committed now. She could not go back. However little she liked it, she was now cabin boy aboard the *Sea Crow*. She set her jaw and slung her pack off her shoulder, settling it underneath the captain's bunk.

"Show me the galley," she said to the crewman, her voice soft. "Sir."

Noémie soon discovered that her ideas about the ship's motion were better founded than she knew. As soon as the ship lifted anchor and clove into the sea beyond the harbor, it moved like a living thing, tossing about anything not carefully stowed. Its turbulent motion spilled Noémie from her feet several times: she envied the crewmen who walked about the ship as if it were as solid as any open field. She waited for the sickness to come; she had heard tales of that often enough.

It did not come. Instead, Noémie began to gain her sea legs, and moved about the ship with a new certainty. She busied herself with duties: she waited on the captain, ran errands and messages, helped the quartermaster with the crew's provisions, and gutted fish in the galley.

The crew wasted no time playing pranks upon her. Noémie learned to look carefully at her plate or bowl for raw baitfish or something else unpleasant placed in the midst of her dinner. Every night she examined her blanket and pack for signs of tampering.

"The crew bedevils you too much, come to me," Captain Signy told her. "I'll stop it." But Noémie stiffened her back and endured the relentless teasing, knowing that she would never win a place if the crew saw her as weak or a talebearer. No word of complaint escaped her lips.

At several times, she glanced around to see Captain Signy watching her. This unnerved Noémie more than the crew's taunts and jokes at her expense; she could not help but wonder if the captain had guessed her secret. Though she slept in his cabin, beneath the shelf which served as his bed, he ignored her completely during their hours of sleep. She attended to her body's needs only when she was sure to be alone, and changed clothes in front of no one. Still, Captain Signy watched her and said no word.

She saw little of Jandith. In directing the crew, he kept far too busy to teach Noémie the things she must learn. Instead, he sent her to follow the orders of any crew who needed an extra hand. She learned to clamber up the limp rope ladders that scaled the mast; to immediately stow any gear left unattended on deck; and to navigate by the incandescent stars which emerged at sunset and blazed across the sky until dawn gently returned them to the night. She became familiar with the shanties sung against the pull of the sail, and heard her assumed name in some of the bawdier verses.

Gradually, the crew's jests lightened, and they began to include her when they spoke among themselves. Most discussions happened in the galley, as some of the men retired from their duties, and others ate before going to theirs. Noémie would serve them flatbread and pickled onions at the long table, and listen without comment. She began to feel as if she were truly a part of this group of men, hardened by work and danger. That feeling of fellowship warmed her even on days when gales buffeted the ship with their vassal waves.

The entire crew venerated both the quartermaster and Captain Signy. "Couldn't ask for better officers," said the cook, a man so tall and bony that Noémie wondered if he ever tasted his own dishes. "Fair, both of them, and the captain has a nose for the wind that a weatherwitch would envy. Best I've ever served." Five crewmates, their long duty shifts ended, murmured assent.

Their opinion on Jandith was less certain. "Not too bad," one sailor told her. "He knows his business, and gets things done. Has a temper, though, and you don't want to rile him."

"And ashore he's a one for drink and for the ladies," one of the deckhands added. "Dodges his work in port. Can't find him unless you ask around town for some pretty lass with too much trust and not a dram of sense."

A red pulse assailed Noémie's temples, and she faced the five other men who occupied the small cabin. This was not the Jandith she knew, or would ever have suspected. She wondered how the crew, each man so close to his fellow on the *Sea Crow*, could be so wrong. She was not willing to believe this depiction of the gentle man she loved.

She drew a deep breath and faced the deckhand. "Doesn't seem like that to me." The galley table held several plates, bowls, cups, and a pitcher. She brought out a clean plate and slapped it hard onto the table in front of him. "He knows his ship's business, but all I hear from him is 'Nim, stow the ropes', 'Nim, get the spyglass', 'Nim, climb up and straighten the rigging'. Not a word of girls or even yet beer."

The men present began to laugh. "Listen to our pretty Nim!" said the first sailor. "He looks so much like a girl, he falls in love with our boatswain just like one!"

Noémie was by now experienced enough to expect this sort of reaction, and to realize that her charade was still intact. "Jealous?" she asked, and grinned at the speaker. His crewmates laughed even harder.

"Got you there!" the cook told him, then turned to Noémie. "Best watch it, lad, you'll find him creeping into your blankets tonight. Were me, I'd take a good sharp knife to bed."

"Why?" The helmsman leaned back and scratched beneath his arm. "You know nobody's crawling into your bed, Cookie. You peeling potatoes in your sleep?"

The conversation took a bawdier turn, as Noémie had learned to expect from the men, cut off for weeks at a time from women. She knew there was no ill will behind the jibes. The crew constantly tested their mettle against each other, both in words and in work. She felt no urge to compete.

During a break in the exchange, Noémie cleared her throat. "Does the boatswain have a wife? A sweetheart? Talks about anyone after he leaves port?"

A deckhand shook his head. "He's never going to settle, our Jandith." He grabbed the pitcher as an ocean swell tilted the room hard enough to send dishes sliding across the tabletop's rough wood. "Though I'd say he looked a bit sunstruck when he boarded last town.

Got some fine loving from the girls there, I'd say. Not a word from him, though."

Satisfied, Noémie let out the breath she did not remember she held. If Jandith's behavior was different than usual at the last port, was that not proof that he truly loved her? She could forgive his past, if he meant to make his future with her.

The galley began to shake, and she felt a long, deep tremor begin, just beyond the edge of sound. A voice above decks called something unintelligible but frantic. Then a clearer voice sounded through the galley door. "All hands on deck! Storm's coming, and worse!"

The men in the galley, including the cook, immediately abandoned food and drink and headed out the galley door to the ladder which led above. Noémie followed them, not sure what to expect. She felt the ship roll under her feet, riding the crests of the waves, then crashing into troughs which the sea had created from wind and water and the ocean's sheer violence. Nimbly, Noémie clambered up the ladder.

She was almost blown from her feet by the wind's fury. Noémie grabbed for a clumsy hold on the edge of the deck, and somehow kept upright, though the wood beneath her glistened with a slippery mix of water and mold. She looked around.

Despite the weatherwitch's protective charm, hanging black from the mainmast, heavy cloud rapidly overtook the flawless sky, filling it with swirling rain-sodden darkness. To the east, she could see a line of calm ocean piling quickly into whitecaps with the force of the western storm.

Captain Signy appeared, followed quickly by Jandith. "Lower the sails!" bellowed the captain. "Kale, get to the wheel and turn us into the wind! Déshant, Thrush, swing that rudder about!"

The next few hours hurled Noémie into a nightmare she could not have conjured from her darkest fancies. The sails swelled and whipped like angry ghosts over the surge of the waves; Noémie helped gather them and lash them tightly to the masts. The foremost sail ripped before it could be lowered, but the sailors drew it down anyway, securing it for the duration of the storm. They could mend it later. Underneath them, a churning chaos of seawater thrust the ship forward in the green-black ocean. Noémie had never realized that water could feel so hard. Each time the ship topped a breaker, it smashed against the hummocks of wave with renewed ferocity, sending torrents of water over the bow. Occasionally the groan or the brittle snap of wood punctuated the tempest's shriek.

Noémie made her way to the rail so that she could see what lay ahead. As she reached the edge, another monstrous wave broke against the ship. The ocean's surge overwhelmed her vision. Instinctively, she raised her arms against it as the freezing water engulfed her with salt and darkness.

Then Noémie felt a hand at her shoulder, wrenching her away from the rail. She coughed and sputtered brine, and knuckled stinging salt from her eyes. When she could blink again, she turned to look for her rescuer; she could see Captain Signy's back as he darted across the deck to aid another crewman.

Suddenly Noémie realized that the previous wave had claimed another. The cook, his bony hand reaching for an insubstantial hold, floated rapidly away from the *Sea Crow*. His mouth opened, but Noémie could hear nothing over the wind's mad roar. Another wave covered him, and he vanished under the sea's foaming shroud. The winds keened through the ship in a fearsome lament.

Noémie called back to him, but she heard nothing, even her own voice. She knew that a jump into the freezing water would prove fatal to the best of swimmers, and she could not keep herself afloat, much less rescue another. A pang of sorrow insinuated itself under her breastbone, where it lodged beneath the fear and desperation she now felt.

Suddenly the wind rose into a howling crescendo then abated. Noémie thought at first that the storm might be finally receding. She looked up and to the west.

A colossal wave reared before them, an impossible mass of solid green, many times the height of the *Sea Crow*. As if time had stopped in the space between heartbeats, Noémie watched it gather and build as it stole its sister waves, creating a deadly canyon directly in front of the ship. She grabbed for the mast, hoping that she could hang on – and that the ship would hold - when they smacked into the trench, figurehead first. The ship screeched like a living thing as its bow hit the water.

Somehow the *Sea Crow* righted itself in time to confront the mountain of water which now curved above the ship, powerful and predatory. Noémie stared at it, determined to face her death, rather than hide from its inexorable advance. And, watching the wave, she saw what the water concealed.

Towering over the wave as if it rode the storm's fury, an enormous wedge-shaped head emerged. Its mouth opened wider than seemed natural to show four rows of teeth, each bigger than Noémie's head. A snakelike neck followed, sleek green shading into sunset gold and red, crowned with a red-gold mane as fine as silk. Fearsome though it was, it possessed an odd grace and beauty, together with an allure which glittered in its eyes, golden as sunken treasure. Noémie stared and could not force herself to move.

The wave broke. An avalanche of ocean cascaded onto the ship, and Noémie held onto the mast with both arms to save herself from the force of the water. She heard a loud crack. The ship righted itself, though it felt curiously limp as it balanced against the sea's face; Noémie hoped that whatever had broken, the *Sea Crow* would manage to keep its precarious seat on the waves. She saw several crewmen who had been washed into the water, and her stomach wrenched as she searched to see if Jandith were among them. If he was, she could not see him.

The monster, its entirety of neck now revealed, lowered its head and picked one of the sailors daintily from the water, tossing the man into the air before swallowing him. His screams were stifled by the tumult of wind and surf.

Noémie released the mast and backed up reflexively. She felt herself collide with some other lucky soul, who had also managed to avoid being washed into the churning ocean. Glancing back, she saw it was Jandith.

Relief and new concern battled each other as she realized Jandith was safe. He ignored her, gazing at the monster with features frozen into an icy shield. Noémie hesitated, waiting for Jandith to recover and to make some decision to fight, or to steer the ship away from harm. Each time the monster moved it shook the ship in a tremulous way that spoke of serious damage to the vessel. Several times Noémie had to again reach for the mast so that she did not slide across the rain-slicked deck.

She was not sure how to fight, but cast about her for something to use as a weapon while the monster plucked another man from the wild ocean waters. They had little time; a creature this size could swallow the entire ship and only blunt the edge of its hunger.

A piece of rail, splintered from its main length, hung with one end severed and the other attached by only a few shreds of wood. Noémie grabbed the free section, twisting it with her arms while she pinned it with one foot, hopping to keep her balance on the shifting surface of the deck. Freed from the ship's tenuous grasp, what emerged was a crude spear. It stretched a little shorter than Noémie's height, with a jagged point on each end.

All the unlucky sailors had now disappeared from the water. The monster whipped its head from side to side, then focused on the *Sea Crow* itself. Poised like a falcon stooping upon prey, it darted its head forward toward Noémie and Jandith. Noémie braced her spear.

Jandith dived for safety under some coils of rope which still clung to the deck from bent iron clips. The creature's teeth snapped at

Noémie. As it attacked, the ship lurched. Noémie lost her balance and fell backward against the mast. Two giant teeth scraped painfully across her chest, tearing open her shirt and gouging her breastbone with two long but shallow lacerations. The cord which held her charm snapped, and the pouch flew through the rail into the ocean.

Noémie doubled over and dropped her spear. She heard Jandith gasp, then cry out, "Noémie!" His gaze met hers, before shifting to the serpent monster. He gathered himself from beneath the rope coils and sprang forward, not to aid her, but to fling himself through the *Sea Crow*'s hatch into the relative safety of the deck below.

Noémie raised her arms to shield her head, though she knew the gesture to be useless. Shadow swallowed darkness, and she could tell that the creature was returning for her. In a long moment of terror, she waited for the crunching teeth to snatch her into the air.

Beside her, rolling loosely, lay her makeshift spear. Suddenly, hands seized it and angled it into the wind. Noémie closed her eyes and cried out.

She felt the monster's mane trail over her arms, but no pain followed. Instead, a scream, like that of angry stallion three times the size of the ship, assailed her ears. The *Sea Crow* began to shake violently. Noémie slit her eyes open, lowering her arms in order to brace herself against the ship's motion.

The monster had pulled away from the boat, and now tossed its head from side to side to rid itself of the wooden sliver that projected from one eye. Beside Noémie crouched Captain Signy, drenched with a viscous red fluid that the rain was already beginning to wash away.

His jaw was set and firm.

The monster swept its gaze back over the ship. Captain Signy poised in taut stillness like a mother eagle warding her nest. Then the monster jerked back, flexed its neck into long, improbable loops, and dived cleanly into the dark water. The Sea Crow steadied, and the clouds above began to dissipate.

The ship was clearly holed, but it seemed that the weatherwitch's charm, or some other magic, had kept her afloat. Jandith emerged from the hatch, and other sailors appeared to converge upon Captain Signy. As each hand saw Noémie, shirtless and without her charm, his eyes widened. Jandith kept his gaze on the deck, refusing to meet Noémie's gaze.

"Good thinking," Captain Signy said to her, his voice still sounding muffled after such a violation of her hearing. "You've more than proven yourself – Nim?" He picked up the tatters of her shirt, tore them into strips, and began, apparently unsurprised, to bind her wounds as if she were merely another sailor.

Now that she knew herself to be safe, Noémie's muscles felt the resulting tremors of danger averted. Grief at Jandith's betrayal followed rapidly, thick and bitter. He had tried to save his own life at the expense of hers; though he could eke tears from his eyes while professing his devotion, he did not love her. Equally as bad, he was a coward. The clarity of disillusionment erased blind adoration; Jandith was not the man Noémie had believed him.

She thought of returning home, and what awaited her there. With surprise, she realized that she not only did not want to return to her father, but would miss her life aboard the *Sea Crow*. The easy camaraderie she had developed with the men might be shattered, but she would miss that bond. Jandith was the only man she would *not* miss.

"We lost several," said Captain Signy. "Can't replace anyone mid-ocean, and I hate to lose a good hand. Will you stay on?"

At first Noémie thought she had misheard, but Captain Signy's words hung in her mind, the same in her memory as in his speaking. Slowly she looked around at the remaining sailors, from whom she had learned so much. Most of them appeared startled, but none seemed ready to contradict the captain. Only Jandith's brows lowered, and his lips narrowed.

Jandith she could avoid. Suddenly Noémie felt free, able to sail her own course without the aid of any man. She could even choose to leave the *Sea Crow* and go beyond Captain Signy's friendly patronage. If she had made her own way here, she could repeat that success anywhere.

But she loved life on the *Sea Crow*, and she had begun to love the rough men who sailed her. She wanted to remain.

"I'll stay on," she said to Captain Signy. "Since you ask."

The captain nodded, apparently satisfied. "Have to work you twice as hard." He smiled faintly. "Good to have you, young Nim."

"Noémie," she said, and warmed his smile with her own. "It's Noémie."

ouse Call

The phone rang halfway through the Black Plague. I jumped, knocking Geometry off the table with my left elbow, dived past a plate of two-day-old spaghetti, and scrabbled desperately through a random drift of papers on Julian of Norwich to find the buried receiver. Catching it on the eighth ring, I jammed it to my ear, silently cursing the detritus of a liberal arts education.

"Joe's Bar and Grill," I said briskly. "Barbeque wings all you can eat every Tuesday and Thursday, eight-ninety-nine."

"Ash, I need your help," said Bob's voice on the line.

That was a surprise. Bob and I had dated a few months previously, but I had broken it off; he was obviously wife shopping, and in my sophomore year of college I wasn't ready to think about credit cards, let alone marriage. In some ways it was a shame, because Bob was sweet, cute, funny, and smart. On the other hand, he was so straight laced that his morals could have gone walking around in his skin, leaving the rest of him behind. And I was hardly a Puritan.

As I hadn't spoken to Bob since the breakup, I wasn't sure why he was calling. I certainly didn't expect him to ask me for anything.

"Okay," I said slowly. "You need my help. Is this a math problem? Because if it is, I need to get into my hazmat suit and grab my waldoes. I don't do math without full protective gear."

"It's not a school problem, Ash." Bob's tone managed to convey a mixture of irritation and something else I did not recognize. Maybe the telephone connection was poor, but I didn't think so.

"Okay, you've ruled out school." My ear was getting sore; I shifted the receiver to my other side and rubbed circulation back into the cartilage. "That leaves – what? Family? Car trouble? Money? You're certainly not going to ask me about your love life."

Bob's voice quavered slightly; with uncertainty, I realized in sudden amazement. Bob was never unsure of himself. "Ash, I've got... I don't know how to explain... I mean, it's not as if..." There was a pause on the line, then a whoosh of exhaled air. "Ash, I've got a poltergeist."

A poltergeist? Plain, ordinary, normal Bob? This was like finding the Holy Grail in a coffee shop. I sank into my chair, leaned back until the front legs lifted from the floor, and propped my feet on the table, dislodging several papers. Julian of Norwich's life skittered to the floor in jigsaw disarray.

I knew that Bob was serious. He was no practical joker, and he did not believe in the supernatural. It had been a point of contention between us, during our dating interlude; he thought I was gullible, and had more than once tried to talk me around to a 'rational' position.

"Assuming you're not talking about a DVD," I told him, "are you sure it's a poltergeist? You haven't taken in any teenage girls, have you? I mean, I know you're repressed, but poltergeist activity is hardly your style."

Bob's voice took on the annoyed edge that had characterized his interactions with me in the last weeks of our relationship. "I'm serious, Ash. I don't know if 'poltergeist' is what to call it, but there's something — something I don't understand — in my apartment."

I was tempted to suggest an exterminator, but bit down on my instinctive response. Bob sounded seriously upset. I drummed my fingers over a dried coffee spill on the tabletop and considered my next words more carefully.

"A poltergeist," I lectured, feeling as if I were teaching 'Paranormal 101', "isn't a ghost. It's a manifestation of something – call it 'psychokinetic energy' or anything else you like – that occurs as an effect around mainly teenagers, mostly girls, and generally kids who are fairly repressed or tightly controlled by their families."

"I haven't had any teenagers in the apartment. Unless you count a nineteen-year-old phys-ed major," Bob said dubiously. "Though I did sublet the place during the summer, so I guess it's possible they had teenagers in here."

"No," I said. "Doesn't work like that. Poltergeist activity only happens in the presence of an adolescent." I blew out a long breath. "What sorts of things are happening? That might help me figure out a few things."

Bob hesitated. I could almost hear his thoughts running in a hamster circle: *This sounds too silly to talk about. But it's Ash, and she knows about these things. But it's too silly to be real, so I can't talk about it. But it's Ash...*

I did know a few things about the supernatural. Once I figured out that some of the things I saw weren't visible to other people, I'd started reading up on anything which might explain why I was so different. Unfortunately, whoever said 'ninety percent of everything is crap' was dead on – except that, in the paranormal field, it turned out to be more like ninety-eight percent of everything I read. After putting my personal studies through an intensive strainer, I came up with a few pieces of what seemed to be fact rather than speculation. I hadn't done much reading in the field recently, though. I was too busy with the Black Plague, Geometry, and Julian of Norwich.

Bob's voice cut through the fog of my reflections. "Things move. At first I thought I was just imagining things. You know, that I really set down my keys on the kitchen counter instead of hanging them on the key hook. That sort of thing. But then it got worse. Things started moving in front of me." I could hear a sternly controlled tremor in his voice. "I tried ignoring it, hoping it would go away. Then things started smashing. You remember those matching mugs you bought me? I really – honestly, Ash, I'm serious – I saw one of them lift up, fly across the kitchen, and smash into the wall. My eyesight is great, I haven't been staying up too late – and I had to clean it up off the floor. I swear, this isn't a joke."

"I know," I told him. "This is me, Ash, remember? The flake?" I was rather sad about the mug – the two of them were a lovely pair, male and female cardinals on a pale green enamel. "Look, I'll be right over. I can't promise that I'll be able to do anything, though. I mean, I don't think I've ever dealt with whatever is bothering you. But maybe I can give you a better idea of what's going on."

"Thanks, Ash." Bob sounded relieved. "Just get here quickly, okay?" The receiver's click ended his side of the conversation.

I plunked down the phone and looked around for my own keys.

Predictably, they dangled on the edge of the table, half-hidden by a napkin and a dirty sock. I grabbed them and headed outside.

My old beater of a car started right up, an encouraging sign. I pulled it out of the parking lot and made my way down the mile-and-a-quarter of labyrinthine streets which snarled their way into the heart of downtown where Bob's place nestled amid the old-forest growth of apartment-converted Victorian houses.

I skipped the front steps and walked around to the side so I could enter the ground floor apartment directly. With a mixture of pleasure and sadness, I remembered the good times we'd spent there, talking, cuddling, and laughing. Last January we'd been snowed in, so we lit up the old fireplace, since the heat had gone out with the electricity. The place had a lot of ambiance, but I'd never seen anything out of the ordinary there beyond the occasional dust swirl or a peripheral movement which might simply have been too much caffeine. Now, some of the other houses in this row were spooky, but I would never have spent so much time in this one if I thought it was haunted.

Bob met me at the door, dressed neatly as usual in a September sweater and pressed jeans. I gave him a good look as I entered, just to see if he really was emitting poltergeist activity. He seemed just the same to me, his dishwater-blond hair a little shaggy over dark eyebrows, and the washed blue of his eyes still keen and perpetually anxious. He might have put on a few pounds during the summer, but it didn't look bad; muscle and tan, rather than fat.

He opened his arms to hug me, and I leaned into him with a surprising jolt in my chest. His embrace felt so good that it was almost like we had never separated. Bob seemed to feel the same way, because he held me for longer than I would have expected, given the way I'd dumped him.

"Better show me where things are happening," I said into his shoulder. It came out sounding like, "Mubber so ee were singz er abbenin." Bob chuckled, so I raised my head and repeated it.

"I'll show you where things have been smashing." Bob finally released me and backed through the doorway into the living room. "Things have been moving all over, though."

"Right," I told him, and concentrated on opening my spirit eyes.

That probably sounds a bit new-agey, but it was the term I'd used for it ever since I realized I had special sight. Many times I'd catch movement, color, light, odd distortions over normal objects or people. When I concentrated, though, I could sometimes see more. Auras were interesting, because so many other people really did see them and convinced themselves it was only a trick of the eyes. In most people, pale revelatory colors extended from dark silhouettes which wrapped closely round the body; but it was easy to attribute both parts to odd lighting conditions. Ghosts, human and animal, were harder for most, but I had little difficulty seeing them, even when they creeped me out.

I saw other things as well. Spirits of all types – and there were a lot of types; the ordinary magics drifting through the world which no one had yet captured and employed; directed magics, more common than many would guess; objects and places which remembered their past; Schrödinger's Cat. That sort of thing.

Seeing was easier when I was exhausted, or when I remembered that the world was really a porous mass of assorted networking atoms. I couldn't go around thinking like that all the time, of course. Life's a balance: you have to juggle what you understand with what you perceive, or you don't function well.

It was a matter of looking past what I knew, to what other possibilities might hover there. I'm not sure where I'm actually looking, but I call it opening my spirit eyes. I've never found a better term.

At first the apartment looked pretty much the same as always. Outwardly, a battered but well-tended sofa elbowed a pair of mismatched end tables we had salvaged from my apartment's dumpster last year. Bob's up-to-date sound system and television occupied most of the wall opposite the fireplace, and a chest of drawers, too big for the bedroom, huddled in one corner like a crouching bear.

Two table lamps trickled light onto the dark wooden floors and white-plastered walls. Despite the stretch of fronting windows, only next door's shadow dripped in through the high glass. These were covered by a gauzy inner curtain, but the musty drapes stood open to block as little of the late morning sunlight as possible. Bob loved the sun.

Four rooms, and the living room was the size of the rest of them put together. The bathroom was a coffin-sized cubicle, the bedroom barely large enough for a bed. Bob led the way to the kitchen, which had little capacity after the appliances had crammed together in a mutual clutch. I followed him in, wondering how he kept the space so clean. The counter was limited to the foot-long area on either side of the sink. Built-in shelves held neat rows of cans and boxes, and the one cupboard over the sink contained all the dishes Bob owned. Including the remaining cardinal mug.

In the kitchen Bob gestured widely to encompass the entire room. "This is the worst of it. Where things are actually breaking. A couple of dishes, a juice glass... and I'm not quite sure whether to count this, because it didn't break, but a jar of pickles hit the floor pretty hard when I was putting away groceries." He paused for a moment, as if trying to remember every incident. "Well, one thing broke that wasn't in the kitchen. Out in the living room a picture fell down and the glass broke. But it might have been my fault too, because I bumped the table." He scratched his nose. "Still, I didn't think I'd bumped it that hard, and it did kind of fly into the air before it hit the ground."

I wasn't sure what to make of the kitchen incidents, and at the moment nothing was moving besides Bob and me. The picture interested me more. "What picture?"

"What?" Bob's brows pulled together to give him an appealing werewolf look. I shook my head to empty the thought. I had good reasons for dumping Bob, however cute he might look with a monobrow.

"My graduation picture." I had it on one of the end tables. I've replaced the glass, and nothing more has happened."

His words ran over me at first like elevator music, ignorable.

Then the import hit me; Bob's picture had been thrown to the floor. I had no doubt it had been thrown; Bob downplayed it now, but he would never have mentioned it if it hadn't frightened him. Dishes were neutral, something to make mess and noise with. The picture sounded more like a personal attack.

"I'm going to go look in the living room." I scanned the kitchen quickly, just to see if I'd missed an elf in the corner. If I had, it must have been a very small elf. I backed out of the room, then turned my eyes toward the pallid illumination of struggling sunlight.

Bob's picture now sat on the mantelpiece, next to a couple of worn model cars. No damage showed to my casual glance. Then I looked at the end table, and my throat closed for a moment.

The end table carried four other pictures. Bob, his parents and sister, his sister's graduation photo, Bob's old dog. And one of him and me, taken that last January, when five of Bob's friends had trekked over to take advantage of the fireplace. It showed the two of us together, bundled in jackets, hats, scarves, and mittens. Our faces shone ruddy with cold, and we laughed at the camera in a cheek-to-cheek pose that was something straight off a television commercial. That picture had not been there when we broke up.

More to the point, it was still there, as were the other three. No wonder Bob was frightened. The four pictures crowded together, almost touching. If Bob had bumped the table hard enough to knock one picture off, the other four should have come with it.

This also suggested that whatever was playing poltergeist in his apartment – which I still had not caught a glimpse of – had personal animosity against Bob, but not his family or me. I wasn't sure enough of that to offer spending a night alone in his apartment, however.

I looked around, unfocusing my physical eyes so that Actuality didn't distract me. I reminded myself that every fuzzy dust mote was not a sign of the supernatural, and that if something was really there I'd likely see it sooner or later.

I almost didn't spot it. It gave off the impression of something that belonged, just one small knickknack on the brick-and-board bookcase. I might not have noticed anything at all if Bob had been in the habit of collecting knickknacks, but he wasn't; almost every small doodad anyone gave him went straight into the cardboard box in his closet.

Very small, it snuggled against the corner of a metal bookend, the sort that Bob preferred because they were cheap and they stacked. My gaze passed over it three times before I spotted what was really there.

It was brown, or perhaps gray; plump except where its body tried to burrow into the bookends. I had an impression of wrinkled skin, more like that of an old man's than natural creases. Large eyes lurked beneath heavy, drooping lids. I was not sure if it looked more like a toad or like a crouching manikin.

It looked me directly in the face and smiled. The smile curved impossibly wide, splitting its face from one ear to the other. On something which was not a cartoon, the smile looked positively macabre.

My pulse beat in my throat, and my vision thinned for just a moment. I had never seen anything quite like this. I took a breath so deep that my lungs burned.

"What is it?" asked Bob, and walked into my view. "Do you see something? What do you see?" He paced in front of me, cutting off my glimpse of the creature on the bookshelf. When the bookshelf reappeared, the Thing was gone.

"I don't know," I said, and released my fear as irritability. "Next time, stay out of my way when I'm looking."

Bob appeared startled. "Sorry. I keep forgetting that you can see the Bump-in-the-night and I can't. What is it? I'm seriously willing to entertain thoughts of ghosts and even the Bogeyman at this point."

I knuckled speckles out of my vision and refocused on Bob. "I saw it. I just don't know *what* I saw. It's not a ghost. It's not any happy shoe-making elf, either. Or if it is, I sure don't want to wear those shoes."

Bob's patience was wearing thin. "Very descriptive, Ash. Can you tell me what it was, and not what it wasn't?"

I stared hard at the bookcase, trying to make sure that the creature was really gone, and not just hiding better. I might not have seen teeth, but I wasn't any too confident it wouldn't creep up on me when I was less alert. "No, I can't," I answered.

"Can we get rid of it? Whatever it is?"

I shook my head, not in denial, but uncertainty. "I have no idea."

Bob sighed in a practiced sort of way. "Great. Maybe I should just move somewhere else. Assuming it won't follow me wherever I go. I mean, the tenants I sublet to during the summer didn't complain of any problems."

"Who were they?" I asked absently. "Friends of yours?"

"No, just three freshmen who were scrambling for a summer place at the last minute. They actually moved out a month early, which was fine with me, because they left the place in a shambles."

Old frustrations began to surface from the oilskin of my renewed interest. "Shambles" to him meant that the toilet paper wasn't replaced, or that a piece of paper missed the wastebasket. My problems with Bob had gone deeper than a simple disagreement about commitment, I remembered; Bob had wanted a wife, but he had wanted one who fit the concept of his ideal helpmeet. When he had decided on me, he had also decided to alter my life to fit into his.

"They left a month early?" I asked, surprised. "I wouldn't expect that, if they were still responsible for the rent. One of them, maybe, but all three?" I laughed. It suddenly seemed funny. "Bob, are you sure they didn't get run off by this creature, whatever it is? I mean, really, do you expect the last tenant to tell you, 'There's some mythical creature throwing my dishes around'? Or the landlord to say, 'By the way, watch out for the poltergeist'? When he can charge three times what this place is worth for the convenience of living so close to campus?"

Bob stared at me for a moment, then laughed too, with considerably less humor. "I see your point. But I didn't have any trouble with it last year."

Amusement drained from me as the discomfort of being alone with Bob – well, except for some sort of gargoyle out of a horror writer's universe – edged me into decision. "I don't know the answer to that one," I told Bob. "And I don't know how to handle this. So I can go away and let it keep throwing dishes, maybe bigger things, or I can call in someone who might know more than I do. Or you can move out. Your pick."

Bob just stared for a long moment. "Move out? I can't afford to do that."

"That does narrow it down." I waved a hand at the living room. "So it's 'live with Dear Friend Gremlin', or let me phone Paul. Unless you've got any other experts on the supernatural waiting in the wings?"

Bob sat down heavily on the couch and leaned forward to study the floor. I hoped he found the floorboards interesting. From the corner of my eye, something flickered; I turned my head swiftly, and caught a glimpse of gray-green eyes, pupils slit like a cat's. By the time I faced the spot where I saw it, nothing remained. I didn't think it was a trick of my eyes, though.

"I hate that term 'supernatural.'" Bob continued to stare at the floor, forearms supported by his thighs. "It sounds so... well, credulous. Like I'm requesting a séance to speak to my dear departed dog." He hesitated for a long moment. "Who's Paul?"

I leaned against the doorway to the kitchen and tried to think how best to explain Paul. I didn't know him well, but he was about my age, and had an aura like lightning. He'd introduced himself in Medieval Lit, and asked, "Does Ash stand for Ashley?" a question I always hate. Ash is my monogram; I can't stand Alicia. Despite that, I chatted with him a few times. We'd once gone out for lunch at the student union, where we got into a discussion on how most people pretended the paranormal simply didn't exist so hard that they couldn't see it if it landed in their living room. The conversation felt remarkably prophetic now.

From my own sensitivities, I was convinced that Paul not only knew more than I did about the supernatural, but had actively worked with it more than once. I didn't ask, but the assumption stretched between us like an extended bungee cord.

"He's in my Medieval Lit class," I said. "Chaucer, Mallory, Dante, and Boethius. He's one of the three people in class who ever bothers to read the assignments."

Bob looked at me as if I'd suggested hiring a hit man. "What do Chaucer and all those other writers have to do with my poltergeist?"

"It's not a poltergeist!" I told him, more annoyed than I should have been with his lack of understanding. "I told you, poltergeists are a manifestation of psychic energy, not some sort of gremliny thing."

"Gremliny?" Bob sat up straight and looked all around the living room as if I'd suggested a serial killer was hiding in the corners. "I have a gremlin?"

"Well..." I tried to think of how best to phrase things so that Bob would not misinterpret what I said. "I suppose you could call it a gremlin. A gremlin is a little spirit that makes mischief, right? But I don't know what this creature actually *is*, and unless I can narrow things down a lot further, I'm not going to be able to get rid of it." I was less worried about physical harm than I was about Bob's state of mind.

Bob leaned back on the sofa, still shivering, though the room was not cold. "How many sorts of gremliny things are there, anyway? I thought you knew about this stuff?"

"Chaucer," I said. "Mallory, Dante and Boethius. Remember them? They're not the only authors I read. In fact, I spend a lot of time at the library. Where they don't have a book called *Who's Who in Wee Spirits*. What, you think I apprentice to a witch in my spare time?"

"With you, Ash, I'm never sure." Bob leaned back and flung his arms out to stretch along the back of the sofa. "So, does this Paul see ectoplasm too? Or does he read tea leaves?" I was surprised by the vehemence of his words; if I hadn't known better I would have guessed that he was jealous.

"You've been watching too many bad movies," I said. "Ectoplasm? You think someone's going to slime you? Breaking dishes isn't enough?"

"Oh, go call him," Bob said irritably. "At this point I'd talk to Genghis Khan if he could clean the spooks out of my apartment. Just do what you need to do to get rid of them!"

This was precisely the type of discussion that we had engaged in during the last few weeks of our relationship: terse, annoyed, frustrated. We'd pretty much stopped hearing each other by then. I'd thought it was mostly my fault, but maybe I was wrong. I decided to step outside and call Paul on my cell phone. That would leave less vexation for Bob. I hated it when he bristled like a porcupine on steroids.

As I left the apartment, the sun canted and spilled into my eyesight, filling me with its autumn dazzle. Here in the center of town I could smell leaf mold, new construction, and ginkgo fruit. I wrinkled my nose at the last and took out my phone. I had programmed Paul's number into it when we had lunch together, though I had never called it.

"Hi?" An unfamiliar male voice answered on the first ring.

"Is Paul there?" I walked around to the front and seated myself on the front steps.

"Justa sec." The voice receded, but I could still hear it in the white-noise background hollering, "Paul! Callforyou!"

Moments later Paul's voice fought with static across my phone, though I could still hear the mild interest in his voice. "Ash? Is that you?"

Since I had never called him before, met the first voice, nor identified myself, Paul was either a very good guesser, had programmed my number into his caller ID, or he knew I was calling. If it were the second case, I was flattered, but the third wouldn't have surprised me either. It wasn't one of my personal strong points, but my mother always knew who was on the line.

I outlined the situation for him as briefly as I could, making sure to emphasize the smashed photo glass. Paul listened without comment as I ran him through everything I knew or guessed about the creature or spirit I had seen.

"So, have you ever heard of anything like this?" I finished, realizing that my tone had begun to rise in pitch, as talking about it ramped up my anxiety level. "And am I completely off in thinking that maybe you know more about this stuff than I do?"

Paul hesitated long enough that I began to wonder if he was still on the line. Then he said quietly. "I have some ideas about it. I'll come on over, if it's okay with you and your friend. Friend, right?"

"Just," I said firmly. "We dated, but it's been a while." I gave him the address and told him where he could find parking.

"Give me half an hour and I'll be there." Paul's voice sounded calm. His unconcern relaxed me just a tad.

"'Kay, I'll see you," I said, and hit the end button. I felt reluctant to go back in, so I remained on the steps, blinking sun showers from my eyes. I heard the door creak behind me, and Bob's hesitant footsteps shuddered a loose floorboard on the porch. I didn't look up, but waited for him to speak.

"Ash, I..."

"Yeah," I said. "This weirds you out. Fine. Just remember, it's not exactly like buying a cheeseburger for me either." I stared moodily out into the street, wondering how long it was going to take for the meter reader to slap a ticket on the illegally parked car in front of the house.

Bob responded with nothing but a sigh. He stood there just long enough to make my neck itch, then turned and re-entered the house, slamming the screen door behind him. I continued to glare at the street.

It took Paul considerably less than a half an hour to arrive. I watched as he rounded the corner of Victorian-era houses, negotiated the cracked sidewalk, skipped nimbly around a misplaced bike rack, and continued steadily up the street.

Compact and wiry, Paul made me think of a gymnast, one of the ones whose muscles hide seamlessly under their skin. Black hair and eyes contrasted starkly with his paleness, despite the patchy remains of a summer tan. The t-shirt he wore over his jeans read, "*Sic biscuitas disintegratum*" above a picture of a broken Oreo.

I could never decide if his features were handsome or simply compelling: either way, I had to stare at him. It did not help that to my eyes, he blazed with a brilliant glow. As Paul neared, I forced my gaze toward my feet and gave him a brief nod. He mounted the front step and leaned on the railing, which gave a paintless shudder before deciding to bear Paul's weight. My pulse quickened to an incomprehensible jazz beat.

"Ash, hi." Paul flashed an irresistible grin. I did not try to resist, but grinned back. "Better show me the crime scene. I need to look at the footprints."

"Footprints, check." I stood up and turned reluctantly toward the front door. "Of course, I didn't see it long enough to tell whether or not it had feet." I waved at the door, where time had etched Rorschach patterns in the wood. "Go on in, Bob's expecting you. Though he may be a little disappointed not to get the beard and the pointy hat."

"I left them at the cleaners," Paul said. "He'll have to make do with mysterious charm."

"Mysterious charm it is, then." I waited for Paul to enter and followed behind, still curious. I felt a little better that I wasn't on my own anymore.

Paul stopped right inside the door and squinted. "Hello?" he called. "Anyone here?"

I let the door swing to just as Bob exited the kitchen carrying a small dustpan full of broken crockery. A cut just above his eye trickled a tributary of blood, and white dust powdered his shoulder. I thought I recognized the broken mug; it had not been broken when I'd gone outside.

"This is Paul." I came up to Bob and looked closely at the cut on his forehead. It was fairly deep, but not dangerously so. "You'd better clean that out if you don't want it to get infected. What happened, Our Friend the Gremlin got annoyed that you called in help?"

As I spoke, I saw a flash of sharp teeth over Bob's shoulder. I shivered, but met its eyes with an unwavering gaze. Then it was gone, like the flash of sunlight on moving water.

"Whoa!" said Paul. "Didn't expect that!"

Bob looked around in alarm. "Expect what?" His hand actually shook. I could see his effort to pull himself together, which must have been hard since he didn't believe in much of anything that was happening in his own apartment. "Ash hasn't really explained much." A frown shadowed his face. "Oh, excuse me. I'm Bob. Thanks for coming." A grudging tone belied the apparent welcome, and he continued to hold the dustpan like a barrier against Paul's presence.

Paul grinned. "I gather this is a little out of your line. A little out of mine, too, but I read a lot."

"You mean you don't know what you're doing either?" I would have sworn that I heard a growl in Bob's voice. "Then why are you here?"

"Chill," said Paul. "I haven't had any experience with this particular situation, but I know of similar cases. Dealt with some. I'm pretty good with them." He gestured at the room's congregated furniture. "Tell me what's happened and show me where? I really need to know why this happened."

I bit down on my tongue, trying not to ask the obvious question: did he know what had happened? Paul was brilliant in more than his aura; his grasp of classroom material made me feel like a first-grader reading Shakespeare.

Bob finally dumped the broken mug into a wastebasket and dusted his hands briskly. Then he gave Paul a walking tour of the apartment, pointing out locations of each incident.

In the kitchen, Paul sat on the kitchen table and dangled his legs like a toddler in a high chair. Bob glared, but kept his mouth tightly shut. "Yeah," said Paul. "You've got a problem all right." He scratched his chin. "Could be worse, but it could be better. At least it's not an infestation."

"What, like swarming termites?" I asked. "Care to let the rest of us in on your Sherlock Holmes world? Or are we playing twenty questions?"

Paul laughed, a genuinely merry sound that would have elicited reciprocal laughter from the Spanish Inquisition. "Ash, I know you tend to put food out for stray cats. I know you were living in your own place, but did you ever do that here?"

That was an easy one. "There was a big gray tom, and a really lovely tortoiseshell who denned under the front porch in bad weather. I put down some blankets for them, and I'd leave milk or tuna or something out in bad weather. Usually milk. They drank it, I can tell you – "

Then I got it, and felt pretty stupid for taking so long. Something was drinking the milk, but it might not have been the cats. "Does Bob have some sort of brownie gone bad? Don't they just leave if they're annoyed at you? And since when do they have teeth that big?"

Bob shook his head and took a step backward. "Please say you two are just trying to freak me out. Brownies with teeth? Are you serious? We're not talking chocolate cake bars or junior Girl Scouts, are we?"

Paul slid off the table and shook his head. "Widen your horizons a bit. There are more things in heaven and earth, yada yada." He walked over to the sink and peered down the drain. "Damn, Bob, you keep this place sterile. Ever thought of subletting to a hospital?"

Paul's wry tone took the sting out of his words. I tried to summon up some indignation on Bob's behalf, but since I'd thought as much myself, a nervous giggle escaped instead.

Bob's face took on his patient and paternal expression, the one which had lived on his features during our breakup. "I only want to know one thing — what is causing these disturbances?"

"OK. It's like this." Paul's arm described a circle around the kitchen. "This is a pretty old house." He walked over to the doorway and thumped the oak frame. "Those are the ones that collect the house spirits. Brownies are just one manifestation, and a pretty benign one at that. We've got a lot in this country, because we have the native ones, and then some traveled over with families from Europe or Africa, or wherever the spirit was sufficiently attached to a family instead of a specific home. Come out here in the living room."

We followed him, and he led us over to the fireplace. Turning to Bob, Paul said, "You dust, right?"

Bob nodded.

"Watch this." Paul drew a deep breath, then blew along the entire length of the mantlepiece. Dust eddied up, saturating the air in a gray cloud. I stepped back quickly. Bob sneezed.

"Sorry." Paul did not sound particularly sorry, but I didn't think he was vindictive, so I waited for an explanation. Paul waited until the dust settled and Bob's sneeze attack stopped.

"Dustier than usual?" Paul asked while Bob walked over to the couch and retrieved a tissue from the box on the side table.

Bob blew his nose, nodding at the same time. "You're right about that. I've asked the landlord to change the filter on the furnace several times, but he swears he changed it a couple of weeks ago." His brows creased together in a confused scowl. "What does dust have to do with anything?"

"I'd say it didn't like you." Paul went and sat down on the couch, crossing his legs in a lotus position. I joined him on the couch's arm, unworried that I would damage it. Bob's furniture was as solid as his character.

My picture of the events was beginning to coalesce. "OK, I put out milk and tuna for the brownie-gremlin-boggart-thingy, and it was happy with us. Then Bob and I broke up, and no more happy spirit, but it left Bob alone. But this summer, when he sublet, this whatever got angry and drove the sub letters out? And then decided to take things out on Bob when he came back to school?"

"This is crazy," Bob said.

"Pretty much," said Paul. It was hard to tell which of us he was answering.

I sighed. "Bob, I saw it. A creature, yea big." I cupped my hands together to demonstrate. "Weird eyes. Nasty teeth. It may be crazy – but it's there. I'm serious."

Bob massaged the bridge of his nose, gathering himself as if he were about to plunge into fifty degree water. "Ash, you've never lied to me." A sideways grin escaped him. "Told me things I didn't want to hear, but you've never lied. I don't think you're hallucinating – and something is breaking my mugs. I'm probably as crazy as both of you, but I have to believe you." He shook his head, then straightened like a felon before a firing squad. "How do we get rid of it?"

"That'd be the question," Paul said. "I'm not entirely sure, but I have some ideas. And believe me, you want to get rid of it. Some of these house spirits can be pretty dangerous once they decide to take against you." He looked up at me and grinned. "Want in on this?"

After having seen the thing's teeth I wasn't sure I wanted to cross it, but Paul's smile warmed like hot cocoa on a winter's day. I wouldn't have turned him down then if he'd asked me to go dragon hunting. I just nodded, all my nerve-endings equally aware of Paul in front of me and Bob behind.

"Great." Paul arched an eyebrow at Bob. "You strike me as the sort of person who'd have a good spice cabinet?"

Bob stared as if Paul had just turned into a leprechaun. "Spice cabinet?" he managed, almost stuttering. "You're going to cook it?"

Paul started to laugh. I wasn't sure whether to join him or kick him; the spice cabinet comment really was weird.

"Paul, really," I said in my most quenching tone. "What do we need to do? Put garlic up on the walls? It'd probably drive Bob out, too."

Paul wiped the grin from his face, though I could see chuckles still trying to surface. "Let me set this exorcism up and I'll tell you both what to do when you need to know. And no," he said to Bob, "I'm not going to cook it, and no garlic, either. On the other hand, there are certain herbs and spices which can be used for magical purposes. A lot of them can be found in the ordinary spice cabinet."

"Magic." Bob shook his head as if trying to loosen some of these new ideas. "Exorcism. Bell, book and candle? I'm crazy letting you do this."

Paul got up from the couch and headed for the kitchen. "Candle, anyway. Do you have any?"

I went after Paul and showed him the cabinet where Bob kept his spices while Bob headed for the bedroom. Paul spun the neatly arranged Lazy Susan, deftly picking out bottles: rosemary, basil, pepper, arrowroot. "Where's the salt?" he asked, as he carried his selections to the table. "We're going to need a fair amount of salt."

"Rock or table?" I knew Bob kept some of the former in his closet so that he could melt his car out of the snow in winter.

Paul actually seemed to consider the question seriously. "Table," he said finally. "It's finer than rock salt, and a little iodine isn't going to matter one way or the other."

"Over the stove," I told him. "How do we use these spices? Boil them together as some sort of potpourri? Tempt it with a poisoned pizza?"

"I hadn't thought of a poisoned pizza" Paul said with a grin. "Have to try that on the next roommate who pisses me off." He scooped up his home exorcism kit and we headed back into the living room.

Bob emerged from the bedroom with a couple of tea lights in his hands. "Will these do?" he asked. "I don't have much in the way of candles, except for emergency supplies. You don't need to use the fireplace, do you?"

"Tea lights are fine. No need for the fireplace." Paul started to push the couch over to one side of the room. I went to help him get the rest of the furniture out of the way. When we had a large space cleared in the middle of the floor, Paul rolled up the rug, revealing diagonal wooden floorboards that were far cleaner than anyone's floor should be beneath the carpet.

Paul opened the salt and began to pour it in a large circle on the floor. Bob made a strangled sound of disapproval, but said nothing. I was proud of him, because I knew how hard he was working to hold back a comment behind those tightened lips.

Arranged in an approximate six-foot circle, the salt gleamed whitely in the refracted sunlight. Paul nabbed a coaster from the displaced end table and set one of the candles on it, placing the coaster neatly in the center of the circle. Opening the spice bottles, he shook a careful portion of each onto the wax of the candle. Then he stepped meticulously back over the salt, taking exaggerated pains not to touch even a grain. I'd read enough fairy tales and fantasy to realize that he was setting defenses against the creature.

"Sit down." Paul gestured to Bob and me, pointing to two locations on the far side of the circle. "Don't touch the salt, and don't let any part of your body lean in, even over its air space."

"I stopped messing up lines during my coloring book days," I grumped, but I knew where he was going. Break the circle, break the wards. That's the way the demon gets you, or whatever supernatural force you're dealing with. I folded myself into a cross-legged position in the spot Paul had indicated, my back to the fireplace.

"Do you need a lighter?" Having decided to humor us, Bob wavered between seating himself and exiting kitchenward. "I mean, that candle's not going to light itself."

Paul flashed a quick grin which flowed over but did not disturb the deep intensity of his expression. "Sit down, and I'll show you a trick."

Bob hesitated a moment longer, than nodded and sat a third of the way around the circle from both Paul and me.

"All right." Paul took a deep breath and closed his eyes.

Bob frowned. "You sure this doesn't have to be done at night?"

"That's window dressing," said Paul, his eyes still closed. "Well, sort of. It helps put people in the right frame of mind, but most supernatural things don't mind sunlight, despite what Hollywood vampires have done to our collective psyche. A few things, yes. But if this spirit is throwing mugs in daylight we can summon it in daylight."

Bob did not respond; I felt tension between Paul and him. I wondered if I was the cause, or whether they simply hit it off as well as two Rottweilers at a barbeque.

Suddenly Paul's aura blazed into a corona of power. As I gasped, the candle lit within the circle. Bob's indrawn breath echoed mine as I blinked away the candle's blue afterimage, adrenaline surging in a tsunami of shock. I was willing to believe three impossible things before breakfast, but Paul had just become impossible thing number four.

Oh well, part of me said wryly. *I did kind of ask for this.* I could smell partially burned herbs as their scent permeated the room. I wouldn't have expected a tea light to crisp them, but then, I wouldn't have expected a tea light to spontaneously burst into flame, either.

Bob's voice, hoarse and nervous, cut into the room's silence. "What do we do? Chant something?"

Paul snorted. "You can if you want. Just keep it down so I can concentrate."

"What do you want us to do?" I asked, hoping that we weren't on the wrong side of the circle. You never know with spirits – at least, that's what I've read.

"Watch for it." Paul opened his eyes slowly. "Especially you, Ash. You've got better sight than either of us. I'm going to call it, but it's got to be in the circle in order for me to banish it. If I go too soon, this will fail, and your friend will have bigger problems."

I responded only with silence, but kept my attention focused on the circle. Bob's tension thrummed through the room like a subsonic vibration, setting up a resonating disquiet within my bones. Still, I stared at the circle while my peripheral vision dissolved into black and white speckles.

Paul mouthed some words I could not quite catch. They whispered into the room like phantom breezes, teasing out the malicious spirit and easing it into tangibility with their persuasive cadences. A flash of white? gray? red? flickered through my vision. I started forward, then caught myself before violating the barricade of salt.

I began to speak, but before I could get the words out, the creature coalesced into complete visibility next to the blazing candle. It was not grinning now, but its teeth showed, yellow and sharp, bared in fierce defiance. Now it seemed like a large, venomous toad decked in mutating colors which made my stomach want to empty itself there on the floor. A toad with a humanlike shape and several extra fingers. And each of those extra fingers bore a nasty-looking talon.

Paul said clearly, "By the power of earth, sea, and sky, I bid you remain within this circle and within this form until you are dismissed." The creature's mouth opened and distended, widening into a tooth-filled gap that was so enormous it dwarfed the thing's head. Unwaveringly, Paul continued, "I bind you by salt, I bind you by smoke, I bind you by fire – "

That was as far as he got. The creature laughed, a high chittering sound, and leapt across the circle at Bob. Bob threw out an instinctive arm to block its attack: over the salt and into the interior circle. At the same time, his knee brushed the salt aside, breaking the line.

Swift as a mudslide, the creature slipped through the break and threw itself on Bob. Its vicious teeth bit deep into his arm, but it was clearly making for his throat. Bob tried to fend it off, but I could see it was much swifter, and that Bob might well lose the fight. My breath backed up in my chest, refusing to allow an exhalation.

Paul jumped to his feet and forward to help Bob. Paul was fast, but the beast seemed to slip in and out of tangibility, and he could not catch it. Bob's sweater arm blossomed red.

A weapon, I thought, *I need a weapon*! But all sharp points and edges in the kitchen were too far. I cast around for anything I could use against the beast.

All I saw was the fireplace shovel – the poker was missing. I grabbed hold of the shovel instead, and leapt into the fray. My sight exploded into overlapping shadows of light and color, almost obscuring the solidity of the room.

Right there, a shifting form of dirty gray, punctuated by flashes of pure darkness. At the juncture where it separated from the auras of Paul and Bob, I brought down the edge of the shovel as hard as I could.

An unearthly sound screeched through the room. My ears echoed with pain. The creature popped out of sight like a disintegrating soap bubble. My vision returned to normal with a sharp jerk.

I looked around, not trusting that something so mundane as a fireplace shovel could have defeated something so dangerous. But I saw no trace of the supernatural. At least, no trace other than Paul and his gourmet cooking show.

Paul pulled away from Bob, and straightened, looking around more carefully than I had done. His cheek bled from a single deep scratch, and he wore a grim expression.

Bob clutched his arm, pain lining his normally smooth features, pulling the sweater free from the injuries. They covered his entire forearm, and I guessed the nasty bites might need stitches.

"What did you do?" Bob asked Paul.

Paul smiled crookedly and looked at me. "Ask Ash that question. She's the one who sent it packing." I must have looked completely bewildered, so Paul continued, "Cold iron. Even the modern ghoulies and ghosties, living among all the stainless steel and iron girders of a modern city, don't like it when they're hit straight on with a few ounces of pure iron."

I blinked several times, trying to assimilate Paul's words. "Will it come back?" Adrenaline catching up with me, I began to shake.

"I doubt it." Paul took off his shirt and began to carefully wrap Bob's arm with it. "Would you, if you'd been insulted, deprived, and hit on the head with a shovel?" He paused and looked at Bob with a speculative frown. "I can do some post-boggart cleanup if you'd like, just to make sure. After we drive you to the emergency room."

"Thanks," Bob said through gritted teeth.

"Ash, got your keys? I'll go get the car." Paul twitched his fingers as if to tease them out of my purse. I scrabbled inside the black hole to find where my dancing moose and spiral keyrings joined. After tossing the keys to Paul, I knelt by Bob's side and waited until the screen door slammed.

"Are you all right?" I asked Bob. "Besides your arm, I mean."

Bob's paper white face met my gaze. He reached out his good arm. "Ash... I know things have been rough between us, but maybe..."

For a moment the old feelings stormed back in like rainwater in a dry gully. All I wanted for that one instant was to hold Bob and be held, safe, protected, and loved.

But it was Paul who had put himself into danger for my sake. It was Paul who had given me respect, honored my vision and my mind, and asked me for my help.

The good times I'd had with Bob were my past. My future was open. Perhaps Paul was in it, perhaps not, but I could not regress into an infancy of dependence.

"No," I said gently. "There's no maybe."

"Well, you can't blame me for hoping." Bob grimaced and elbowed himself to his knees without asking for help. I did not offer.

Rising to my feet, I gave the room one last look. Nothing quivered at the edges of my sight, and the sunlight poured onto the floor as usual.

I knew I wanted to learn what Paul could teach me. I'd kept myself ignorant for too long, trying to fit into what I thought was a normal pattern.

My car horn blared outside the door as Bob rose. I caught his arm and steadied him.

"Come on," I told him. "Paul is waiting."

And more, I thought as we left the house. Much, much more.

Guardian

Night wrapped the countryside in a frayed blanket marred by the pinpoint holes of stars. The moon, a sliver of claw on the western horizon, warmed the heart, but provided little light by which to see. From inside her cave, the golden dragon stirred, stretched, and came forth, as silent as a dream.

First the dragon looked at each face of the steep mountain around her, then down at the rocky fields which bordered the mountain's foot. Satisfied that no mortal thing would disturb her flight tonight, she spread her wings, tested the wind with a sail of hide, then launched herself into the air with a wild delight. Tonight was for flying only.

She twisted and danced on the wind's currents in fierce gladness. Far below, she saw fires hastily kindled, by shepherds and farmers who knew what they saw, but not the meaning of her dance. Tales were told in human lands of nights like these, when dragons rode the wind. They feared for their sheep and cows, crops and children. The dragon snorted softly, knowing that their tales arose from ignorance, not malice. Still, ignorance led to malice, and the dragon must always be wary of those who came to kill her, naming her thief and murderer. So she flew only on the darker nights, and let the full moon reveal the expected; fields drenched in white moonlight and the sad cry of owls on the hunt.

Flight was her joy and release from the burden she shouldered.

The craft of humans outstripped their wisdom, and in folly they made many powerful things, some too powerful to trust to any but the purest of heart. It was the dragon's task to seek the golden and magical weapons, the jewels over which wars were fought, the cauldrons which might have banished hunger but instead bred strife. These she took and piled secretly in her hoard, dreaming upon it of the one to whom each treasure could be safely given.

One weapon in particular troubled her mind. It shone in her imagination, a long sword forged from the heart of a star, with the power to lead men and women in battle. Its power was great, as was its potential for misuse, and the golden dragon feared its theft by one who would use it for private gain. She knew its future master; a young man with flaxen hair and a gentle voice, who never would wish to wield the power he carried. She pitied him, but knew that the sword must be given to one who did not value what it brought, yet would be strong enough to use it.

By starlight she shook her body from crown to tail, letting the cool air flow over it with quiet pleasure. Light glinted faintly off her burnished scales, sending spears of illumination far into the night. Below, herders swore or prayed with the intensity of those who feared what they did not know. The dragon saw more fires kindle and knew she had betrayed herself. With a soft flap on the air, she rose high, hiding herself in a drift of passing cloud.

As the stars wheeled around the sky, those who lived below the mountain relaxed and laughed, joking that the beast had been frightened by their neighbors' faces. But they did not forget the fear of the stone cliffs and what dwelled within, and resolved to keep their children safely at home. What dwelled in the mountain they had no desire to see closer.

All but one boy, who looked out of a cold stone window casing, brushed flaxen hair from his eyes, and dreamed of dragons.

astery

Frissan joined the summer festival just as nightfall stained the last of sunset's bloom a perfect black. Wrapping his walnut-framed harp in an oilcloth, he hummed a small spell of protection so that no one would accidentally trip over it in the silhouetted darkness of night. Then he laid it carefully on the grass and stepped onto the Hightown common. Flame spread streaks and quavers of light over the green as the enormous bonfire in its center danced in its own storm of twisting wind and embers, and sparks fireflied their way upward to lose themselves among whitely glittering stars.

The leaves of a maple whispered in the moonless dark above and behind Frissan's head, and he sighed in contentment. It was very good to be home again after completing his minstrel year of wandering throughout the Freelands. Traditionally, this tested a minstrel's skill and dedication as he spread news, taught lore to the young, and connected the independent towns, tying them together with their common history. Most importantly, within the month he would become the youngest minstrel ever to earn the position of full bard. A confused feeling of pride and humility tangled together whenever he thought of the honor for which he had been chosen.

By the light of the festival bonfire, he looked about to see who else had arrived. Young and old spiraled and intertwined in dances more ancient than even the bards remembered, patterned steps to call the sun back to the sky and ensure a bountiful harvest in the coming year. Two pipes in counterpoint blended the dance with the rhythm of a single drumbeat on the far side of the fire.

Frissan saw well in the dark as long as he remembered to keep from facing the fire full on, and the shapes of several young girls were emerging on the side of the green nearest Hightown. Giggles trickled like water from the far end of the common. Then three silhouettes against the flames resolved into girls of Hightown, heading across the green toward Frissan.

Frissan knew the girls well; Bid, the tanner's daughter, her younger sister Tamrath, and Bid's best friend Clover. He had spent his youth with these girls, though his year of wandering had left a gap between his memory of their childhood and their flirtatious presence.

Clover stepped forward, swirling her skirts and stepping sideways so that her legs were visible in the ruddy light. Frissan kept his expression still, but inwardly he grinned; he knew this game, and was not averse to gaining a good look at Clover's strong, slender calves. He licked his lips as she tossed curly dark hair over her shoulders and pulled her skirt back into place in an innocent fashion that did not fool Frissan in the least.

Tamrath followed, trying self-consciously to imitate Clover's skillful flirtation. Shyer than the other two, she looked at Frissan, giggled, blushed, then looked at the toes of her shoes. Frissan discounted her; Tamrath was twelve, and still a child, though she was clearly developing an interest in men.

It was Bid whom Frissan watched the most closely. At sixteen, she was no longer the young girl he had left in Hightown a year ago, whose limbs outstripped her body's growth, leaving her struggling for poise of both body and mind. Instead, Bid stepped forward with the allure of a woman comfortable with every part of herself, and with the knowledge of how her poise affected others.

The fire limned Bid's hair with flame. Spots of light danced on her nose and cheeks. Her eyes were recessed whorls of shadow, seeming to flicker with their own embers whenever her head turned. Her voice, musically clear and precise, carried to Frissan's ears as if the other girls merely chirped like summer crickets. Bid's lips curved into an enigmatic half-smile. Frissan's breath caught in his throat.

"Have we surprised our bard without words?" Bid teased, and put her hands on her hips. "Did you forget them when you awoke this morning? Or have you simply left them in your spare breeches?"

Frissan was not about to let anyone, even Bid, best him in his own arena of words. He gave her a long, slow look, and chuckled. "Bid, though you are the darling of my heart, and my life has no meaning without you, I must tell you – I seldom speak unless I have something of merit to say."

Clover laughed with a high tinkle, like carillon bells.

Bid was not intimidated. She replied, "What, you have so few words that you must hoard them? When you cast a spell with your music, do you merely hum along with your harp?"

Frissan's pulse speeded with the dual emotions of annoyance and excitement. "Heart of Oakwood," he said, his own expression bending into an answering smile. "Bid, you sound like a smitten woman. Am I to take it that you have developed a fatal passion for my own admittedly marvelous self?"

Bid's half-smile did not alter. "You'll know that when I let you, and no sooner," she told him. "Don't think too highly of yourself, Frissan. You're not the first skilled minstrel there ever was, and you won't be the last. Prove your worth before you accept your praise."

Apparently irritated at the lack of attention, Clover put her hands on full hips and swirled her skirt once again, looking at Frissan with a sidelong, but unsubtle gaze. "Bid's moody today. Perhaps it's the tides of the moon. It would be a shame if that kept you from enjoying the bonfire." She emphasized her words with a slight twist of her hips which drew Frissan's attention away from Bid and back to Clover's lovely figure and features.

"Nothing could spoil this for me," he told Clover, quite sincerely. It had been a long time since he had spent a festival at home, and the one that marked the beginning of summer was the most important. Many of the bards, minstrels, and music apprentices would be here, as well as a large complement of priests and acolytes, and every soul from Hightown. There they would thank the Freelands' patron, the goddess Kawerycan of Oakwood, for their survival through another year, and the beginning of summer's bounty.

It was also the one time of year when trysts between unmarried young adults were not only condoned, but encouraged. Frissan was looking forward to this especially.

"Don't expect too much," Bid warned him, her half-smile still concealing her true thoughts. "It's too much to fancy every woman in Hightown will fall into your arms. You may have to settle for a paltry score or so."

"Perhaps fewer than that," Clover added, licking her own lips slowly. "One might suffice to hold your attention – if she were sufficiently attentive."

Frissan felt the beginnings of urgency in his groin. Clover seemed eager to have him without any great opposition. He considered whether the dark girl might prove a pleasant diversion.

Tamrath might not yet be of age, but she was not so young as to be entirely unaware of the flirtation among the other three. Striking a tentative pose rather like Clover's, she said, "Of course, sometimes the harvest is best when the corn is young." She then spoiled the effect of her clever words by giggling and looking back down at her toes.

Frissan allowed a small smile to flit over his lips. He enjoyed this sort of competition for his attentions. As a young and handsome man he experienced such situations frequently, the more so since his brilliance had become as apparent to townsfolk as it had always been to the bards. Linnuad, the Chief Bard, had cautioned him more than once about arrogance and the tendency to use people for his own benefit rather than mutual need, but Frissan thought the cautions unwarranted. He had never forced a woman nor harmed a man, and if he knew his own self-worth, was that a cause for shame?

Determined not to distress Tamrath by dismissive words, Frissan smiled at her gallantly. He decided to temporarily ignore the more interesting possibilities, and offered an arm to the younger girl. "Tamrath, my darling, it will be a notable harvest indeed, but I do not wish to spoil its bloom by garnering it prematurely." Tamrath looked up just in time to meet Frissan's most charming smile; she looked back down again immediately, blushing with frantic embarrassment.

"I do, however, need a dancing partner. Would you honor me?" He liked Tamrath, and a dance with her would not harm his chances with the other girls. Tamrath first looked startled, then nodded anxiously. Frissan took one hand and put the other on her waist, like a brother. Tamrath gasped, and a breathless laugh escaped her as they swept into the knot of dancers.

Frissan found himself pleasantly surprised. Tamrath danced very well, and one dance soon became three, before he led her off to the other side of the fire. Here most of the young unpartnered girls congregated, presumably so they could discuss the young men. Frissan let go of Tamrath's hand and bowed to her with a friendly grin and a wink.

Bid and Clover now stood amid four other girls of similar age. It was clear to Frissan within moments of his reaching them that all of them were competing in some degree for his attention. He had rather expected it. His position was unrivaled by any of the unmarried men in Hightown. Adding this to Frissan's own looks, it was natural to expect the women to compete in the hope that not only might he choose them for this night, but that he might consider a marriage alliance should he be sufficiently satisfied.

Quickly dismissing one girl as younger than Tamrath, he looked over the rest of the cluster. It was easier to see them, this close to the light. Clover shone from among them, from her glossy hair to her red ruffled skirts which accentuated the slenderness of her waist and the fullness of her hips. She had woven wild rose in her hair, and her bodice was laced tightly, so that the space between her breasts appeared deeper than it actually was.

Clover laughed a tinkling laugh that sweetened the night air. "Frissan! Are you going to dance with me next?" She twirled in place, sending her full skirts flaring. "Have you some steps to teach? I am always willing to learn from a master." She shook her head back so that her hair cascaded in a shining fall behind her.

Frissan took an appreciative glance, then turned his attention to Bid. In the young minstrel's mind, Bid's lush body and bright hair crowded out Clover's more conventional prettiness, and the boldness of Bid's tongue and spirit both attracted and fascinated Frissan. He had never loved any woman with whom he had lain, but Bid made it difficult for him to think of anything or anyone else. If this was love, he wished to explore its possibilities. Tonight would seal his knowledge of the girl and enable him to understand his own heart. Wooing her would be a matter of deftness and skill, and Frissan had ample experience. Frissan felt the slow burn of excitement as he considered the chase before him.

Frissan briefly considered taking Clover first and Bid later. On consideration, he decided against this approach; Bid was not the sort of woman to brook competition. He eyed Clover a little wistfully, and thought that he might make closer acquaintance some other time, when Bid was not around to complain.

"Indeed, I am ready for another dance," Frissan said, an undercurrent of laughter staining his tone. "With the right partner I might learn some steps of my own. Is there anyone here who can keep tempo to my beat?" He looked straight at Bid as he said this, hoping to ignite an answering spark in her cool gaze.

Tamrath, apparently missing the innuendo entirely, put her hands on her hips and nodded her head. "Wasn't I a good enough dancer for you?"

Two of the other girls giggled. Bid sighed, and leveled a warning gaze at Frissan, who spread his hands wide to indicate that he was innocent of Tamrath's error. The corners of Bid's mouth turned down, and she shook her head.

"Better not strain your tongue by flattering her." Bid gave him one of her half-smiles. "Clover will be unhappy if it isn't working properly."

"You are very good," said Frissan to Tamrath, annoyed at the older girls for laughing at the younger. "But I would like some time with others as well. Perhaps we can dance again when the night is older." He smiled his most charming smile at Bid. "Bid, would you accompany me?"

"Perhaps," Bid said in an amused voice. She turned away. "But there may be others who wish your company more than I. Clover, for instance, who seems hot for the dance."

"Never would I wish for better company than yourself, Bid." Frissan tried unsuccessfully to catch her glance. Her graceful poise caused Frissan's pulse to throb heavily in his wrists and throat. Silhouetted against the fire, Bid's hair appeared dark with an edge of flame. Frissan imagined what it would feel like to caress it, and to explore the plentiful curves and soft skin of her body. His breath quickened and the feeling in his groin intensified. "Your graciousness alone would do justice to the finest herd of goats Hightown has ever seen."

Bid's mouth twitched as she turned back to Frissan. "Ha! I am not a harp, for you to call forth the tune of your choice. Dance with whomever you want; you haven't yet persuaded me that you are my best match this evening."

Frissan determined that she would speak quite differently later on, but for the moment he had leisure to enjoy the attentions of the other girls. "Very well. Clover? Will you dance?"

Clover's eyes sparkled, and she nodded. Frissan took her hand and led her out into the darkness of the field. Here Clover pressed close to him, clearly wishing to impress him with her lush womanhood. Though he did not object to the feel of her lithe body against his own, it merely heightened his desire for Bid. His breathing deepened, and he swirled Clover off her feet, startling her first into a shriek, then into a delighted laugh.

Later he would pursue tonight's goal. But first he would share in the joyous revelry of the music and the dance.

The stars had wheeled midway through the sky before Frissan caught Bid alone. The fire subsided from a conflagration into a smolder, with an occasional lick of flame. With its absence, young folk separated into couples, dispersing into trees, barns, or the soft tall grass which spread everywhere the goats could not reach. Finally accepting Frissan's inattention, Clover had departed with Drothan, a well-set but unmarried townsman several years her elder. Tamrath's mother herded her home, properly determined to protect her younger daughter from the profligate lovemaking until she came of age.

Bid stood near the edge of the green, her head tilted back to look at the night sky. With muted excitement, Frissan approached and put one hand possessively on her shoulder, stroking her hair with the other. It was as soft as he had imagined, and smelled faintly of lavender. He bent to nuzzle her neck and to lick her ear with the barest tip of his tongue.

Bid shook him off impatiently. "No, Frissan," she told him, her voice a little faint. "Not tonight. I'm very tired. I do like you, but – not now. Give your favors to some other girl."

Frissan smiled in the dark. The chase was on, and he knew this game well. "Why Bid, my love," he said, as if she had spoken an endearment instead of a rejection, "how can I seek another girl, when the sweetest and loveliest is before me now? You outshine those others as the moon outshines its reflection in a clear pool. Even your shadow betrays you; it stretches more shapely than any other. Where else could I possibly find such a masterwork?" He reached back out for her hair, sifting it through his fingers like cool water. The pressure between his legs intensified.

This time Bid jerked away, turning to face him and tangling her tresses as they pulled free from Frissan's reaching hand. He could not see the expression on her face, but her voice sounded as cold and damp as the nighttime dew. "I want none of your flattery. I do not intend to be one of your conquests, Frissan. Go away and leave me alone."

Frissan frowned; this was not the way the game was played. "I know you want me, Bid. You made it quite clear. Why else did you tease me until I was half mad?"

Bid snorted. "You have me confused with Clover. Go find her. If you're lucky, you may be in time for Drothan's leavings. I don't want you, Frissan. Go away. Is this clear enough for you?"

"Quite." The flame which fueled Frissan's desire exploded into fury. "You wish me to dog your heels, but you have no intent of giving me what you promise. I won't be teased into submission, Bid. I won't follow you in hopes that you will drop me some morsel of your affection."

"Think what you want," Bid said flatly. "Just go."

His pride smarting, Frissan pivoted away from Bid and walked rapidly off without another word. He had no intention of begging, and Bid would learn this soon. If she intended to keep him on her leash, she was gravely mistaken. Frissan had too much pride to grovel for the affections of any girl, no matter how much he desired her.

But as he walked, Bid's lovely voice, her intelligence, and her sensuous body would not leave his mind. If anything, her words heightened his hunger; fury and fascination melded in his mind, intensifying to a ferocious passion. His body ached with desire. That this was certainly Bid's objective enraged Frissan as much as it enticed him. Bid was no common woman; but neither was Frissan a common man, and he would prove it to her.

He returned to the spot he had left his harp, unused throughout the long night. The magic he had placed on it kept it free, not only from careless feet, but from the dew which shimmered everywhere in the reflection of pale stars. He picked it up and brushed off droplets of water which clung to the frame and strings but penetrated neither. Then he sat down in the wet grass, cross-legged, to think.

He knew Bid's mind better than she believed; he understood her wish to master him, something in which she would never succeed. That he would never accede to her domination she had not yet learned. Frissan was no hapless village lad for Bid to beguile with her charms. The anger grew in him as he contemplated her seductive rebuff.

He stood with a single decisive movement. Bid would take Frissan on his own terms or not at all. She would learn that playing with his affections was useless. With his harp in his arms, he went to look again for Bid.

She stood watching the stars just as she had when Frissan had left her a short time before. This time Frissan made no sound as he approached. Only when he was close did he lift his harp to his shoulder, settling the straps so it would stay where he held it.

The magic he had learned was the magic of the mind and of the heart; it held the power to sway others to feel or think what the bard willed. Frissan had long been taught never to use this power to coerce another, for that was against the bardic code. It was a helping and healing magic only, not a means to power.

But Bid wanted Frissan as much as he wanted her. She had made no secret of that attraction. And Frissan would not coerce her; he would only help her to express the longing they both felt for each other. It would be good for Bid to shed her need for domination and control.

He began a soft tune, threading it with the harmonies of magic and his own need. *Come*, it called, *join with me in glorious union.* The allure of the tune pulled at the core of Bid's will, teasing out every scrap of longing she felt, every stirring of lust and bodily appetite. He could not make her love him in this way, but the spell would last at least until morning. And once they had coupled, Bid would see no need to continue with her charade of indifference.

At the first note Bid's head snapped around. She began to shiver, and though Frissan could not see the expression on her face, he sensed that she might flee. Quickly he caught her will with his magic, prisoning it within a flurry of notes and the deepest urges of his own soul. Beyond the harp music, he could hear Bid's breathing deepen and grow hoarse.

Frissan played continually until he perceived that she was caught; the magic had tangled her consciousness and laid her bare to the deeper instincts which Frissan awoke. He let the music fade, laid his harp gently on the grass and went to her, knowing that now she would receive him as they both wished.

Bid's eyes seemed to stare past him into a darkness greater than the night. But when Frissan touched her shoulders, her movements were sure and definite. She drew his face to her own and kissed him with the furious passion of a wolf on its prey. Frissan explored the kiss, letting the throbbing tension flow through his body to kindle the ecstasy he sought. When he reached to untie the laces of Bid's dress she crowded closer and groped to remove his shirt, her fingers exploring the contours of his chest to awaken a thrill of sensation. His heart drummed under her touch.

They lay down together on the wet grass, the urgency of their lovemaking raw and exposed as their naked bodies. Bid arched her back, and he kissed her throat, taking one small breast in his hand to marvel at its perfection of form.

Like a blind woman, Bid continued to search the sensitive nerves of Frissan's skin with her fingers, lips, and tongue until the pressure grew to unbearable force within him. Frissan's ardor burst into almost painful release as he entered her, the experience transcending everything he had hoped for. He knew then that he would no longer be satisfied with any other woman.

Throughout the night they made love again and again. Toward morning they fell asleep, spent and exhausted. Frissan's dreams brimmed with Bid and the passion they had shared. Even deep within his slumber, he was aware of Bid's head pillowed on his chest.

He awoke to the dazzle of mid-morning sun. It was Bid who had roused him by violently jerking her head from his body. As Frissan tried to orient himself, Bid scrabbled to her feet, her long snarled locks the only clothing she wore. Her eyes gleamed wildly. Frissan sat up as fast as he could and looked at her in confusion.

Bid immediately snatched her dress from the ground where it lay a short distance away, and held it before her like a shield. "Come no closer!" she said in a strained tone which held equal parts of bitterness and fear. "Don't you dare touch me!"

Frissan frowned. "Bid, my dear love – what is wrong?"

"You should know," she said, her voice growing rougher as she continued to speak. "It was you who forced me, and I will see you pay the full price for what you have done!" Tears squeezed from her eyes, but she lifted neither hand to wipe them away.

Frissan sighed. He would never understand women. "You wanted me as much as I wanted you," he said patiently, as if explaining a difficult concept to a young child. "If you regret it now, in the morning sun, that is not my fault, and I take no responsibility for it."

"Oh, you are responsible," Bid said in a low voice. "You don't understand what you've done? Whether you used the force of your magic rather than the force of your arms makes no difference." The tears tracked into her ears and down the sides of her nose. "You are a danger, Frissan, a danger to every girl in Hightown and the Freelands."

Frissan merely stared at her, dumbfounded. How she could so misunderstand after what they had shared, he could not fathom. "I took nothing from you that you did not wish to give."

Bid shook her head violently, shaking droplets of tear into the air. "You made me want you – and even then, only my body and not my heart. I hate you, Frissan: You seem to be a man, but you are only a charming rind filled with rotten fruit. I don't care if you are the

201

flower of the bardic school or the lowliest weed that grows by its door; you will suffer just the same." She backed away into the trees which bordered the green, still holding the dress before her until she melted from Frissan's sight.

"Bid..." Frissan clambered awkwardly into his breeches and pulled his boots on without bothering to first don his socks. Snatching up his harp and leaving his shirt behind, he darted into the trees after Bid. She was gone. Frissan leaned against the rough bark of a hickory and stared blankly into the air. How matters had come to this he did not understand.

The summons which came that day from the chief bard was no surprise. Frissan returned to the bardic school just before dusk, carrying his harp as the old man had requested. He knocked on Linnuad's door, his stomach heavy and sour. Perhaps there was still some chance to remedy the damage of Bid's twisted version of last night's events. It would take considerable explanation, but he might avoid a heavy punishment for his conduct if he used the right words.

"Come in," called the chief bard clearly. Frissan opened the door and entered. Linnuad sat waiting for him, his snowy hair and cobweb wrinkles belying the youth of his voice and his cloudless black eyes. He sat in one of a pair of intricately carven chairs, and held his legendary harp, Ashthorn, on his lap. The chamber was clean and bare, set with a large window that looked onto the forest of Oakwood. Sunset limned the trees with a fire of rose and melted gold.

Frissan seated himself in the other chair and set his harp on the floor; Linnuad did not keep great formality. An expression of perfect blankness guarding his face, Linnuad caught and held Frissan's gaze for a moment of eternity. Frissan met the old man's eyes directly, waiting for Linnuad to speak so that Frissan could defend himself.

"I have only one question for you," Linnuad said finally. "Did you use the magic we have taught you to induce Bid to lie with you?"

Any idea of denying Linnuad's words died beneath the chief bard's penetrating gaze. If he faced the accusation squarely, thought Frissan, the consequences would likely diminish. He set his jaw, took a steadying breath, and answered one word: "Yes."

Linnuad closed his eyes, then opened them, his only sign of emotion. "Bid came here this morning to have words with me. I know truth when I hear it, Frissan, and it was truth that she spoke. And you have answered truth for truth. I am glad of that at least." His expression transmuted to one of great sadness. "I have worried about you greatly in the last few years, Frissan. Your gifts are great, but so too are your flaws. There is a difference between justified pride and arrogance."

Drawing a deep breath, Frissan launched into his defense. "It wasn't like she told you. Not at all. Bid may not have lied, but she must have distorted the truth."

"You know so much of what she said when I have not told you?" Linnuad's tone was soft but implacable.

Frissan began to speak again, but something in Linnuad's manner silenced him. Instead he settled back in his chair, watching the old man for some sign of what was to come.

Linnuad remained silent for a long time, searching Frissan with his gaze as if he saw into the younger man's heart and soul. With a gentleness more unnerving than violent anger, he asked, "Do you even understand what you have done?"

Frissan sought for the right words, the ones that would explain how Bid had teased him, led him on, met his loving with the fierceness of her own desire. Under Linnuad's dark stare, explanations washed away like river clay. All Frissan could think to say was, "She wanted it as much as I."

"And have you learned to read the hearts of others so surely?" Linnuad's expression hid within his wrinkles like a partially unraveled face in a tapestry. "You cannot even read your own heart, Frissan." He took a deep breath and let it out slowly. "Frissan, what you did to Bid was rape. No matter how you try to justify it, she was unwilling and you forced her. That it was magic instead of might makes no difference. You compelled her as surely as if you had bound her with rope. Except that your ropes were the skein of your power, not cord or tether."

The impact of Linnuad's explanation shook Frissan's understanding of the night before with jarring power. Was Linnuad's interpretation correct? Frissan felt his insides twist like a wet washrag. Could he have been so wrong about Bid? Could he have done something so terrible without comprehending the magnitude of his actions?

One thought stood out so clearly and cleanly that Frissan grasped at it with desperation. "Bid did want me," he told the chief bard in a voice that barely escaped the narrowing prison of his throat. "My magic would not have worked otherwise. I only brought her own desire to the fore, so that she could see it as well as I."

For a moment Frissan felt as if Linnuad had gone elsewhere, leaving only his unmoving form of living stone. Then the bard spoke, his words echoing into the silence with the precision of harp notes. "Frissan, it may be true that Bid wanted you. I know what magic you used, and you speak some truth. But that truth turns on its own tail; you understand less than you should, or you deliberately deceive yourself. Either way, your magic has become a danger to those who possess none of their own.

"What you seem not to perceive is that only part of Bid wanted to lie with you; and that part was not most of the whole. You are a handsome young man, but attraction does not mean that every girl will submit to your charms. Frissan, Bid may have *wished* to lie with you, but she did not *will* to do so, and that is the difference. It was her will you forced, not her body. And that is an even graver matter."

In horror and the sparks of anger, Frissan's mind denied Linnuad's explanation. He was not such a monster that he would force a woman, even if he needed to employ such coercion! No, Bid had willed their union as well as desired it; she had teased him and taunted him, and long experience taught Frissan that those wiles were only used on men when a girl invited a lover. Linnuad could not be right. And how could the chief bard believe such a thing of the school's best pupil?

Frissan shook his head vigorously from side to side, trying to shake Linnuad's words like droplets of water. "No," he said tentatively, and then, more strongly, "No. I did nothing wrong. I gave Bid what she wished and what she willed. Her story to you speaks only of Midsummer morning's regret over the abandon of the night. She wishes, by this tale, to control me, perhaps to force me into an offer of marriage." As he spoke, Frissan considered the plausibility of his explanation, deciding that it made more sense of Bid's actions than anything either he or Linnuad had previously said.

Grief etched itself onto the old man's countenance. He shook his head.

"Perhaps you will never understand, Frissan," said the bard quietly. I had hoped that you could see what you had done and were willing to make amends. But it seems that you are so trapped within your illusory net of power that you do not understand what it is to be a bard." Linnuad ran a finger up the side of his own harp, as if touching a talisman. "We are the guardians of the Freelands. In our heads and our hearts we hold the knowledge, the lore, the history which would otherwise be forgotten. Our magics protect that knowledge, and allow us to impart it in a living fashion to those who must remember what has gone before. There is no place for any bard to use his power to impress his will upon another. No matter what his reasons may be."

Frozen dread seeped into Frissan's limbs; he could not move. He waited, like ice, for what Linnuad would say.

"We have taught you ill, and we must bear some of the responsibility." Linnuad placed his fingers over Ashthorn's strings, as if to play. "But you are a man, and it is a man's business to act with restraint. You have proven that you are unfit for the power you wield." He hesitated for a long, chill moment. "Frissan, nothing has saddened me so much for longer than you know: You may not become a bard. I revoke that privilege. Your harp I take from you, and your magic I forbid."

He played a dark sequence of notes on Ashthorn, which rang throughout the room. Frissan felt a cold pressure settle over the warmth which held the core of his magic and power. Where it sat on the floor, his harp shivered, frosted, and shattered into myriad fragments which then collapsed into dust. Frissan made a strangled sound of protest, which Linnuad ignored.

"Gather your things and leave this place," the bard told him. "From this time forward you have no leave to pretend to any bardic status. And never forget that you have brought this on yourself." His face stiffened into the semblance of unyielding stone.

Feeling hollow as a rotted oak, Frissan rose. He said no word to Linnuad, but turned and exited, pride the only thing keeping him standing. The emptiness inside of him yawned into a frightening chasm into which he feared to fall. The contrast between last night's delirium and today's humiliation was almost too much to feel at once.

Upon leaving the school, a kernel of heat trickled into Frissan's emptiness. As he walked, it collected into a pool of dangerous anger, replacing the shock and defeat with one impulse: revenge. Bid and the bards would suffer for his suffering. He vowed that he would work to that end, even if it took years.

In the west, the sun gleamed with a final shaft of radiance. Frissan turned his back on its light and walked forward into the livid darkness.

The Bone Box

Oddments and trinkets spilled over the merchant stall's shelves, an assortment of items purchased from everywhere within trading range of the Kaelennar marketplace. Marritt picked up a silver ball ornamented with a spiral wave pattern, and was surprised to hear it tinkle quietly as he tilted it. He smiled and set the ball down; it was a child's toy, similar to one he had recently bought for his own three-year-old son.

The merchant, a man of middle years with a dark complexion and unusual amber eyes, finished haggling with a hard-faced woman in lace and pearls. He turned to Marritt. "Anything you like?" he said with a smile. "I've trifles from the Isle of Kait, baubles from the north, or if you prefer, magical novelties. What are you looking for? A gift for your lady?"

Marritt shook his head. "I'm not looking for anything in particular." He tapped the silver ball with a forefinger, listening with pleasure to its silvery chime. "This is a nice toy, but it's overpriced. And my son already has one." He smiled again as he thought of little Gard, with his shining blue eyes that saw the world as if everything in it had been created just for him. Suddenly his throat tightened, as Marritt remembered how much he missed his son.

The merchant nodded. "A family man, eh? What about this?" He took a metal bird, sparrow sized, down from a high shelf and placed it on the table in front of him. Marritt looked at it with mild interest, noting the exquisite detail on its blue enameled feathers and the facets of its jeweled eyes.

"It's faldren crafted clockwork. Watch." The merchant turned the tiny key in its back twice.

The bird jerked, then hopped forward. Its beak opened, and a trill emanated from somewhere within its metal body. It hopped once again, then stopped in mid-trill as the key wound down. In all, Marritt thought, it was an impressive piece — clockwork was rare and valuable — but not one he wanted to give to a three-year-old. He shook his head and turned to leave the stall in favor of finding some pastries for an early lunch.

Raising his voice, the merchant asked, "Sir, are you from around here? Or your wife? How many children have you?"

Marritt sighed and considered ignoring him, but manners forced him to turn back to the stall. "One child," he said. "A boy, three years old. My wife and I were both raised in Harfal-on-the-lake, and studied here at the mage's college. She's back in Harfal, with our son."

He wondered if Adrah might like the bird. She certainly deserved a lovely gift. Despite his own considerable proficiency in magic, she could not only outspell him, but managed their growing household with the ease of a great lady. It was due to her skills and management that they had amassed a fair fortune in ten short years. She had not lost her beauty in that time, and would never lose her considerable grace and charm.

Adrah had been tremendously angry when Marritt proposed returning to Kaelennar for further study. "Our home is here," she had said, in acid, cutting tones that he barely recognized. "We have family here, friends, our entire life. We can't just drag Gard around with us on a whim. It's not fair to him." So Adrah had stayed behind with Gard, and Marritt had come to Kaelennar. Thinking of them brought a catch to his throat.

"Ah." The merchant scooped up the clockwork bird and returned it to its shelf before Marritt could look at it again. "A mage? I may have something which would interest you. Do you like puzzles and mysteries? I could use help with a mystery of my own."

This was certainly a different approach; Marritt found himself curious as to what mystery this purveyor of novelties might have to offer him. Putting aside thoughts of Adrah and Gard, he raised his eyebrows expressively.

This time the merchant removed a small casket from its place behind a line of tiny carven dolls. The box was a little shorter than Marritt's forearm, and half as wide; finger-length bone plates the color of ivory covered its surface, and only pale brown lines suggested the wood beneath. It was a beautiful piece of craftsmanship. Marritt waited for the merchant to open the box, to display the secret within.

Instead, the man sighed. "This box has given me more trouble than anything else I have ever bought. I had it off a man from just south of the Kurtish Mountains. He said it was magical – well, it is, at that. The strongest magic I've ever come across." He frowned at the casket. "I have gone to a score of mages, and all of them say the same thing; the box can't be opened. Whatever lies inside, it must be precious indeed, to warrant such powerful protection." He met

Marritt's gaze squarely. "I am at the end of my resources. If any mage can open the box, I will give him a third share of whatever lies inside."

Intrigued, Marritt reached down to pick up the box. It tingled slightly in his hand, warming to the temperature of his skin. The bone plates were smooth and worn with age, and despite polishing, some of the brown lines melted into aged black near the seams. Yes, there was magic here; he could feel it spilling over the box like rainwater over stone.

"I expect," he said to the merchant, "that you have tried to open it without magic." The man nodded, and Marritt continued, "And you have tried to discern what magic holds it so tightly closed, and what treasure is hidden in the box?"

The merchant puffed his cheeks and blew out a frustrated breath. "Repeatedly. Every one of them says the box is so tightly bound with outer magics that they can tell nothing of what lies within. Nothing. If it's not going to open, it might as well be a potato or a piece of shoe leather. I'm certainly earning no coin from it."

Marritt looked back at the box, smoothing its surface with his thumb. He liked the feel of the piece; it seemed to radiate something comforting just beyond the range of his senses. What the merchant said was true. No one would put such magic on anything which had no value. Whether or not it was something that could be sold in the marketplace was another question. But it cost him nothing to attempt the feat, and might well gain him a considerable fortune.

He nodded. "Do you have someone to watch your booth? I don't want to try anything in the middle of the marketplace, in case it contains something dangerous. Besides, it will be harder to concentrate here."

"Yes." The merchant walked to the opposite side of his booth and bellowed into the crowd. "Kemmi! Get over here and watch the booth for me!"

A very young woman who shared the merchant's dark skin and amber eyes separated from the near side of the crowd and entered the booth by sliding beneath the counter. Her shrewd gaze skewered the box, then Marritt. "Another mage?"

The merchant nodded. "I'll be back in a bit, just you be sure no one makes off with the merchandise. If I find a single gewgaw missing, I'll take it out on your hide, girl!" Kemmi grinned, obviously not intimidated by the threat.

The merchant exited the booth by the same route as his daughter, and took the box back from Marritt. "An inn?" he asked. "A quiet one?" He scowled at the casket, then at Marritt. "I'll buy you lunch, though merciful Kyaan only knows how much money I am going to end up spending in getting this cursed box open."

Nearby was an inn that was not too shabby, but had little custom at midmorning, due to the poor quality of its food and ale, and the headaches of its guests. The merchant secured a table in a small dark nook facing the door. They ordered two flagons of what turned out to be weak beer, and sipped quietly for a moment or two. Then the merchant set the casket on the table between them. He seemed a bit resigned, and it was obvious to Marritt that he had few hopes that

Marritt would succeed where so many others had failed.

Marritt reached out with a charm that enhanced his magical senses and might help him learn the box's purpose. He was a good diviner, and was usually able to trace the outward shape even of magics that were inwardly too great for his abilities. Expecting some sort of protective spell, he touched it with a mental finger, trying to see where the spell gave and where it remained firm, so that he could pinpoint the best place to apply magical pressure.

At first, all he could make out was the sheer exuberance of the magic. It rushed and eddied, swirling over the box in great waves of power. Something different at the places where the plates joined caught his attention, but he could not focus on them, due to the force of the magic. Marritt was not certain he had ever felt something quite so powerful contained within a physical object. The power was almost elemental in its strength.

This box was beyond him, he knew already; but he had said he would try, and so he would. Like a thief inserting a pick into a lock, he tried to angle in spells of opening and unbinding. Little to his surprise, it remained tightly shut. Working at the spells, he tried to find any crevice where they might gain greater purchase, but he could find none.

If only Adrah were here, perhaps the two of them might find a way to open it together. She might also have some better suggestions for an approach. Marritt felt the catch of pain, like a sudden cramp, that still caught him off guard when he thought of how much he missed her. Her image, complete with tumbling chestnut hair and cheerful brown eyes, flashed through his mind.

The bone box opened.

Inside was a rudely carven bear, jointed, and mounted on a tiny pedestal. Short strings anchored it to its base. It appeared to be nothing more than a simple child's toy, made to dance by the interaction of the strings and manipulation of the pedestal.

With a startled gasp, the merchant reached out his hand to take the box. It snapped closed immediately, as tightly as before. The merchant uttered a particularly nasty epithet, and picked it up to examine it; from his expression, Marritt guessed that it was again fully sealed.

"What did you do?" the man asked finally. "What sort of spell does it open to? You must have done something different from all those others. How?"

Marritt knew he had done nothing to force the box; his spells were ineffective on this strange artifact. He had no answer to the merchant's question; it was unlikely that Marritt's magic had been the catalyst.

But if not that, what? Marritt wished again for Adrah's precision, her perception, and her common sense. Her absence was like the want of a hand or an eye; Marritt could more easily have done without both. He thumped the table with a loose fist, frustrated by his inability to puzzle out the solution. He was a mage, and one of a mage's greatest strengths should be in piecing together disparate information into a whole.

Out of the emptiness beside him, the answer crystallized, sharp and clear. It was not simply Marritt's spell that had unlocked the casket; it was his longing for Adrah. Not alone, but in conjunction with his opening magic, at the precise moment when he had touched the box. Somehow the combination had triggered whatever power held it closed, and momentarily coaxed it into giving up a small portion of its secret. It was unsurprising that no other mage had managed to pry open its jaws. Even beginning students were taught to clear their minds at the beginning of a spell, so that nothing could distract them and cause them to lose their tight focus and control.

"Oh," Marritt said, a little startled. "That's it, then."

The merchant's mouth pulled into a downward arc, and he wrinkled his forehead. "What? Can you do it again? I don't know what that toy does, but it must be valuable, however it looks." His mouth briefly crooked upward. "And, I confess, I want to know what it's for."

"As do I." Marritt blinked his eyes, sipped more of his beer, and stretched his back out before leaning forward to again touch the small container. He closed his eyes, and reached out his forefinger to tap one of the plates. Keeping thoughts of Adrah in his mind, and how much he missed her, he eased into the opening magic, as gently as a moth alighting on a leaf. A picture of Adrah and Gard playing at jackstraws drifted into his mind.

The bone box opened.

This time neither Marritt nor the merchant moved. Seen closely, the carven bear looked forlorn, as if it longed for a child's touch. One of the ears was chipped, and there seemed to be a tooth mark on its left paw.

"What does it do?" whispered the merchant, as if even his voice might again cause the box to shut forever. Not sure if that were indeed true, Marritt kept his own voice low.

"I don't know yet," he answered. "Finding its purpose might be tricky. Anything might trigger its magic." He looked at the box, assessing his options. "What are you for?" he said, half to himself. "Why do you hold such a strange treasure?"

An intense wave of feeling answered him; Marritt felt his throat constrict as if with deep sorrow and longing. His breath quickened, and black spangled his vision with a vertigo of the spirit that made him feel as if he were no longer anchored within his body. Tides of emotion drowned him in their intensity, until he was swept away.

Marritt found himself within the mind of another man, feeling each emotion and sensation as if it were his own.

His hip hurt. Every time he twisted or bent, fresh pain stabbed at his thigh and jabbed with a sensation like sharp splinters up and down the outer right part of his leg. Movement of any kind, even the smallest twitch, was agonizing.

As he was unable to work, his wife had assigned him to care for their young son, while she labored in the fields to support them all. He hated to watch her toil so hard for so little; she was slight and not strong, and her wages barely kept food on the table. Not that times were easy for anyone these days, but they need not be as hard as this.

The gods only knew when his hip would heal, and he could work again.

The two sat inside a roughly built house with a dirt floor and wall planks smoothed by the passage of years. The father sat immobile in a crude chair, while his son rolled about the floor, acquiring a film of dirt over his clothing and pale hair.

His son was a joy. Three years old, healthy, and bright as a summer day, he was too young for his parents' unhappiness to cloud his childhood. The father watched as his son played with a toy whittled just for him; a cunning jointed bear, whose strings would make the creature jump and dance when the base was pushed. The child was still young enough to find repetition a surprise; he laughed and crowed whenever the bear moved.

Listening to his son's laughter simultaneously lightened the father's heart and touched him with sadness. There would be no more children. His wife had nearly died bearing their son, and the healers said she must never have another. So the parents accepted the will of the gods, and mourned the children they would never raise. All of their heart's love, that settled in the throat with a passion too deep for words, was given to this one boy.

After a while, the boy put down his toy and smiled up at his father. "Please, Papa!" he said, his tone light and exuberant. "Can I go outside and play? Please, Papa, please?" He jumped up and ran toward his father, who put out his hands to intercept his son before the child could climb on his lap, and waken the sleeping agony which waited for him to rouse it with motion.

The father first laughed, then winced, as pain knifed through his hip. He held his breath for a moment, trying to ease it as much as possible. Letting the breath free, he touched his son's hair lightly, then bent carefully to drop a kiss on the top of his son's head. "Certainly you may," he said. "But keep close to the house, and stay away from the barn. I will call you when we eat."

The boy nodded enthusiastically. "Yes, Papa! Thank you!" He ran to the door, and pulled its heavy frame open with an effort, just enough to squeeze himself through. The door banged behind him like a quick report of thunder.

Here, Marritt's immersion in the man's experience lightened. An overlay of thought intruded atop the scene. Like someone commenting on a long-past tragedy, the father's thoughts spoke: "This was the last time I ever knew happiness."

A heavy knock rattled the door in its frame. The father rose with effort and dragged his way to open it, each step jolting his hip with a torturous shock. As he lifted the latch, a small man tumbled in, his face the color of whey. His hands were stained with dark red.

"Do you have a son?" the small man asked, his tone seeming to plead and demand at the same time. "A small son, three or four years of age?"

A sense of dread settled in the father's stomach, and his limbs trembled; the blood on the stranger's hands boded evil. He nodded, feeling a wash of vertigo flood through his head. "I do," he answered. The sound was raspy, hoarse.

"Coran's mercy," said the smaller man, paling even more. "A boy ran in front of my horse. It kicked him in the head. I swear that I meant no harm, but – " He stopped abruptly, and swayed.

The father barely heard the words; his feet seemed to carry him out the door without waiting for conscious consent. The pain in his hip did not slow him; he could feel little else but the knotting of his stomach. Outside, mild autumn spilled harvest colors from the trees and fields, but the father ignored them, seeking only the color of pale hair atop a tiny figure clad in homespun brown.

Not far from the house he saw the horse; a sturdy gray work animal, its shoulder the height of a tall man, with hooves the size of a human head. A splayed form lay to one side.

Bitterness rose from the father's throat as he knelt beside his son. The child had been lifted and laid on his back, most likely by the owner of the horse. The child's forehead was staved in from the hairline to the brow; it was clear he was dead.

Time ceased, as the father tried to make sense of what had happened. His mind attempted to rewind the day's events like thread on a spool, or to deny its reality and recreate it as a terrible dream from which he would soon waken. No tragedy he could imagine was worse than this.

The smaller man joined the father, who glanced at him to see tears staining his cheeks. The father had no such consolation; his loss left him far too desolate for tears. Within him, winter settled, its frost leaving no hope for any spring. He lifted his son gently and carried him to the house, cradling him as if he could still protect the child from mortal pain.

In a blur of memory, perspective shifted, and time collapsed the next hour into mere moments. To Marritt's watching eyes, the horse's owner was suddenly gone, replaced by the mother, who knelt by her child.

Her skin was gray-tinged, and her limbs trembled. "No," she said in a voice like the scraping of bone against bone. "He's not gone. The gods cannot be so cruel." She shrugged away the father's touch. "I should have died before him." She brushed the child's head delicately with her fingertips, as if she hoped her fingers would discover life where her eyes could not.

There was no comfort the man could offer. He knew how much his wife adored their son; so often when the child slept, she had touched his hair like this, as if she feared he was as fragile as spider's thread. There had been five long years before she conceived, and she had prayed each day for a son on whom she could lavish all her devotion. He ached to hold her, but she was clearly neither able to give solace or to receive it.

He blamed himself. He had not been able to care for his son, and he was not now able to care for his wife. Now that he had lost the one, the other was everything to him. All he wanted was to wrap himself in her scent and her body, to alleviate the pain by sharing it between them. Yet she saw nothing but her child.

Marritt sensed the passing of months. They flowed by as if he had lived them, while simultaneously folding half a year into moments of perception.

Nothing could console the grieving mother. She would sit in her chair and stare at the wall, as if she saw something invisible to her husband. She did no housework and no cooking. As winter settled its frozen breath over the land, there was no labor to be done in the fields. She spoke little, and purpose drained from the deep of her eyes. Only her hands expressed her pain, stroking the air as if she caressed the head of a young child.

His own grief walled behind frozen battlements, the father settled into a routine of care for his suffering wife. His hip healed so that he could move without agony; the agony in his heart was unending. He cooked, cleaned, and tended to his wife's simplest needs, from brushing her hair, to feeding her the scant food that she would consent to eat. Every day he awoke listening for his son's laughter.

On the third day of each week, the man rode to market in his neighbor's cart, to buy what supplies he had been unable to save for a hard winter season. Each coin was precious, and food was dear. The man wondered if they could last until the spring, but he kept his thoughts to himself, sheltering his wife as best he could.

One market day, late in the season, the man returned to his house carrying a sack of dried meat and fruit that had cost three times its autumn value. He struggled through drifts of calf-high snow, redistributed since that morning by a stiff western wind. Though his hip still twinged occasionally, he ignored it; there was no one who could work for him. He stepped through his door, set down the sack, and looked for his wife.

She did not sit in her chair, nor, when he checked, was she in her bed. A deep dread knotted his belly. He dropped the sack on the floor, and called his wife's name, so loud that she must hear and answer. There was no response.

Fear rocked the husband with disorienting force. He ran outside, calling for his wife, looking everywhere for her pale hair and even paler face. No response came; it was as if the wind had blown her into oblivion. Then he saw the tracks.

Wind had scoured them as well, but a few still remained, where the house had sheltered them in the lee. They moved inexorably toward the old barn, which had housed no animals in years. The husband followed them to the structure, whose loose boards and sagging roof made a perilous haven from the worst of the weather. He hesitated a moment before flinging open the door, his wife's name on his lips.

Her pale hair fluttered in the gusts that blew through the barn's chinks and holes. The man thought at first that she still breathed. He ran to where she had hung herself, fumbling with the slipknot that her passionate fingers had tied in the old harness rope. He knew, even then, that she was dead, and that only the wind gave her the semblance of a living woman.

Her weight sank into his arms. Her skin was icy to the touch. The husband brushed her lips with his own, and gently carried her from the barn into the house where they had once been happy. His tears were dammed by the ice of overwhelming loss. At least his wife was at peace.

Spring came early that year. As soon as sun thawed the ground enough for a spade, the man buried his wife alongside their son on the tiny farm which had once held their future. It seemed to him that spring flowers clambered over the graves almost before he had laid the last shovel of earth. Most were pale white or yellow, like the hair of his wife and his son.

He kept the toy, and would look at it sometimes, unable to shed his pain in tears. At times he thought of joining his loved ones in their earthen home. He was not sure what held him back; except, perhaps for fear that if he did not remember them, they would fade forever from the living world.

Years passed. The man repeatedly contemplated the small bear he had once carved for his son. As he grew older, his memories softened, though he never shed tears. Finally the grief, only blunted by time, transformed into something new; poignant love, and a deep regret that his child would never grow to a man, and that his wife would never know the treasure of grandchildren.

The man held the dancing bear in age-withered hands, remembering his son's innocent joy as the child played. A sad smile pulled at the corners of his mouth. The man would die within a few years, and no one would remember his graceful wife and their beautiful son. He could do nothing to commemorate the lives they had once lived, and the love they had shared.

As he smoothed the places where his fingers had polished the toy over so many years, an idea formed. At first it was an idle thought, but it rapidly built up force, until he felt driven to act. He knew what he could do to keep their memories alive forever.

Taking his shovel, he looked for the blossom-covered mound that embraced the body of his wife. It was not deep; he had lacked the strength to fight the still-cold ground when he had buried her. He found her shroud, tattered with decay, but still clinging to her white bones, the color of her hair. "My love," he whispered, and reached into the grave to take a bone. After resettling the shroud as well as possible, the man replaced the earth over her resting place, even settling the flowers back into place over the mound. His son's body he left alone.

In the barn, he carved a wooden box, just the size to hold his son's favorite toy. With tremendous care, he shaved off thin slices of bone, sanding and planing them until they fit smoothly on the entire surface of the casket.

As he worked, the dammed tears finally came free. They flowed like a silent river down his creased cheeks, dripping over his fingers and onto the whole of the box. All the years of loss, pain, and grief, seemed to contract in his chest and to pour up through his throat, to find release through the channel of his eyes.

Images formed, clearer than memory, behind the watery blur. His wife giving birth; his son's first steps; his wife singing lullabies until their son drifted off to sleep; their laughter as the toddler danced to his own tuneless humming. There had been so many happy times, all of them precious in recollection, no matter how ordinary they had seemed at the time. The pain in the man's chest became the mingled pain of grief and joy, to be expressed in the one thing he wished the world to remember: They had lived.

The box snapped shut. Marritt jerked into awareness, feeling as if he had lived a lifetime in the few moments the box had opened to reveal its story. He understood now. The magic on it was not the studied spell of a mage, but the more essential enchantment of the heart, coalescing out of years of concentrated grief, pain, and love. Such magic was rare, and Marritt had never come across a more powerful example.

He reached out to stroke the bone plates, remembering the woman whose joy and grief had been her only child. The spirits of all three were mingled here, crafted with love, and bound by bone and tears and the innocent joy of a small boy, who would forever be held in the embrace of his mother. His chest ached, and he thought of Adrah and Gard, so far away in Harfal. How could he have left them?

The merchant shook his head, a dazed expression on his face. "I can't sell it," he said. "It wouldn't be right."

"You must ask it to open," Marritt told him, finding some respect for the merchant as he agreed with the man's assessment. "It won't be forced, but it wants to tell the story. That's what it's for." The merchant could actually sell this for a considerable sum; some mages would value it for what they could learn of its magic. But it would be like selling a man's heart.

The merchant cleared his throat uncomfortably. "I offered you a third share, but there's no money I'm willing to make from this." He paused, looking down at the casket, before reaching to touch it with a tentative finger. "Do you want the box?"

Marritt considered. He felt privileged to have experienced the box's enchantment, but he did not desire to relive it. Perhaps Adrah would feel differently, but he thought she would not want to suffer the loss of a son, even in such an attenuated way. He shook his head. "No," he answered quietly. "Keep it."

Nodding, the merchant continued, "I owe you, and I pay my debts. Choose one item from my stall, and you may have it without cost." He flashed a white smile, and took a sip of beer. "At the very least, you have saved me from spending more of my money on other mages, and I thank you for it."

Marritt thought of the clockwork bird, and nodded. Adrah would love its delicate enamel, and the melody it sang. He would bring the gift when he returned home.

And that would be soon. Though knowledge and study was important, it need not be here and now, in Kaelennar. It might take longer, but the things he wished to learn he could find in Harfal; there were always options for a determined man. The time he spent with Adrah and Gard was irreplaceable.

Gard would have grown; children changed so much at that age. Marritt imagined his son's bright eyes shining at his father's return. Adrah had been right.

Downing his beer, Marritt began to plan the trip home.

228

Jewel's Price

The mirror reflected the paradigm of Jewel's face, young skin taut over sculptured bones, eyes and lashes darker than her father's heart, cascade of ebony hair eclipsing the translucency of her face. It mocked her, showing as it did a reflection of her mother's face the way Jewel had never seen it: the extraordinary beauty that had captured the attention of the young duke and caused him to swear that he would wed no other woman.

Jewel's mother had died three years before, forsaken by all but Jewel. Age clawed her face deeply, and her parchment skin hung loosely over bones that had long since lost any hint of grace. Even the courtiers and servants had neglected her, concerned only with the duke and his comforts. *He* had long since abandoned Jewel's mother, going openly to other women to slake his thirst for beauty; he had never cared that her mother possessed wit and intelligence, talent, warmth and humor. Only Jewel had sat by her side, listened to her last rattling breaths, waited for final words of love or wisdom that never came.

Jewel took her brush and began to brush her thick raven hair. She must look her best tonight; Lord Beichan was to offer for her hand this very evening, and Jewel wanted to make certain that he was truly snared by the allure of her face and slender body. She wanted no loveless marriage such as her mother had endured.

She dressed herself in brocade of black with threads of gold, adorning her hair with a fragile chain of gold and winking diamonds, settling gold and diamonds into the hollow of her throat. She looked regal, a princess. She felt as empty as a tree, leafing on the outside, rotted at the heart.

Her eyes fixed ahead of her as she went to dinner in the great hall. She remained conscious of no fear, simply a gulf inside where her emotions should be. She followed torchlight and candlelight and at last emerged in the great hall as light on her feet as the wind which blew through her soul. Great weapons adorned the walls, a reminder of the history of her father's house. Most had not been used for centuries, but remained, rusting into legend to feed the duke's desire for glory. Helmets of all sorts lined the mantle over the great open fireplace which fed more draft than warmth into the hall.

The others were there already, her father, Lord Beichan, and his mother. Jewel greeted her father first, as was proper, curtseying like a dancer and rising back to her feet while touching his hand as little as she could manage. He was a heavy man, but not soft; the years had aged him less cruelly than his wife.

Next it was Jewel's responsibility as chatelaine to greet their visitors with proper ceremony. She turned to Lord Beichan, feeling the emotions spilling back into the cavity of her body. He was so beautiful, a strong godlike young man with golden hair and a smile that could melt mountain ice. He was no fool, either; Jewel knew that he spoke with her father of politics and philosophy. To her he wrote exquisite poetry with excellent rhyme and scansion. His smile cradled her, made her feel safe and loved.

"Lord Beichan," she said, a smile curving her lips into a

crescent. "Welcome to you and yours." She turned to Lady Beichan, the smile freezing. Lady Beichan was a nothing, a shadow appendage to Lord Beichan's blazing light. Courtesy was required, but nothing else. "Welcome, Lady Beichan."

"Greetings, Lady Jewel," Lord Beichan responded, his gaze fixed upon her face. "You are as lovely as ever, maiden. It is a good night to speak of alliances."

"Sit to dinner, Lord Beichan, Lady Beichan." The duke snapped his fingers and a page appeared from the recesses of the room as if he had grown there. "Business can wait until the meat is upon the table."

The page first seated the duke, then Lord and Lady Beichan, and finally Jewel. Servants hastened to bring them their dinner, supplying them with knives, trenchers, and blue china fingerbowls which Jewel's mother had brought to her marriage with the duke. Conversation came to a momentary lull as the steward brought in wine and poured some in each goblet. Jewel sipped lightly, listening to the conversation in which, though about her, she might take no part. Instead she dropped morsels to the dogs which milled about the table through the fresh rushes which the duke had ordered laid just for this occasion.

"Her dower is extensive," said the duke as if Jewel could not hear. "Her mother's jewels are hers, and I am not niggardly; I intend to add gold as well. And she is my only child; her husband will inherit the duchy after my death. Can you fulfill such a task and manage your own lands as well?"

Lord Beichan set down his goblet in front of him. "I cannot fill your shoes, if that is what you ask. But I will endeavor to serve my responsibilities as best I may. Your land will not suffer."

Jewel listened to him with pride. Surely Lord Beichan would be a great duke someday. And she would labor beside him, giving everything she had to him. He would be sure of her love and of her worth to him.

Lord Beichan laughed. "Besides, even if you said that your daughter was to have no dower of jewels, gold, or land, I would still ask for her hand in marriage. Her beauty is the only dower I need. You are most fortunate to have sired such a daughter."

Jewel felt as if her heart dropped from her body altogether. She had heard words like those before. What had her mother told her? *I care not if you have dowry or rank or land*, had said the young duke to Jewel's mother. *Your beauty is the only dower I need.*

Lord Beichan could not possibly mean the same. Could he?

Jewel knew that she was not strong enough to endure what her mother had suffered at the duke's hand for so many years: the loneliness, the abandonment, the years of growing older and seeing the man she loved turn away from her for young beauties. She would do anything rather than endure that.

As her father and Lord Beichan spoke of the marriage contract, she determined that she would find some way to keep Lord Beichan's eye and heart from wandering from her ephemeral youth and beauty.

A nurse had once told Jewel a tale of wishes fulfilled through the courage of body and spirit. *Deepest in the woods, Love, lies the castle*

tower, the nurse's hoary voice asserted like a wraith in Jewel's memory. *Terrible, those wolves – they will tear your flesh like parchment and the ravens feast on it after. But should you win through the gates, covered over with thorns to rend armor swiftly, and gain the fountain at the base of the tower, there sits a cup chained to the fountain's lip. Drink from that and you will have a wish such as you never imagined. Only whisper that one wish in the cup and it will be granted, no matter how great.*

Even at eight Jewel had been suspicious of what sounded too simple. *The thorns, the wolves, the ravens? That is all between anyone and their greatest wish?*

The nurse hesitated, then answered, *I have heard more. That the wish may exact a price, and that price may be too heavy for bearing.*

Later, when Jewel grew too old for nurses, she put the story away with her childhood toys and other foolishness. The story of a wish meant little to her in her daily routine of becoming an accomplished young woman. Her mother taught her the womanly arts of sewing and embroidery, weaving, riding and hawking, the running of a household, the playing of the harp. From her mother Jewel also learned the less womanly arts of reading, writing, and mathematics, as well as the caution that she should never parade her accomplishments before men.

But now, with Lord Beichan's love the stakes, Jewel remembered.

Wondering if she chased moonshadows, Jewel dressed for the journey at the midpoint of the darkness. Clad in a divided skirt, warm wool coat, and high boots, she clandestinely descended the stairs to the scullery. There, amid the snoring of the servants, she took some bread and cheese, stowing them in a leather pouch at her belt.

Creeping into the great hall, her heart pounded so hard she could not think why no one else could hear it. She had no skill in weaponry, and knew it would be futile to carry anything beyond a sharp knife, so she made no attempt to wrestle down the hundred-year-old halberds or swords from their roost on the walls.

Instead she looked at the rushes for the dogs. They also slept, sated with the meat, enough for two-dozen, that four could not eat. The duke spared no expense when it came to arranging his daughter's marriage. Jewel kicked through the rushes, looking for what the dogs had left. Several bones and two large cuts were the reward for her search; she carefully placed them in the pouch with the bread and cheese, wiping her hands on the rushes. It was not as good as fresh meat, but it might serve her well.

Her last indoor stop was the fireplace mantle. She could not reach the helmets, and did not wish to make noise in knocking one down. Instead she wrestled one of the heavy chairs from the table to climb upon. Selecting a helmet of small and simple design, she tucked it under her arm and climbed down again, leaving the chair where it was. They would know in the morning she was gone. Whatever success she might have would not depend upon secrecy.

The horsemaster and his boys were drunken somnolent, something Jewel would not have let pass at another time. As it was, she was glad; it made her task easier. On impulse, Jewel snagged a sturdy length of rope off the wall before attending to the horses; it might serve her well. Saddling and bridling the lovely gray gelding, calmest of the beasts, she led it silently out of the stable and into the grounds surrounding the duke's keep. Then she mounted, turned its head toward the forest she could see black and massy to the east, and began to ride.

Jewel had no idea how she was to find the mysterious castle tower deep within the forest. At first she attempted to follow paths that crisscrossed through the trees, but darkness blinded her and many of the paths did not seem to be true paths, but only the trails made by some foraging animal. Branches tore at her hair and clothes with fingers leafy and clawed by new summer growth. Finally Jewel simply turned her horse's head toward where she thought was the center of the wood and loosened the reins. She clung tightly to the gelding's mane to glean what comfort she could. *For Lord Beichan*, she chanted in her mind. *For Lord Beichan and our marriage that is to be.*

Every sound she could not recognize terrified her; Jewel began to wonder why she had come here to follow a child's tale on nothing else but a fear and a distant hope. She shivered within her coat, shrinking like a snail into a shell. *I will never find my way home. They will find nothing but my bones.* Even her father's indifference seemed to blaze like a hearthfire in her mind and memory. Lord Beichan's image shone golden in her heart.

It was that image which brought her out of the cold fear of dark and abandonment. Nothing else in her life had ever made her feel as had Lord Beichan; his strong arms, his warm smile, his love, were all that made Jewel feel like a young, vital girl and not like some ageless statue looking out from behind eyes of marble and alabaster. She needed his love to live; she would not become like her mother. She would not!

I must go on. I will pay any price for what I seek. Her nurse's warning was years behind her, and desperation overrode caution. *If it be there, I will find it. I must, or die – and death at the teeth of the forest creatures is better than the slow death Mother endured when Father turned from her.* Salt stung on her lips, and Jewel realized with surprise that she was weeping.

Before her the trees fell away and sky instantly darkened. The gelding stopped, snorting uneasily, and Jewel patted its neck. "Good horse," she told it, feeling a frantic rush of warmth toward this, her only companion, as she tried to make out what she saw.

Gradually, light spilled in around the edges of Jewel's vision as dawn woke to rouse the rest of day. Ruddy edges tinged the massive spectacle before her; a great black castle with a tower that loomed over even the oldest and tallest of the forest trees beyond the clearing. Its walls, too, were massive, of black stone nearly twice as high as the walls of the duke's keep. Jewel sat just outside the gates, ironwork which curled and looped its way around rose vines covered both with bloom and thorn. Though the gates stood open, the vines laced them tightly together, preventing the entry of anything larger than a house cat.

Jewel stared at them, wondering how she was ever to get through the thorny vines into the grounds beyond. She would not have to worry about wolves and ravens if she could not pass this first test. It seemed an insoluble barrier; even if she had brought one of her father's swords or halberds she could not have hacked through the thickness of these vines. They must have grown for a hundred years.

As she sat and pondered the hindrance, dawn dipped the sky with the paints of morning. A thread of question, fine as spider silk, wound its way into her mind: how had she found this place so easily? She could have wandered for days, even weeks, and never found her way to the heart of the woods. But the question slithered away as she contemplated the problem before her.

Perhaps there was another solution. Jewel looked at the rope coiled over the horn of her saddle. She did not like the thought of climbing over the wall, though she thought she could gain easy purchase on the brambles that cascaded over its top; the thorns would cling to her as easily as to the rope.

Instead, Jewel looked carefully at the gates. Were they to open, they might well pull the vines out of place, leaving room for her horse and herself to squeeze into the courtyard she could see only dimly beyond.

She slid out of the saddle and approached the gates, watching carefully for windblown tendrils of vine. She could discern no lock, nor could she tell in which direction the gates opened. Pulling her hand inside the arm of her coat, she gingerly reached out a fabric-coated hand to take hold of the ironwork of the gate. Sharp thorns slashed at the wool and stabbed her through its bulk; Jewel winced and drew her hand back quickly. Blood puddled onto her sleeve, staining it with red. Hesitating a moment, she reached out a second time even more carefully, determined that she would not shrink from pain this time. Though the roses stabbed at her hand and arm, jolting all the way up to her shoulder like spears of ice, this time she grasped the gate firmly between the vines and pulled as hard as she could. It did not budge.

Jewel nodded to herself. She had half-expected this. Retrieving the coil of rope from its perch on her saddlehorn, she returned to the gates. Ignoring the painful slashes and cuts she received, she laced the rope through the bars of the righthand gate. By the time she finished, her sleeves were ripped and her arms bleeding profusely, but the rope was tied. She took the other end back to the gelding and secured it around the saddlehorn, taking up the slack in another coil. Then she mounted and urged her horse backward.

This time the gate gave, groaning with each step the horse took. Jewel walked the gray horse to the right, steering its steps until the gate hung open most of the way, and glad that she had chosen this one of all the horses in the stables. She dismounted once again, and took the extra coils to wrap around the masses of creepers hugging the wall. This was harder, and before she was done, much of her clothing, face, and upper body was torn and stained with blood. Tightening the rope as best she could, she looped it off the saddle, and waited to see if it would hold. For a moment the gate swung crazily, then settled into a position facing straight outward.

By now all the scratches and gashes hurt like the intense prickling that signaled the onset of a fever. Though some of the vines had fallen back over the entry, far fewer barred her way, and she thought she could lead the gelding inside without too many lacerations.

The horse balked at the first touch of the thorns, but Jewel spoke soothing words, and then he followed her, though not willingly. She felt for it, but she could not leave it outside the gate, alone. This time the barbs caught at her hair, attempting to tear it from her head, but Jewel shook her head and plunged through as swiftly as she could.

Once inside, she could see that this had once been a great castle, fortified and built to last any siege, were it to last a thousand years. Now stone crumbled and grass grew over the flagstones of the courtyard, but the tower still lofted, strong and impossibly high into the sky before her. It shone the ominous black of a dark dream, and Jewel shuddered. *The fountain*, she told herself. *I need not enter the tower. I seek the fountain only.* She cast about for any signs or sounds of water in this place.

In relief at having negotiated the terrible thorns, Jewel had managed to forget the castle's other dangers. A monstrous howl reminded her of them, sharply. Jewel scrabbled to pull the slabs of meat from her pouch as two enormous wolves careered around the tower's edge toward her. She threw the meat as hard as she could, one toward each wolf. They turned to sniff the offerings, while Jewel hauled on the reins and began to run. Then, without even tasting the food, the wolves turned back toward Jewel.

Jewel's breath rasped in her throat. She could not outrun these creatures, and she could not fight them. She could only distract them. In terror, she drew her knife and hacked as hard as she could at the spot on the gelding's throat just above the life-vein. Blood gushed out, soaking her instantly. Jewel felt sick, but did not stop to indulge herself. She ran toward the far end of the courtyard as hard as she could.

The wolves did not follow. They stopped at the horse, which tottered on weak hooves, eyes glazing. Jewel did not know how she was to return home without her horse, but knew she had not had a choice.

Shadows speckled the morning sun's pattern on the grass. Jewel looked up and saw ravens gathering in a flock. She wondered what she would do now, if these birds attacked. She had nothing to give them but bread and cheese, and ravens were not fond of bread and cheese. She felt suddenly weary, as if she had spent a hundred years in this place. She could not leave soon enough.

But the ravens seemed to have something else in mind. They streamed away sunward, scarcely above Jewel's head, around a corner of the main castle. Suddenly intrigued, Jewel followed.

And here it was: the fountain, a pure spring bordered by a black marble wall the height of Jewel's chest, and heaped with wildflowers which grew almost to its lip. Jewel walked forward, a little afraid now that her goal was in sight. She leaned against the fountain, one hand on the stone, one in the wildflowers. Then she touched bone and started. Looking down, she saw a pile of human bones, almost completely covered with wildflowers. Vetch adorned his empty ribs, and clover grew through the hollows of his eyes.

Perhaps the wolves killed him, thought Jewel hopefully. *Before he tasted of the cup.* It was small comfort for her, standing beside naked death as she was, but it gave her the courage to look for the cup. The vessel sat on the opposite side of the fountain, chained to it by a chain of marble. Had she not been in such pain, terror, and exhaustion, Jewel might have marveled at such craftwork. As it was, she merely wanted to gain her hard-earned wish and leave.

Ravens settled on the stone lip of the fountain as Jewel progressed toward the cup. By the time she reached it, they ringed it like gargoyles, only the space needed for her to drink unoccupied. Jewel hesitated a moment, wondering what it meant. But she had not come all this way to be stopped by a vision of ravens. She took the cup.

Dipping it into the fountain spring, she came up with a drink of the purest water she had ever seen. It seemed to hold all the hopes she had ever possessed, back before her mother's death and her father's indifference had stolen them. Tears sprang to her eyes as she looked upon the magic waters. "Eternal youth and beauty," she whispered into the cup. She drank.

A wild vitality leapt through her veins. Jewel felt all the hurts of her flesh mend, and health filled her, as did the water. *Lord Beichan will never leave me now.*

The ravens fluttered up like a cloud. Several descended on her shoulders, her hair, her arms. Others wheeled into the sky in a dance of dark jubilation. Jewel stretched, feeling as if she had been ill all her life and now she was well. She walked back toward the main courtyard, then turned toward the gate.

The gelding was dead, but the wolves had left it. It lay, torn and bloody, on the grassy flagstones, a sacrifice to Lord Beichan. Jewel gave it a somber look as she passed to reach the gates.

The ravens scattered as she reached the gate. It was still stood open, vines reaching thorny fingers to rend any who dared breech the opening. Jewel ducked down and tried to pass under the roses. But instead of thorns, she met with a firm resistance like strong hands holding her back. At first in surprise, then in shock, she tried harder and harder to force herself through the gate, finally throwing herself at it so hard that, had it been a wall, she might have injured herself. Though she landed on the ground, there was only the firm, gentle resistance, like a parent forbidding a child to leave its room.

"No," said Jewel. Tears squeezed from her eyes as if pulled directly from her heart. "No. I did not mean this to happen. It was for Lord Beichan, so he would love me forever. Let me go. Let me go!" She did not know to whom she spoke, but pled with it as if it were a living, thinking creature. But nothing responded, and still she could not pass the gates.

Now Jewel remembered her nurse's words. What was more useless than a wish which could not be brought back into the world? Someone had left an irony in the castle keep to snare the hopes and perhaps the spirits of those foolish enough to wish on the fountain. She wondered about the ravens: were they the spirits of those who had died here, bound in death as in life to this place? And the bones beside the fountain; had he had gone there, hoping beyond thought for a second wish of freedom? He had died there, but what of her? In alarm, Jewel remembered her own wish; "eternal youth and beauty". Did that mean she was chained here for eternity, as the cup was chained to the fountain?

She turned back to the gray gelding and the knife that lay beside him. Her limbs felt heavy and slow. Kneeling, she let the tears fall as she took up the knife. Trying not to think of what she did, she drew the blade it across one wrist. It made no impression; her wish had armored her as well as trapped her. She dropped the knife and stared into the space beyond life where she would never be able to go.

Alone forever? Despair choked her; she tasted ashes on her tongue.

Ravens settled again in her hair, comforting her with their presence. *Not alone*, that presence said.

Jewel turned and saw the wolves padding toward her, their yellow eyes gleaming. A faint optimism returned. *They are the guardians of this place. If anyone can give me peace, they can.* She bared her throat to them and closed her eyes. She hoped it would not hurt too much.

A wet nose thrust itself into her hand and a tongue splashed across her face. She opened her eyes to see the fierce guardians of the keep licking her like puppies.

Not alone," she said, her voice hoarse as a raven's. "Not alone."

Wind Child

Ttane danced in a vortex of whirling, spiraling wind. Within her gauzy garments swirled the remains of last year's leaves, a sprinkle of soil, and a number of insects who rode her wind with the joyful abandon of creatures with no sense of individual lives. A moth flapped upward in a helical intoxication; a scatter of bees surfed the air in furred delight; and a lone grasshopper reveled in the chance to open its wings in true flight.

A few more turns, and Ttane was done for the moment. She carefully set down the creatures so that they would not be injured by falling from the heights. Unlike some of her sisters, she cared for the welfare of the living things that crossed her path. And she was so lonely, even the grasshopper was company.

She was not sure how long she had been there; all she knew was that the season had not yet turned. Whether it was days or months since she had danced over the mountains she could not remember. The ecstasy of the storm took her kindred that way, obscuring both thought and memory. When she thought of the night she had come, all she could see was driving rain and the violence of the dance spiraling into the sky.

When she had crossed the mountains, accidentally flung by her powerful oldest sister Sshessh, she had first felt the heavy weight of the land tugging at her feet. It resisted her chaotic nature with a heavy solidity, a drag on her dance like the anchor of a ship. It robbed her of strength with an active hostility to her kind. Every time her feet touched the ground, Ttane could feel a tug as the land sought to draw her into its ponderous order. There was a malice in it, but she was unsure of its reason. She had no gift to speak with earth spirits, and any wind spirits who had once passed through had either blown away, or been pulled into the claustrophobic vortex of the land.

To the sight it was beautiful; a mountain valley, inexplicably low and flat, a soft scatter of grasses and low trees over its rocky bones. Ttane would have fled, but she did not know how to cross the mountains which encircled this place. More importantly, when she chose a direction by way of the sun and arrowed along its line, she found herself slowing gradually, sinking toward the green-furred skin of the earth's face. It was as if the land itself did not want her to leave. It had begun to frighten her: would she ever be freed to rejoin her brothers and sisters, or would she succumb to the deep pull of the land, sinking forever into its unyielding oppression?

It frightened her as she had never been frightened before. Her kind did not fear the creatures that occupied land, water and sky. Only elemental powers of earth, wind, water, and fire could harm or destroy such an ethereal creature as Ttane. But among the company of her more powerful sisters she feared nothing, protected by their furious strength and wildness. Alone, she was vulnerable.

Ahead and below her, a village straggled, strewn among the fields like a handful of loose stones. Ttane usually ignored human dwellings, finding no commonality with the heavy creatures. But today, something drew her; she felt a pull toward the settlement, as if one of her sisters were calling her. Startled, Ttane's hair lifted and whipped around her, calling small clouds from the clean skies and darkening knolls and hummocks with little smudges of darkness.

The pull led her to a dwelling on the outskirts of the town, a small cottage of whitewashed plaster, thatched with long grass and fenced by a low stone wall. Smoke puffed from its chimney in short, apologetic hiccups, indicating that someone was home. She eagerly stretched out her senses to catch any hint of a sister on the wind. All she felt in the skies was a flat stillness. She sagged, defeated. None of her kind were there.

As she hovered in the air over the cottage, the door opened, ejecting a pair of human girls into the warm evening. The younger had a mass of white-blonde hair, which tumbled down her back in untamed tangles. The elder had a sharp, angular face.

Looking at the children, Ttane again felt a pull of kinship. She did not understand; humans had no bond with the wind's children, could not even see the smaller powers unless they revealed themselves. But there was something that spoke to her of air, though trammeled in earthborn flesh.

To test her perceptions, Ttane touched down next to the two girls, stilling her motion as much as possible. She was not much taller than they, but she was much less substantial. She had danced with insects and birds, but those were partly of the wind; she had never been so close to humans before.

Their eyes did not move toward her form. Ttane reluctantly decided that she was mistaken. Perhaps her desperate longing for her kind had caused her to seek out something that was not there at all.

Perhaps loneliness and fear was driving her mad. Bitterness suffused her, and she sagged, letting loose a sweep of breezes. They flowed through her hair and whipped the children's clothing in a sudden rush.

The younger girl started, then turned around twice, as if searching for something.

"Mona, what is it?" The older girl frowned. "Are you chasing shadows again?"

The younger — Mona — blinked. "I keep on seeing something out of the corner of my eye. It's like somebody is standing there just out of sight. Only when I look, I can't find her. Why is that?"

Ttane felt a sudden lifting of her spirits; the girl knew she was here! Perhaps there was some connection between them after all. Her feet trod out the steps of a quick dance, and she raised her arms to the sky. "Sister!" she half-sang, in a voice like rustling reeds. "Little sister!" She moved backward and began to twirl in a large arc, raising the winds as she did so. The grass rose upward, and bits of loose earth twisted into her orbit.

"Oh!" Mona's eyes, as blue as autumn skies, widened. "Look, Frell! A dust devil!" She launched herself forward in Ttane's direction, moving more lightly than Ttane had thought possible in the earthborn. Then, to Ttane's startlement, Mona grabbed both her hands and danced with her, matching her step for step. Exhilarated, Ttane lifted Mona off the ground, and a safe height into the air. Mona shrieked with joy.

Frell's answering shriek was less joyous. "Mona!" she cried, her voice laced with fear.

Suddenly realizing that the older girl was frightened, Ttane set Mona down gently. She was not herself entirely sure what had happened, only that something had enabled the child to dance with her, if only for a few halting steps. Among her own kind, those would have been considered baby steps. For a human child, it was magic.

Mona tumbled backward, laughing. Running forward, Frell caught her up in her arms. "Mona? Are you all right? Are you hurt? What happened?"

"The dust devil danced with me!" Mona seemed oblivious to Frell's distress. "Did you see? She danced with me!"

"She?" Frell's face seemed to pinch together. "What do you mean, *she*? All I saw was a dust devil dragging you into the sky!" Her cheeks were flushed and mottled, and she was breathing hard. Tears leaked out of her eyes and dripped down her nose.

Ttane was not sure why Frell was so frightened. There had been no danger to Mona; Ttane had kept tight hold of the child. Even a daughter of the wind knew that to drop an earthbound creature from too great a height could extinguish their breath. True, the greater cousins did not always care, but they knew what they were capable of.

"Let's get indoors," Frell said, her voice flat.

"I would not harm her," Ttane said as loudly as she could, hoping that at least one of the children could hear her voice. "She, at least, has something of our kindred about her."

Mona cocked her head as if listening. "It's like a voice," she said to the older girl. "Like someone is talking very softly, and I can't quite make out the words." She scowled. "Like listening to someone talking in the next room with the door closed. I hate not being able to hear it!" She stamped her feet.

Ttane found a laugh bubbling out of her for the first time since she had parted from the others. Mona seemed so much like a young breeze, passionate, temperamental, and joyously spontaneous.

Frell's features pinched together even more. Without another word, she grabbed Mona's hand and dragged her toward the house, shutting the door behind her with a slam. Her alarm was like fire, obscuring the air with smoke.

Ttane could have followed them inside; all she needed was a small crack or chink to seep in through the walls or the roof. But she hated being within walls; though not as frightening, it was still a little like the weight of the earth upon which the house stood. Instead, she would keep watch over the cottage, and hope that, with time, she and Mona might speak, and perhaps play again.

The earth was growing stronger, or perhaps gaining more power over Ttane. Twice more she tried to flee, and each time felt heavier and heavier, like a cloud preparing for rain. Her gossamer swirl misted into opacity; her dance slowed. Each time she tried to loft into the air, it was harder. For the first time, flight took effort. The sky seemed to lower overhead, the blue ceiling of a prison.

Exhausted by her efforts, Ttane fled to the house where Mona lived. She peered into one of the windows, trying to find the child. What she saw was an older woman, even more pinched than Frell, dressed in a smock and cooking something over a fire. The woman was sweating, but she did not so much as fan her face to keep cool. It was as if she refused to stir the air even for the sake of comfort. Ttane felt the first stirrings of anger; even the smallest of drafts should be free to dance.

Unsure if she was in the right place, Ttane tried to find any other movement. There was a smaller door opposite the main one, but it was closed. The table and benches that filled one side of the room looked heavy, chunky and graceless. Nothing seemed scaled for a small girl. Ttane decided to check some of the other outlying houses in case she had forgotten the route. Human dwellings appeared much the same to her.

The facing door squeaked just as she was about to leave, letting Mona and Frell into the room. Ttane stopped her winds motionless for a brief moment while she tried to assess the likelihood of drawing Mona outside.

"Frell!" the woman said sharply. "You haven't scrubbed the floor yet. Send Mona out for the water, and get to work!" She gestured toward a bucket tied to a rope that sat by the door.

Ttane felt a moment's sympathy for Frell, even though she had no real understanding of the girl's pinched, sour nature. Frell sighed and turned to her sister. "Take the bucket and get water," she told Mona every bit as sharply as the older woman had spoken to her. "And don't dawdle!"

Mona nodded without rancor, took the bucket, and skipped outside. She headed toward the back of the house and continued down a long path which led to a stone-rimmed well with a low and heavy lip. This was Ttane's chance; she followed her with excitement, hoping that Mona could still sense her dance and her words. She sent a breeze ahead of her to tousle the girl's hair playfully. "Sister?" she called. "Do you know me?" She swirled ahead.

Mona stopped and squinted into the sun. "Is that you, dust devil?" She scrunched her face into an expression of thoughtfulness. "The earth priests say that your kind are evil demons, sent to make us fight with the land." She reached the well and sat down on the low wall. "Perhaps I'm bad, but I don't think you are evil. I think you're beautiful." She turned to let the bucket down into the well, pulling it up hand by hand back to the surface. It sloshed over the rim and onto Mona's dress.

"Do you want to play?" Ttane asked her. She did not understand what a demon was, and she knew she was not evil. Mona's words made little sense to her.

"Oh, yes!" Mona said eagerly. Then she squinted again, as if trying to see. "That's funny. I heard you ask if I wanted to play. I'm sure I did." She frowned. "I think I did."

"I did," Ttane responded gently. "Leave the bucket and come."

Mona frowned. "I can't take the bucket." She set it on the ground and coiled the rope beside it. "Just for a bit." She spread her arms and ran at Ttane, whooping with laughter. Ttane caught her gently and spun her around.

From then on, Mona would find ways to creep from her house

and be with Ttane. It was the only lightness that Ttane felt in this land. The affinity between the two was growing, though Ttane was still unsure if the child could truly see and hear her. She was confident that Mona sensed her; the little girl spoke to her, almost as if she expected an answer. Ttane was sure that Mona had some ancestry among the daughters of the wind; it happened sometimes, though seldom. Children born of such unions were usually deposited with the nearest members of their father's kin. Many did not survive.

The evenings were growing colder and shorter. Sapped by the chill of approaching autumn, Ttane fled her fear of the land and went to find Mona. Looking through the window of the house, she hunted for the girl. Mona was in the main cottage space with Frell; the two of them were kneading bread. Ttane tapped on the window, then sent a soft puff of dandelion seeds whirling by to catch Mona's attention.

Frell looked up first. "Mona!" she said sharply. Everything about Frell seemed to be sharp. "Don't you dare go outside!"

Mona frowned. "Just for a minute, Frell? Please?" Her voice took on a wheedling tone.

"That thing is waiting for you." Frell scowled ferociously. "You know it is, and you're going out to meet it." Young as she was, lines were already grooved into the skin of her face. "It's wrong. The land doesn't like it. You're challenging the land whenever you consort with that thing. It's unnatural and evil! It won't even show itself so that we can pray it away."

Mona's sky-colored eyes filled with tears. "She's not evil! She's not! She's just something that's not – not part of the land!"

"That's exactly what I mean." Frell's grim pronouncement was certain. "Anything that is no part of the land is evil. You know what the priests say. The land says the powers of wind and water are evil, and so they are. If you told one of the priests what you said to me, he'd switch you until your skin was raw. Haven't you been switched enough times?"

Wiping her eyes, Mona glared at her sister with a certainty that seemed much older than she. "The priests are wrong."

Frell slapped her. "Don't you *ever* say that!" Tears leaked from her own eyes. "Do you want them to send you off a cliff into the wind?"

Ttane felt shocked. Was this what the land wanted: that anything which it did not claim was extinguished, like earth covering a flame? She could not understand why the land was so hungry for ascendency over all other powers. A thread of anger blew through her: it was wrong. But it did explain why the land was trying to pull her into itself, to stifle her little breezes under its unyielding surface. The anger strengthened.

She would not give up Mona; Ttane would find some way of keeping her safe. A fierce rage and a wish to shatter those who would even think of harming such a young and helpless sister whirled through her. She sensed in the girl a need for the same freedom that she herself longed for desperately. Ttane could not bid the earth to loosen its grasp, but she could try to keep the winds alive in Mona. The child must not turn into a creature like Frell, bound to the land so tightly that she seemed flattened and deformed.

When Frell looked the other way, Ttane sent another puff of dandelion seed awhirl on the wind. Mona nodded, and Ttane knew that she would find a way to come so that she could dance again with the wind's daughter.

Her sisters were seeking her; Ttane knew it in all her breezes and gusts. Though she could not sense them near, what air that was allowed to move over the land brought her the whispers of kinship. They were looking for her, and sooner or later, they would find her. The hope was enough to keep Ttane's feet in the air. She needed them to come soon; the land was wearing on her.

The more powerful of her sisters could challenge this land's supremacy. In force, they could do tremendous damage even to its lazy strength. She held so little love for this land, and so much rancor toward its will, that she hoped for destruction; she wanted them to break it open and send its pieces flying to all directions. She wanted the earthborn priests who worshipped the land disbanded, shattered, unable to switch children whose dreams flew, or to send those who could not fly into the wind. Ttane wanted violence.

It was a strange thought for a simple whorl of air. She had always been one of the gentle ones, those who left no real damage behind them as they spun. She had never before wished harm to living things.

There is a need, she told herself, *to open the paths of the air. There is a need to challenge the reign of this oppressive land.* She could not do it, but perhaps her sisters could.

The whispers grew stronger one night, under a clear sky. Ttane felt a vibration in the air, a presentiment of something borne on the wind. A surge of energy pulsed through her. Her sisters were coming.

The earth beneath her seemed to growl in angry response; a low, slow note that held fury beneath its seeming passivity. Ttane felt a tug at her feet as it pulled the very air beneath her, trying to bring her down so that it could swallow her whole.

No! Ttane told it. *I will not bow to your mud and your rock and your weight*! She had anger of her own, born of the long exile in this hostile place. *My sisters are coming*!

A cold wind whistled down the sky, an icy, questing lance. Even more strongly now, Ttane could feel its breath and the lightning which shivered through it. Clouds sent fingers into the night, streaks of dark and light that engulfed the stars. They swelled as they came, full of storm and fire.

Ttane lifted her feet to the growing gale. The dance was everything. She had not felt so free to spin in almost two seasons. She reached out her arms to their fullest extent, reveling as the misty garments she wore belled out and away from her. This was what she was made for.

Then, with a crack of thunder and a lash of lightning, her sisters came.

They spiraled down from the sky, their skirts full of rain. The violence of the storm broke over the stultifying immobility of the land, drenching it with floods of rain. Almost immediately, Ttane heard the land complain as runnels of water washed through it, loosening the soil and carrying it into placid rivers which became torrents. The winds, loosed, screamed and moaned, and before her most powerful kin, roared. Vortices of wind tore into the ground, churning it into mud. Streams of earth and grass lifted from the plain and funneled into the air, creating black cyclones that rushed through the countryside.

They reached Ttane soon; they were traveling so fast she could barely see them. A few of the weaker sisters crowded around her. They took her hands and danced, their happiness at finding her apparent with every movement. There was no need for words.

Others danced around the great ones, their steps making small circles and helixes. Ttane knew that against these, the engulfing gravity of the land was lifted for a time. "Oh, my sisters!" she cried out, feeling such a wave of relief and joy that only her feet could express it. "My sisters!"

There were five of the most powerful elder sisters, and they were clearly minded to revenge themselves on what had held Ttane for so long. She watched as they sped through trees, wrenching their roots from the ground and tossing them onto their sides. Insects fluttered on the wind, trying to fly, though they were helpless against the winds. The wind's children plowed through grass and bushes with an easy strength, their hair spinning around them. Then Sshessh, the oldest and strongest, headed toward the town, shrieking in delight at the destruction in her wake.

Ttane snatched her hands away from the dancers and followed. She had no love at all for this land or its people, but she was beginning to realize what her sisters' rescue meant. This would hurt everything dependent on that land; the insects, the few sleepy birds, even those that crawled on the ground or swam through the waters. Her sisters would have no mercy on the power that had kept Ttane prisoner for almost two seasons. On this night, they were a pure force of destruction.

Ttane reached Sshessh as her sister flung out a cloak of wind into a wide circular path. The cloak touched the houses at the town's edge, tearing at the roofs and lifting the corners of the boards that framed them. Fingers of wind pried at the shutters and even prised a few stones from the foundations. As Ttane watched, their roofs lifted entirely off of the houses, floating away as easily as leaves in autumn. A body lofted into the wind, whether alive or dead Ttane could not tell. The shrieking of the gale masked any sound from those within, but she could imagine them, terrified and defenseless. As terrified and defenseless as Ttane was before the heavy weight of the land.

Sshessh turned toward the house where Mona and Frell dwelt.

Ttane danced toward her, fighting the instinct to merge with the storm and immerse herself in its wildness. She could not allow harm to Mona. The child was akin to them all, a small sister sheathed in flesh. Ttane loved Mona. That was more powerful even than the storm. She caught a glimpse through slatted shutters of Mona and Frell crouching beneath the heavy table; Ttane knew it was not enough to protect them from Sshessh.

She reached the house first, and spread her arms wide across it. "No!" she called to Sshessh. "You must leave them alone!" Then she remembered that the people of these lands were Mona's sisters and mothers, friends and cousins. Suddenly she wished to defend them as she defended Mona. The understanding was a revelation. "Touch none of them!" The protective urge took her by surprise.

Sshessh looked at Ttane, disapproval in her expression. Thunderclouds clung to her dark hair and lightning trailed from her fingers. Her winds whirled and howled with force that Ttane could not begin to stand against. Still, she must try.

"No!" she called again. "Turn aside!"

Her sister frowned. "You know that I can blow them out like a spark, Ttane. You know that I can blow you out like a spark. Why do you stand against me? We are here for you."

"I know," Ttane said softly. "I know. I love you all, and I have missed you desperately. But – " She searched for the right words. "There is a little sister here. A sister even though born of the earth. You must not harm her."

"You are the only sister here." Sshessh's words were furious. "We care nothing for the creatures of this place. The land held you here. The land will pay the price."

"No." Ttane's words were even softer, but she knew Sshessh would hear. "You will not. I will stand against you if you try."

Her winds recoiled almost immediately upon her words; no one defied Sshessh. So old and so strong was Ttane's sister that she could tear through this land by herself and leave a long, dark trail of destruction that would take years to heal. Her cloak now spread almost as wide as the town itself, and Ttane knew that she herself was in danger. Sshessh might have come to free Ttane, but the wildness of the winds was on her, and she might do almost anything.

Sshessh spun even faster, her hair and cloak whipping around her. The vortex she created scraped grass and dirt from the ground, mingling it with the planks and tiles she had torn from the roofs of the town. She was a truly terrible and beautiful sight. "No!" she howled. "I will have all of them! This land must learn that we will avenge our own!"

Ttane thought quickly; Sshessh would not whirl in place for much longer. What did she know that could turn her sister aside?

It was the land that angered them all, the land which forced servitude on every power in its scope. It was the land with which they must deal, not the earthbound creatures held in its sway. They must prevent the land from returning to its hungry ways once they were gone. They must open a path for the air to blow cleanly from one end of the land to the other.

"I will not move," she told Sshessh with quiet determination. "I will defend this little sister against you." As her elder sister surged forward in fury, Ttane flinched back, but held up her palm in negation. Her winds shivering with fear, she spoke again to the dark, swirling power before her. "I know another way – you must listen!"

For a long moment, Ttane thought her sister would sweep her up in the maelstrom of her anger. Sshessh's winds wailed and screamed. The edges of slate tiles flapped. Ttane knew she was lost in her sister's madness. Sshessh might extinguish her entirely.

Then Sshessh stopped spinning. Perfect stillness blanketed them both.

Hanging in the air, even Sshessh's dark hair hung motionless. "What way?" she asked slowly.

"We can – all of us – open the paths of the air." Ttane spoke swiftly, aware that she must convince Sshessh now. Ideas tumbled into her mind faster than they could tumble from her tongue. "The land is circled with power that sucks everything into it, especially the wind. That is why it could trap me. It holds its creatures captive to its need. But if we all work together, we can crumble the power that deadens the wind, open the ways, free the air. The land will not be able to hold us. The land's creatures will be able to breathe." And to dance, she added to herself. Mona might be able to grow free and whole.

Sshessh sucked in a breath full of earth and grass. Ttane tried to quiet her own winds into patience. Then her dark, old sister looked at her, eyes glimmering with the banked fire of lightning.

"We can." Wonderment suffused her tone. "We can open the land. We need not break it. Not if we work in union."

They had never done such a thing, but Ttane knew that their combined might was stronger than anything they had ever done singly. Sshessh would persuade them, even if Ttane could not. Perhaps even the land could learn, if it were opened to the air.

Sshessh reached out a hand to Ttane, her face broadening into a smile. Her winds overlapped with Ttane's; Ttane gladly resumed the dance, happy to again have the joy of orbiting her stronger sister. She would come back once they had opened the land. She would see

Mona again. And Mona would grow up free from the fear of air. She would be a creature of both.

"Yes, sister," she told Sshessh. "I will rejoin the dance." The exile had strengthened her in a way she had not expected. In pushing against the land, she had also grown.

She had never felt so free.

# Green Thumb

Kallie found the first green tendril of ivy growing through her window frame.

Entering her apartment building after work, she rode the elevator to the third floor, skirted the incinerator and stopped to pick up the newspaper in front of her door. Safely inside, Kallie threw her purse on the futon and glanced around the room at her potted plants. "Hi there," she said to them cheerfully. "Hope you had a good day. Mine was all right."

Looking down at the paper, she routinely checked to see if there were any interesting headlines. "Roots Undermine Rec Center Foundation" was the main story. She quickly skimmed the article; apparently a part of the downtown recreational center had collapsed from poor management of the pair of ancient oaks which framed its front entrance.

"Interesting," she said aloud. "Someone's falling down on the job." First there had been the well-publicized warehouse disaster, then the barely averted catastrophe of the post office, and now this. She wondered how the city could ignore such an obvious hazard as enormous trees next to a building's walls. Personally, she sympathized with the trees.

"Oh well, not my problem." She looked around the room, which was covered with her plants. Philodendrons and spider plants draped from the ceiling in pots secured by well-anchored hooks; African violets and coleus dotted the room with color; two towering dieffenbachias stood guard on either side of the window. In smaller pots around the apartment, Kallie grew aloe, oxalis, gardenias, and a number of others she had either rescued or received as gifts. In the center of her coffee table was her pride: an enormous Christmas cactus with a spread nearly three feet in diameter.

She went to the window to draw the drapes against the evening light. That was when she saw it; a tiny thread of ivy which seemed to have broken through a crumbling corner of the frame which the landlord had not yet fixed. Kallie laughed. "How did you get here, my friend?" The ivy on the outside wall was almost as scraggly as the poor trees tethered by the front walk. "Did you sense a kindred spirit?"

She touched it lightly with her forefinger, stroking it as if it were an animal. "I suppose I should tell the landlord about you, but if she hasn't fixed the frame by now, she probably never will. And you'll at least block the draft." She empathized with the vine, trying to survive amid the sterility of a hostile city. "That's settled, then. You can colonize my home any time you like."

Her words echoed oddly; Kallie felt as if someone were in the room listening to her. Adrenaline jolted through her, and she spun around reflexively, though she was positive no one was there. Sure enough, she saw only her familiar green oasis.

"Too much caffeine," she muttered, and went to fetch the watering can.

A little breeze blew through the room, rippling through leaves and blossoms in a tiny wave. Kallie stopped for a second, still a little unnerved. Then she shrugged and continued with her after-work routine. She would not let imagination hold her evening hostage.

Something tickled Kallie's cheek as she lay on the bed. Sleepily, she rolled over to bury her face in the pillow.

An insistent tickle on her ear roused her again. Her mind still full of sleep, she scratched at it groggily. Her fingers met something solid.

Startled, Kallie woke up fully and swatted at air. Her hand caught in a vine and ripped off part of a leaf. Sitting up precipitously, she stared at it, her comprehension still motionless from the night's dreams. The heartleaf philodendron which hung over the bed had dropped a pair of long tendrils which dangled all the way down to the bed. It was one of these which had caressed her.

She could not figure out what had happened. The plant had not been nearly that long when she had gone to bed; it could not have grown that much. The ends of the vine still swung, as if they were the tentacles of some arboreal squid. Kallie shook her head back and forth, trying to clear out the confusion so that she could fit the vine's length into the correctly labeled box in her mind. It was too disconcerting to remain unexplained.

She stood up on the bed and peered into the planter. Perhaps some of the vines had tangled together, and a gust of air had dislodged them. She could find no evidence that this was the situation, but the explanation calmed her. It was not beyond reason, and it made sense.

The clock read 6:10 in the morning, and sunlight had already pooled on her floor. She jumped out of bed.

"I guess I'll be starting a couple of new cuttings," she told the philodendron, and went to get her smallest pruning shears. On her way, she glanced around the room at the three other pots which adorned it; an amaryllis with a scarlet bloom that stood two feet above its terra cotta pot; a thick patch of mother-in-law's tongue jutting up from an enormous ornamental crock; and a small, recently started aloe vera. Kallie could almost believe that they were taller and thicker than when she had gone to bed, but that could not really be the case.

"I need breakfast," she muttered to herself. "My eyes aren't seeing properly." She snipped the vines and wandered into the kitchen to find a tall glass to root them in. On the way through the living room, she thought again that all the plants looked thicker and fuller than the previous night, but Kallie was determined to have no more of these forays into fantastical thought. She had merely failed to notice how much they were growing, she told herself.

She put the cuttings on the kitchen windowsill alongside several others, and readied herself for work. Right now, Kallie needed to focus on what was real, not dream-fed imaginings.

The golden pothos which overlooked Kallie's cubicle at work had grown, cascading down both sides of the divider. It was usually a healthy plant, its spade-shaped green leaves streaked with bright yellow, and its strong vines curving slightly up at their lowest extent, which now stretched a good two feet below where it had been the night before. Kallie took one look at it and shook her head in disbelief. It was one thing for her surroundings to seem odd when still battling sleep, and another to come to her carefully controlled office environment and discover the same thing. Though Kallie worked in the office of a small theater, she did not expect dramatics from her workspace. She blinked twice, hoping that the strangeness would clear from her eyes. It did not.

From the other side of the divider, her co-worker Emily called out, "Kallie? Is that you?" Emily sounded uncharacteristically nervous. Ducking around the edge of the cubicle, Kallie saw her friend sitting at the desk staring at a spot before her.

A tiny old lady cactus, its fine white hairs sticking out of a rounded body ordinarily sat on Emily's desk. "Because I forget to water plants," she had told Kallie the first day. Now the cactus had grown two sharp spikes a good foot-and-a-half tall. Bright red blooms dripped down the sides of one spike, while sharp, stumpy leaves speckled the other. There was no way the cactus could have grown such features naturally.

"How?..." Kallie began. She stopped speaking when she realized that there was no answer to her question. This transformation was so unnatural that she could not explain it away.

"I don't get it." Emily continued to stare. "Cactuses don't grow that fast. And the shape is all wrong." She shook her head. "I wonder..." She slapped the desk hard enough that Kallie jumped. "I know what happened. One of the directors is playing a practical joke on me. You know how they get." She laughed, and the tension sloughed from her shoulders. "Had me going there for a little while. I'll have to tell them they got me good. And then get back at them."

Wishing she could accept such a pedestrian answer, Kallie picked up the pot and examined the cactus carefully. She did not recognize the species; it looked like an amalgam of the original plant and at least two other unusual types. Before this morning, she might have passed it off in the same way as Emily, but the troubling events were adding up, and she was growing increasingly disturbed.

She brushed it lightly with one finger. Like needles piercing her flesh, knowledge pierced her mind, forceful and shocking. Without question, she *knew* that the cactus had retreated into two past stages of its evolution, so far back in time that the first human ancestors had not yet risen onto their hind legs. She gasped for air, and would have dropped the pot, but something beneath consciousness made her lay it carefully on the desk instead.

Kallie could no longer deny that something of great power and significance had entered her normal life and was changing the world into a new shape. Terror began as a jolt in her spine, and continued as an acidic bite in her midriff. She felt dizzy and sick.

"Kallie?" Emily laid a hand on her arm. "Are you feeling all right?"

"I don't know." Kallie walked back around the divider to her own desk. "I need to sit down." Dropping gratefully onto her chair, she leaned over the desk's surface and pillowed her head on her arms.

She must gain control over her emotions; whatever had entered her life was something she must confront and defeat. Whatever force was attempting to hijack her reality, she must fight back. She could not depend upon the world to be sane and safe.

Emily put a comforting hand on her hair. Kallie turned her head to smile up at her.

It was not Emily. The touch came from her golden pothos, which had grown several more inches and whose leaves were spreading to become hand-sized. Tendrils descended from it as she watched, dropping to stroke her skin with tiny green hooks. Kallie scooted the chair back from the desk explosively, her eyes widening in fear. This could not be real.

"Going for air," she gabbled at Emily. With all of her courage, she grabbed the pothos, and trailing leaves and vines, headed for the outside door. She would have to leave Emily with the cactus; she could not easily carry two pots.

A gust of wind blew her hair back as she left the office. She stood before it, a gray three-story structure flanked by gray ten-story structures. Any pretense at gardening had long been abandoned, and nothing grew in the gray gravel under the windows. The small placard on the door read 'El Dorado Theater'.

"Why?" she asked the plant, as if it could answer. "Why me? Why are you doing this?" It wrapped around her and clung loosely to her skin, almost like a pet python. As if she were in a horror film, she envisioned it encapsulating her in an air-tight cocoon or squeezing the life from her. She would have dropped it, but this time her fingers refused to straighten. "Please let me go," she pleaded, though it seemed ridiculous to beg a vine for mercy.

Part of the vine uncoiled and stroked her cheek as if in apology. Kallie stopped walking and stared at it.

"You can understand me?" she asked in disbelief.

The vine snaked around her the nape of her neck and patted her gently and firmly on the shoulder.

"I don't believe this." Kallie's vision swam with confused and frightened tears. "If I promise not to leave you here, can I put you down?"

There was no answer, but she decided to try it anyway. She leaned over and placed the pot on the ground. This time her fingers worked.

"All right," she said to the plant. "You don't mean me any harm. You want me to understand you – somehow. You want something from me. I still don't understand. And why all the other plants? What is the connection? Why are all of you growing, and growing out of shape?"

She was not actually sure it would not answer; her understanding of the possible was rapidly shrinking. She was not even sure whether she hoped it would.

The answer, when it came, was not audible. Kallie's sight collapsed into a tunnel of dark; she could feel herself sinking through the concrete and into the ground below. Earth soaked into her clothes, filled her vision, worked its way into the pores of her skin. Her fingers and toes felt as if they branched into roots, growing and spreading out widely in the starved soil. Kallie's heart pounded with terror; she was not sure if she was hallucinating, and her perceptions were very immediate and tangible. She thrashed, trying to escape from the suffocation that must inevitably happen.

Moments later, Kallie realized that though she did not seem to be breathing, she was not suffocating, either. She closed her eyes so that she the blindness was not so frightening. Then someone folded arms around her from behind, though she could not see who or what it was. Nerves screaming as her voice could not, Kallie bucked and tried to throw off whatever had taken hold of her; there was an invisible horror beneath the earth with her.

The arms restrained her gently without hurting her in any way. The touch was so eerie that Kallie stopped thrashing. She was still alive, after all. It could have harmed her if it wanted. That thought was comforting. But what did it want?

Who are you? she asked in her mind, as she could not move to speak. Though calmer, she was still frightened, and not sure that she wanted an answer.

A vision of green poured across the back of her eyelids. At first it was only a dim smear, but the color soon multiplied into dozens of divergent shades, each tinged a little differently from all the others. Like a leaf unfurling a figure resolved, created from the patchwork of greens. It sprouted arms in profusion, and its roots ran inextricably deep in the earth.

A presence so ancient that Kallie could not comprehend it surged through her; eons whirled in her mind like a handful of days. Great fans of green sifted light from the sun, transmuting it into growth and change. Spores and seeds danced on the wind or swirled through the water, blowing and drifting to new places, new homes, new existence. Seeds sprouted and fruits fell; heat and cold slowly altered one growing life into another. Colonies of plants devoured great patches of land and sea; single plants eked out thousands of years in barren and solitary spaces.

But always, throughout immeasurable years, was the green. Adapting and changing, it grew new shapes in a constantly altering world, while retaining its essence. It had been part of the world so long that it had developed a memory and a will greater than any human consciousness. Sometimes allied with human interests, sometimes a bitter enemy, it owed no loyalty to any creature. Still, it could feel, it could care, it could hate, and occasionally it could love.

And it wanted Kallie.

A resurgence of terror attacked her; she began to struggle again. She could not bear any more of this living entombment. *Let me go*! she begged the green consciousness. *Please let me out*!

Something abraded her chin, and she snapped her eyes wide; she lay on her stomach, her chin on the concrete walk. A smudge of blood showed where she had scraped the skin. Slowly she sat up and discovered that the golden pothos had attached itself to her hair and was braiding both together.

"That can't be – " She stopped as she realized that none of it was possible. She also knew that she had not suddenly gone insane. That was as unlikely as anything else about the whole experience: which left her with the mind-shaking truth. Looking down at her hands, she saw that she was shaking with reaction. Drawing a long breath and expelling it in an equally long sigh, Kallie finally admitted to herself that the world had turned upside down.

"I need to take you home," she told the vine, her voice quaking. Though she was in the habit of talking to her plants, the sense that they were listening was something new. "Please don't draw attention to yourself. I don't know what other people will do to you if they get scared." *Or what you will do if they get scared*, she added silently. The previous day's newspaper heading flickered through her mind; those trees could have killed.

She felt several tugs on her hair, then the vine dropped back into the pot. Kallie breathed out, trying to calm herself. Striding back into the office, she headed toward Emily's cubicle.

"I've got to go home," she blathered at her co-worker, hoping she did not sound completely incoherent. "Not feeling at all good." She waved her hand at the cactus. "Do you want me to take this home and take care of it? I'll help you hunt down whoever swapped them later." To her own ears, her voice sounded high and foolish. Tears pooled in her eyes, but she fought them back.

"Oh, would you?" Emily scooped up the small planter and put it in Kallie's free hand. "I wouldn't know where to begin. You know me – I'm lucky if I can keep an air fern alive." She gave Kallie a long, hard glance. "You are kind of pale. Go home. I'll cover."

Kallie refrained from mentioning that air ferns were neither plants nor living, but instead took the cactus and walked out of the office as fast as she dared to go.

On the bus home, her heartbeat was ragged; she was afraid that her admonishments would hold neither of the plants. They seemed to have some sort of good will toward her, but she was not sure whether that would hold true for the other thirty people who rode with her. She knew what plants could do over long stretches of time; she was less sure what they might be able to do when they grew as quickly as both of the ones she now held. She also did not want to become the target of a terrified riot. *Please*, she said in her mind, *don't give yourself away. Don't risk it. Not here. Not now.* If it came to a battle between humans and the green, she was not sure which side she would be on.

At least carrying two plant pots kept anyone from sitting next to her. At her stop, Kallie jumped up and exited quickly, hoping to get home before anyone noticed. She was not sure why she had become the focus for this green invasion. She just wanted it to stop.

The saplings that shaded the front walk had grown a foot taller and a bit wider since that morning; their tethered stakes dangled, unanchored, from the trunks as if they had been pulled from the ground. Petunias in every imaginable color spilled from their lava rock beds and spread thickly into every possible crack of concrete. A pair of bemused maintenance workers stood talking in hushed tones; one carried a hose, the other a pair of shears.

Kallie darted past them and into the lobby of the building. Even here the green was spreading; the normally spindly fig tree which occupied a corner by the mailboxes had split its pot, and its roots were beginning to dig into the tile floor. Now Kallie was beginning to wonder what had been unleashed, and why she was the epicenter.

The elevator was still working, though she had some doubts as to whether she should use it. She hugged both plants to her, very aware of how the cactus thorns seemed to shiver away from her so that she would not be impaled on their spikes. It seemed surreal, yet Kallie knew it was tremendously real. And tremendous was an apt word for it, as the ordinary plants the city tolerated were changing their nature in revolt.

A man she vaguely recognized as living several doors down stood by the incinerator, five potted plants at his feet. All of them showed signs of explosive growth, and one philodendron clutched at his ankles as if in fear. Kallie felt the blood drain from her head; this was what she feared the most. If the green consciousness was rising in rebellion, how could anyone stop it? The implications were dizzying.

"Help me!" the man called to Kallie. She stared for a moment, then tucked the cactus under her other arm and grabbed the philodendron.

"Let go!" she hissed at it. She was almost unsurprised when it did, uncoiling from the man's legs and wrapping its extra length around Kallie's forearm. "Don't burn them!" she called to the man, hoping he would listen. She did not know what else to do for him.

Darting down the hall to her own apartment, she did not know what to expect. She placed the three pots down and fumbled with her key, managing to insert it into the lock with shaking hands. She opened the door.

Inside was a jungle. All the plants she owned had spread to cover the entire set of rooms with green. On every wall, she saw ivy rippling in an invisible wind, plastered over every clear inch of paint. Her gaze went to the window where it had first entered.

That was it: her words the night before. *You can colonize my home any time you like*. But she had not known what those words would mean. She had invited the green into her home, and that meant into the city itself. Remembering the news stories of late, she guessed it had been laying siege for some time, waiting for just such an opportunity. Before she had spoken, it had been forced to use ordinary means to achieve its goals. She had changed that.

But what did that mean for the hundreds of thousands who lived here? And what did it mean for the green things that would be destroyed by all those people? A war between man and nature could not be allowed; it would leave no one the victor.

She was responsible. It was she who had unwittingly opened her door to it, and it had not harmed her in any way. It must be channeled, controlled, aimed only at what was necessary, not given license to eat away at the foundations of humanity. There was only one solution she could see, and it horrified her. She swallowed hard, and tried to summon the courage to speak.

"All right," she said aloud to the green consciousness. The words came out garbled by a suddenly dry mouth. Her chest hurt, and she noticed that she was breathing very hard. "You want me. Take me, then. Use me. But only if you work with me and not against me. Let me show you what needs to be done."

The words exploded in the room as if someone had dropped a

stone in a still pool. Kallie heard them catch in the leaves and whisper around the room, like sounds borne on the wind. She knew, without a doubt, that the green consciousness was listening. The sense of monumental age beyond any comprehension swamped her mind. Then she heard something else, swirling in the leaves and carrying far beyond the room: an answer. *Yes*, it said, and again, *Yes*.

Sharp pains assailed her head, as if something were sprouting from the inmost core of herself. Her vision brightened until sight was an agony. She felt a tickle in her fingers, and looked down, surprised that she could still move her head.

Curling from beneath her fingernails were the first green tendrils of ivy.

bout the Author

Inspired by authors such as J.R.R. Tolkien, Lloyd Alexander, and Madeleine L'Engle, Beth determined to become a writer when she was still in grade school. That path meandered through an attempt at astronomy, a linguistics degree, and a brief flirtation with anthropology, but during it all, she worked on her writing, producing numerous short stories, and even completing two (unpublished) novels while in high school and college. Since deciding to focus on her writing, she has published a number of fantasy short stories (and a lone science fiction piece) in various magazines and anthologies. *The Herd Lord*, a novella about a war among centaurs, was published in 2011, and her first full-length novel, *Etched in Fire* was released in 2015. Beth's ideas are sparked by music – Celtic folk, classical, and classic rock – and she sings, plays guitar and harp, and writes songs as well as dabbling in jewelry-making and other assorted crafts. But it is her sons, Dylan, David, and Alex, who keep her striving for excellence, so that she can make them proud of her.

Seeing Green is her first short story collection.

Check out Beth's webpage at: *http://firedrake1.wixsite.com/etchedinfire*
On Facebook: *https://www.facebook.com/etchedinfire*
And find out about the Centaur Homeland at: *centaurspace.weebly.com*

www.ingramcontent.com/pod-product-compliance
Lightning Source LLC
Chambersburg PA
CBHW070548120726
47909CB00007B/2288